VICIOUS CYCLES

How to Stop Attracting the Same MEN!

By Daphanie Howard

Forward by Dr. K. M. Howard

Vicious Cycles
How to Stop Attracting the Same MEN

Type of work: Biography / Autobiography
First edition: 2021
ISBN: 978-1-955622-76-9

Cover Design: Author's Dream
Cover Photograph thanks to: Author's Dream

Printed in the U.S.A.

Contents

Foreword by Dr. K. M. Howard

As she entered my office I knew that there was something eccentric and moving about her. Sometimes when entering a person's space you must pay attention to the space instead of the person.

She moved with calculation of accomplishing what she set out to do. It was apparent that the goal was clear but the direction was foggy. This was the first encounter that I had with Ms. Daphanie.

We began to discuss her vision for this book, that it would enlighten the reader to start their stop. To begin bringing to an end the CYCLES of life they do not desire. To begin a new leaf on life. Stop making wrong choices again and again giving people relationships, covenant agreements, the power to enter and cause damage to their life.

Daphanie has found the penmanship to place on paper the right words to support and help anyone that finds themselves in a spinning web. The person that once like her are foggy with the direction.

This book contains the most uplifting and revealing aspects of relationships on many scales. It will take you on a journey of a young woman's life and the root, cause, and effect of choices.

It is detailed in its concept of giving you the blow by blow details, so you don't miss a thing. Sometimes the reason why we make the same mistakes over and over, is because we miss the small signs.

Daphanie has with great style delivered a message to the soon delivered reader, on how to break the Cycle! By recognizing the root, then eliminating the cause, that will stop the effects.

Your life has just begun, because your Cycles have just ended.

—Dr. K. M. Howard

"*Integrity is doing the right thing,*
even when no one is watching."

—C. S. Lewis

Life is a Mirror

By Lucretia Robison

I suspect I am a mirror to the rest of the world.
You do not see me. You see your perception of me.
Your perception is yours based on your experiences.
It's not me.
Some look at me with love.
Some look at me with hate.
Some look at me with disdain.
Some look at me with disgust.
Some look at me with fire.
Some look at me with fear.
Some look at me with bravery.
Some look at me with pity.
Some look at me with empathy.
Some look at me with envy.
Some look at me with gratitude.
Some look at me with appreciation.
Some look at me with pride.
Some look at me with laughter.
Some look at me with sadness.
Some look at me with surprise.
All who look at me see through their own perceptions.
I am just here: existing, living, breathing, feeling, and experiencing
life the best I can with the knowledge and abilities I currently have.
When I know better, I do better. I am human. I am a spirit within
the flesh. I am energy. I am a creator.
Regardless of what else I am, I am a mirror of an element in
yourself that challenges you. It would be wise to accept and love
that element of yourself.
Whatever feelings arise in you, I will carry on with my life's
work. Find your purpose. Do the best you can. Then do better.
Life is nothing but a mirror. Illusions are meant to be shattered
with the shining of the light of truth.
Time to awaken.

Verbal or Non-verbal

Communication is the key to any good relationship. It's beautiful when you are honest about what you want and expected early in the relationship. An individual can choose to stay or exit quickly. Often, we know our truths but don't have the courage or confidence to express them because we don't want to be labeled as arrogant or overbearing. Society has changed the perception of traditional relationships. It's perfectly fine to be in a monogamous relationship. Each person needs to discuss exclusivity.

Values

Throughout my years of and social engagement I've noticed there is a breakdown of values to include religious, moral, social, work, and political values. Normally, values are passed down from one generation to the next generation. This is not happening today. Parents are not communicating with their children. In turn, the children are left to figure it out on their own spending many years in the same cycle of mistakes and regret with any guidance to make a better life for themselves. I learned I keep attracting the same guy throughout my dating history. For example, I keep attracting liars, cheaters, bullies, and controlling men. They all have the attitude it's all about them.

Personal Methods for Healing

Each person has to find their own method of healing. What might work for someone else may not work for you. I recommend developing your own daily routine first thing in the morning. You can start with prayer, reading a few verses in the Bible, meditation, yoga, practicing martial arts forms, listening to gratitude affirmations, spiritual music, two-mile walk, taking my vitamins and hydrating the body with water. It is best to start with something rather than nothing.

Counseling

Professional counseling might be the best alternative if you need to discuss confidential difficult times. Recognizing you need help and getting counseling is not bad. It becomes bad and shameful when you decide not to do anything.

Chapter 1

Leaving Home- Summer 1985

The promise of the new day's light is barely peeking into the window through the blinds in my room. I turn over, to readjust myself. I hope I can go back to sleep. There's a break in the silence, and I can hear the creaking noise in the living room. My grandmother, Clara Rosa, is pacing the hardwood floors.

This day feels rather haunting because she operates like a well-oiled machine. She doesn't use an alarm clock. She wakes up every morning at 3:00 a.m. to start her day. Her daily routine begins with a prayer, reading the Bible, and listening to gospel music and sermons on the radio.

Today, the house is filled with no singing in the kitchen or music on the radio. There's no smell of biscuits baking in the oven. I can't hear the bacon sizzling in the skillet or eggs being cracked on the kitchen counter. There's no sound of the broom sweeping the floors or residue of the foot passage from the previous day. There is evidence of customers being served moonshine in the designated room of the house. I call it the relaxation room where people would come to drink, smoke, listen to music, and dance their cares away.

I remember as a child, being awakened in the wee hours of the morning by a knock at the back door. I would hear a car engine running in the cornfields. The sounds of a baritone voice are echoing in the backyard. Sometimes, I would get up from the bed, walk on the pecan hardwood floors that lead me to the kitchen vinyl flooring, and peep through the cracked door. I would see darkness.

A glimpse of light would redirect my vision toward the dashboard of a vehicle. I adjusted my young eyes and saw an old model car. Listening intently, I could hear movement. The trunk of the car was open; a few clear gallon jugs are delivered to the back screened-in porch. An exchange of money is made. "Thank you, ma'am," I brushed up against the door, and it made a squeaky noise. My grandmother and the male's attention were directed toward the door. I quickly made my way back to bed and pretended to be asleep.

Throughout the years, I've heard those noises but not last night. I've watched years of my grandmother attentively placing the charred apples in the clear liquor to change the color. I've helped her serve her clients. My grandmother would look at me time and time again, repeating her words of wisdom and warning.

"This is a business"; "I don't drink, smoke or do drugs and never will." "You can't make a profit if you're drinking your product"; "Men will drink with a woman in the streets, but rarely does he want to take a drunk and promiscuous woman home to wife"; "Be a respectful woman"; "What you and your man do, keep it behind closed doors, it's private." There were times I wondered was she talking about the mistakes she made. Was this guidance or a warning? "Never mix business with pleasure"; "Don't lay where you make your bread"; "Do you see me dating these drunks?"; "I smile and grin with them"; "This is my business"; "I got to take care of my family"; "Baby, you got to remain sober at all times"; "Baby, you got to remain sober at all times."; She would always repeat that saying twice and then.... Do you hear me?"; "Keep your eyes on your money at all times"; "This stuff, I am selling will kill a person."

Today feels like someone has died. The intense energy of mourning is felt throughout the house. I am trying to figure out who has died? For an intense overcast is in my presence. A familiar Bible verse reminds me to prepare for the unknown.

"To everything there is a season, and a time to every purpose under heaven: A time to be born, and a time to die: a time to plant, and a time to pluck up that which is planted; A time to kill, and a time to heal; a time to break down, and a time to build up." Ecclesiastes 3:1-3 King James Version (KJV) Bible.

I am dressed in my black two-piece sweatsuit sitting on the edge of the bed with my purse and bag. *"I'm a big girl now,"* I say this aloud, I stand up, take a deep breath in and a slow, deliberate breath out. I slowly walk from the bedroom to enter the living room. I proceed to open the thick beige heavy-duty curtains, to let the daylight in from the two large windows. The moderately furnished home was immaculate. It was free of clutter. No newspapers or magazines were laying around the house. The wood-paneled walls are adorned with generations of family pictures and memories. I notice the glass walnut wood cabinet was unlocked and a rifle is missing. The case typically displays five shotguns and rifles.

My grandmother startled me, *"Good Morning, Baby."*

I'm a little baffled, but I reply, "Good Morning, Grandmother. I see you have your rifle in your hands. Are you going hunting?"

Clara Rosa believes in firearms. She has several handguns, shotguns, hunting rifles and the ammunition stored throughout the home. She has stored her expensive weapons in the cabinet. The firearms are always loaded and ready to shoot. I've often watched her clean, load, and polish the firearms. I learned how to load and shoot a gun before I was ten years old. My grandmother was a small, framed, strong, fierce, and courageous woman. She would stand up to anyone no matter who they were with or without a gun. I admired that about her. I always felt safe with her, but today I'm not sure of our safety. I wasn't sure why she's holding a rifle today pacing the floors and guarding the front door in her long white robe.

"Why do you have your rifle out today?"

"Oh, no particular reason." I might have to kill some wild animals today. Especially the ones that don't know their place. You got them on lockdown." She goes on, changing the subject without noticing my level of discomfort.

"D'Alise, you should stay here and start your master's degree program." Your mother and siblings will be lost without you."

Her words touch emotions I haven't had in years. *"I feel as if I'm being backed up in a corner."* It reminds me of when I was ten, and fifteen elementary kids were taunting me asking if LaRosa was sick? I couldn't give them an answer that would satisfy them. My grandmother wouldn't be satisfied, either.

"Grandmother, I am tired. I am leaving the family in a good place. I have been helping with the family ever since I was five years old. I've been cooking the meals and cleaning both houses. I've been helping with my three siblings for a long time."

"What can I do to make you stay?" Her reply I expected and have an answer prepared.

"Nothing." I hear my mother's voice in my head.

"Darling, it's dangerous in the city, people stealing, killing, and robbing on the street. It's just isn't safe."

My mother always had a fear-based mentality ever since I was a child imprinting her insecurities on me.

"Baby, stay." As my grandmother's tone softens, I understand my need to be determined.

"No, Clara Rosa. I need to leave." The sound of the phone interrupts her next comment.

"Hello, yes, I will be leaving today and will be at the Greyhound bus station waiting for you to pick me up at 6:00 p.m. Thanks, Goodbye," I spoke quickly. My grandmother was waiting for the call to end.

"Baby, please don't leave." I was a big girl and didn't need her to change my mind.

"My bags are packed, and I have my Greyhound bus ticket right here in my hands. Thank you so much for the blue thirty-inch footlocker trunk. It's sitting at the front door. I appreciate all the advice you've given me throughout the years. You have trained me well and prepared me for life."

"I know your cousin invited you to move to Louisiana, but he has a wife."

"Yeah, she seems to be nice. She's called me a couple of times, and we've talked on the telephone. I don't know what to expect with two grown women living in the same house. John has always looked out for the family. I've always looked up to him. He's the first in the family to attend a community college, and he has a career. For me, this is a once in a lifetime opportunity to leave this small, depressed town. If I don't leave now, I'll be stuck here barefoot and pregnant like all the other girls."

"That's not true D'Alise. You are a different kind of girl. We kept you out the streets. I tried to give you everything. Don't leave." She is pleading for me to stay.

"John sent me the money to purchase this ticket. He wants me to come. I am leaving. I liked his ex-girlfriend. She was genuine, kind, and kept a clean house. She made the best southern fried chicken and seafood. I don't know his new wife's moral qualities or character. I trust his judgment in discerning a person character. I'm certain; I'll like his new-wife." I'm beginning to feel as though there will never be a reason that she will accept. I know it's now or never. *"Why can't she understand?"*

"Make sure you carry your own weight D'Alise; find a job."

"I will. I've been helping the family with my part-time income for years."

"When you find a job, open a checking and savings account at a bank. The savings account will come in handy for rainy days. I want you to give your cousin and his wife rent money to cover your shelter. We raised you well purchase food, cook and clean up after yourself. Always remember your daily prayers. I want you to find and join a good church in the city. When John comes home, give the couple a chance to have quality time together. Don't be in the couple's space all the time."

"John works overseas. He comes home one week out of the month. Trust me; I will not be in the way. I'm looking forward to this new adventure."

The taxi horn blows. "Grandma, my taxi is here. Come here and give me a hug and a kiss."

I kissed my grandmother on the cheek. As I struggle with my purse, bag, and footlocker, I manage to exit the door. I never gave a second thought to the screen door until it slams in my grandmother's face. The struggling continues, I am determined to do it on my own. My grandmother is standing in the door, mourning the loss of her oldest granddaughter with a sad face and teary eyes. She calls out from the screened entrance.

"I can help you."

"No. No, thank you, ma'am." I find the strength to make it to the car. I'm determined to prove to myself. *"I am a big girl."*

"You can always come back home if it doesn't work out in the city. You'll always have a place to call home here in Alabama. I love you."

It's been a long time since I heard those words. Maybe, they're resonating today. I recall my basic needs being met daily. I was always fed, clothed, and had a warm place to sleep.

As I walk down the long red brick walkway, I recall helping grandmother lay those bricks in the summertime. The aroma of the roses and flowers smell pleasant. Looking back at the house as I walk away. I will always hold onto the bittersweet memories of home.

I will hold onto the memories:

"I have no regrets leaving the big white southern planta-tion house with black shutters. On the 4th of July, the long front porch accommodated many family members and filled the three-swing set for gatherings. The fellowship, food, games, and live blues being performed by uncles made me proud to know I had professional entertainers in the family. My grandmother loved making baked beans, potato salad, fresh corn from outback, and her secret Bar-B-Que sauce.

The porch extended five feet from the ground and contained different shapes and sizes of flowerpots and planters. I helped my grandmother fill those planters with dirt. I sat on those steps of the property listening to many adult conversations as a child. I gained lots of wisdom and knowledge. The house had lots of curve appeal. The flowers looked lovely around the property. I pulled the weeds and helped plant many of the flowers. The lawn was well manicured. The two large oak trees at the entry made the home look like something out of a magazine with the black antique car parked on the side. During the gatherings, at least eight vehicles could easily be parked on the lawn.

My brother once tied a rope around a black cat's neck and swung the cat from one of the trees at the front of the home. Bruno was a rebel, always getting in trouble.

Chapter 2

Traveling Alone

I jump in the back seat of the yellow taxicab and wave good-bye. I tap on the headrest.

"To the Greyhound bus station on Greensboro Ave, Sir."

On the ride to the bus station, my thoughts run rapidly.

"This day is finally here. This day is finally here. This day is finally here. Thank you, God. I am leaving. I am leaving this place."

I think about my brother and his first proposal for us to run away.

"I plan on running away. I'll never stop nothing, or no one is going to keep me down. D'Alise, if you come with me, we can plan on how we will survive. You got the brains, and I got the streets, smarts."

I never gave his plan any serious thought. I lived in a different reality. *"Bruno, I can't go. I don't know anything else but here. We're just little kids."*

The ride isn't long. I watched the road without any thought and finally gave in to my new life once the driver slowed down, preparing to park in front of the bus station.

"Ma'am, we are here." The taxi driver parks close to the curb. He gets out and assists with my luggage. He opens the glass door and brings all my items inside the bus terminal. He sits them down by the ticket counter. I pay the driver and give him a tip. Now, this is the first time in my life I have felt empowered. I'm ready to concur the world. I approach the window to give the ticket

agent my ticket. I look around and notice everyone is traveling with someone.

I went on my first vacation to Iowa on the Greyhound bus with my grandmother and brother. The motorcoach had reclining seats, overhead storage, and an onboard bathroom. This was the first time I had an opportunity to see how other people lived. We stopped in Chicago, Illinois. I've never seen so many people in a bus station traveling. I played on the escalator and purchased souvenirs. We each had a packed lunch from my grandmother's kitchen. Fried chicken, sliced white bread, pound cake, and soda. *"Hmm, Hmm, Good!"* The best-fried chicken in the world. When we arrived in Iowa, my uncle picked us up from the bus station in his old model vehicle. He's happy to see us.

I get the feeling my uncle, and my grandmother have a good relationship. He's telling us all the places he wants to take us. We went to his home in the historic area where he and his girlfriend lived. I had never seen such a big house; it had two-stories, stairs, and a basement. I enjoyed playing games in the house. My uncle is proof that people can change their lives. In the past, my uncle drank, smoked, and was a womanizer. Once we got settled in my uncle gave us a tour of the city and took us to visit the state capital in Des Moines. We had an opportunity to visit other relatives. While on vacation, my grandmother is not letting anything go to waste. A rabbit got hit by a car. She picked it up from the street and made rabbit stew and noodles. That was my first-time eating roadkill. Now, I am traveling alone. *"I am a big girl now."* I am no longer in a box that defines me. *"I can breathe."* All I have ever seen was the funeral home at the top of the hill, the corner stores, and the church in my neighborhood. I love the vacation memory of my grandmother and brother.

Now, I get to see how other people live again. My hometown is located off Interstate 20 west. I was born and raised in a rural area in Alabama in the 1960s. The economy wasn't that great. A major tornado hit the state and destroyed everything in its path. The storm was an adverse event. The city is now part of the revitalization area to improve the economy and struggling neighborhoods.

I've had many storms in life. I want a new beginning and a new life. I was born in a time where John F. Kennedy was the president in the 1960s. The non-violent freedom movement is remembered for social change through protest. Martin Luther King was one of the big players during the civil rights movement. I remember my grandmother and my mother playing Martin Luther King's Last Speech: "I've Been to The Mountain Top." Dreams do come! I am leaving home.

The ticket agent stamps my ticket tags my footlocker and places it on the opposite side of the counter for placement on the bus.

"Ma'am your bus will be departing from terminal A. Please wait and sit in that area." The ticket agent points to the area I should sit and wait for the bus.

I follow where I think her finger was pointing, and then I see the sign. I spotted an empty seat, but I need to ask to be sure.

"Hello, is it okay if I take a seat here?" I saw the lady and her baby. I hope this seat is available.

"Help yourself." She smiles and adjusts herself next to me.

"Your baby girl is beautiful." I smile at the two of them.

"Thank you." I can tell she's proud of her little girl.

"Is this your first child?" Babies fascinate me. She is a beautiful golden brown. Her eyes hold the wonder of the world. She's got me mesmerized. I'm curious about her features.

"Yes." Her mother is not put off by my questions. She's enjoying the attention.

"Is she mixed?" I hope she doesn't take offense to my questions.

"Yes. Do you have children?" My questions may have given her the wrong impression. I just love little ones.

"No, I recently graduated from college in May." I pause and think to myself. My father was never involved in my life but attended my graduation. He was never present for my struggle as I didn't meet him until I was eighteen years old. His words were, *"I don't ever want you to ask me for nothing. Do you hear me?"* I always remembered those words and respected his wishes.

"Would you like to hold our baby?"

"It's been a while since I held a baby. When my cousin stayed with my grandmother in the summertime, I babysat and changed his diapers. I also help with my younger brothers and sister. *"Thank God that's all over. Too much work for one, that's for sure."*

"Here, take her." I reach for the precious bundle without a second thought. To my surprise, holding the baby feels so familiar.

"She is beautiful. Look at the springy ringlets. She has naturally curly hair like you."

"That might change once my daughter gets older." She runs her fingers through the dark curls.

"Why do you say that?" I couldn't imagine the curls being any different than the thick curls her mother had.

"At one time, I didn't embrace my natural curly locs. I wanted my hair to be straight. The heat from the blow dryer and flat iron damaged my hair."

Our conversation is a comfort. We could talk the way I couldn't speak at home. Not many understood the worldly life I had encountered.

"Really? I can identify with you. When I was in elementary school, all the girls had chemically treated hair. I wasn't allowed to relax my afro-textured/kinky hair. The kids teased me about my hair making it difficult for me. I was encouraged to embrace my natural hair. Sometimes, I would beg my mother for a press and Shirley Temple curls. The process of pressing my hair required lots of hair grease. I suffered the consequences when my mother used a straightening comb heated on the stove. Often, I left the chair with burnt ears and burns on my neck. The scares took time to heal, but I was happy with the results of my hair straightening. My sophomore year of college, I received my first Bantu relaxer."

"I like your earrings."

"Thank you. I've been wearing cheap clip-on earrings and getting allergic reactions for years. When I start working, I'm going to get my ears pierced and purchase real 14K gold earrings. When I lived at home, I was never allowed to get my ears pierced."

I was rambling on about myself. I wanted to know more about her angel.

"How old is she?"

"She's two months old."

"Did you have a full-term or premature baby?"

"I had a full-term birth at home with a midwife and my husband. We didn't have a lot of luxury items as a hospital does."

"My oldest brother was born at home with a midwife." My mother said she wouldn't do that again."

"That sounds nice to hear someone else had a baby at home. Now were you a full-term or premature baby?"

"I was born prematurely at HCD Hospital. My mother said the natural vaginal birth was easy. The hospital room was comfortable and well-equipped from the time she arrived until the day she went home. I had to be placed in an incubator to sustain my life for several weeks. The heat from the light dried my skin out and changed my skin color. My mother often laughs, claiming I looked like a dried-up prune. My mother said I was the ugliest baby she ever had in her life."

I smile. *"Have I embarrassed myself?" I hope not.*

"What is your name?"

"Danielle Alise' James. You can call me D'Alise James."

"We're Mr. and Mrs. Baker." She points to her husband, who nods. "From what we can see, the ugly duckling has turned out to be a beautiful swan." She giggles, and he smiles.

"Thank you. I see you have lots of toys and books in your bag."

"Yes, we want to create happy memories for our baby girl. We want her to be creative and provide a safe environment."

"That's important. Start early by keeping your eyes on your baby at all times. It's lots of predators in the world."

I can't stop smiling. I have flashes of being very happy. I recall memories from my development stages of birth to age five. Those stages were significate in life. I was a creative child. I enjoyed laying on the green grass in the backyard looking up at the clouds and stars. I enjoyed coloring and drawing nature pictures. I expressed my self through abstract art paintings using the primary colors. I enjoyed making scratch art pictures, painted stones, and used them for paperweights. I sang and remembered all the nursery rhymes. My favorite nursery rhymes were; Itsy Bitsy Spider and Mary Had a Little Lamb. The yellow easy baker oven I received from my grandmother ignited my love for cooking and baking.

"I see you have the nursery rhyme Mary Had a Little Lamb. Can I read it to her?"

"Yes. Let me get the book for you." Mrs. Baker reaches into her bag and pauses to hear the announcement airing on the intercom.

"The bus for New Orleans, Louisiana is at terminal A. Passengers please go to your gate at terminal A and begin boarding now."

"Let me give you your baby girl back. Mr. and Mrs. Baker it was nice meeting you."

"It was nice meeting you D'Alise."

"I got to go now they are calling me for my gate departure. Goodbye." I waved goodbye to my first set of strangers.

The signs look confusing. I'm following the crowd hoping they too are headed to Terminal A. I see a man in uniform. He looks as though he's taking tickets.

"Is this the gate for terminal A?" I ask feeling unsure of myself.

"Yes." He replies dryly.

I reach with my ticket in hand. "Here's my ticket."

"The bus ride is eight hours and fifteen minutes with occasional stops. Ms., you can board now." He speaks as though he is programmed to do so.

"Thank you. Sir." I stepped past him, hoping I didn't sound as automated as he did. The bus interior hasn't changed much since I traveled with my family to Iowa. The modern changes are noticeable.

"Ma'am. I can help you get your items overhead." I'm glad a man offers to lift my bags over my seat.

"Yes, thanks." I continue to stand watching over each bag as he places them tightly between the other passenger's items. He turns and smiles.

"You may be seated." The man is just a passenger helping to store carry-on items.

"Oh, uh, sir, I am going to take a window seat."

I sit and get myself comfortable in my seat.

"Ma am. Do you need help with your jacket?"

I pause, giving his words a moment of thought. "No, I'm good." I am putting it on because it might get chilly on the bus.

I pull out my pen and journal from my bag and place them in my lap. The voice comes over the microphone blasting its next announcement.

"Passengers, please be seated; we will be leaving the bus terminal in five minutes."

Now, that I am situated in my seat a certain calm has come over me. The chaos and all that was included being my family's keeper that once overwhelmed me is fading. I am glad I was able to get a window seat. My thoughts begin to take me places. In a matter of seconds, my mind flashes memories and gives me visions of what my future may hold. I allow the memories to fill my mind. Recalling the memories of my past make me want to cry.

I remember everyone in our neighborhood was envious of
what our family had. Willie Haywood adopted my brother
and me. He was a tall man; he had a light skin complexion,
brown eyes, and a mustache. He smoked cigars. He was a
good provider for the family. From the outside looking in,
we appeared to be a picture-perfect family. We took nice
family pictures, wore nice clothing and our mother was very

attractive. She was something nice to look at, a natural beauty. The family occasionally went to church on Sunday's. This wasn't the perfect family because the man my mother married was a monster. We were the poster family for domestic violence and abuse behind closed doors. At the age of four, I lost my innocence. I was repeatedly molested by my stepfather. The theme for my life became guilt, shame, denial of my power, lack of trust, and a closed heart. The closed heart came about because of the rape.

Some people might think Willie Haywood displayed narcissist characteristics because he was dictating how my mother should look and what she should wear in the early stages of the relationship. He did not mind my mother working but really didn't want her to work. He only started controlling her when she did not want to be a submissive wife. He was abusive verbally, and then he became abusive physically. It started with a gentle push. Then increased to a fist in the face and then he started hitting her in the mouth when she talked back. He forced himself on her sexually because he wanted to have sex all the time, and she didn't. Willie Haywood was a mean angry man because LaRosa did not disclose all of her health issues with him.

My mother was dating a man that worked at the same company as Willie Haywood. The man was always talking about my mother to him and how he enjoyed her company. The conversation spurked an interest in Willie Haywood wanting to date my mother. Since the man was dating someone else, Willie Haywood asked if he could date LaRosa. Willie Haywood told LaRosa he knew he wanted to marry her the first day they met. He picked the ring, wedding dress and made all the arrangements for the marriage. He even told her he was a man that wanted to have children. Clara Rosa didn't consent to the union because Willie Haywood was controlling prior to him asking for her hand in marriage. His ex-wife's sister came out of the cracks and begged LaRosa not to marry him because he was already a married man. The couple had a short engagement and got married quickly. The nuptials were held at her home in a small back yard ceremony. The church pastor performed the ceremony in an evening wedding with approximately 100 people in attendance.

My stepfather had been married two times. He never divorced his first wife. His second wife was upset because he was molesting his own daughter. She started treating him badly because of that behavior. My mother LaRosa was his third wife. He liked all of the woman in the neighborhood and would have dated them, but it was inappropriate. While I was outside playing in the grass, I would see him with women driving by the house every day in the light blue car. He was not a faithful man because he wanted sex all the time. In my room, I could hear the night fights. The beating, screaming, yelling, and crying. This man was a hell-raiser. This man was never pleased at the beginning of the relationship because he wanted everything he was dissatisfied. A lot of times, he was upset because LaRosa did not want to cook for him. My mother's pinky finger was practically sliced off fighting with him. The doctors were barely able to sew her finger back in place. Black eyes, busted lips. He slammed her to the floor and almost broke her neck. She wore a neck brace for almost a month. Everybody was asking her what was wrong with her. She was telling people she slipped in the kitchen and hurt herself. Willie Haywood was still living at the house. The house of abuse and the drama. He told her no one would want to be married to a woman with two children. She stayed and endured because she didn't have anywhere else to go. We were human sacrifices. Everyone has a back story, and he was abused by his father because he did not have any self-control. He was a pedophile, an abused child, and he was adopted by a family member. The family member wanted to help him but didn't realize he had so many issues stemming from his childhood.

I recall the day my mother stood up for herself. I was outside playing. The sky was blue; it was so bright outside. The pretending was over. My mother came out of the house, screaming and crying. I could see the tears falling down her face and the mucus running from her nose. The blue car was parked on the side of the street with my stepfather in the car. I saw my mother began to pull the red brick pavers from her rose and flower garden. She threw the bricks one at a time at the blue car. She busted all the windows out of the car. She was coming for him. This was my first time witnessing my mother having a nervous breakdown.

I recall my mother's psychiatric care. I recall her telling the family she hears voices and noise. Sometimes her hallucinations, schizoid personality, seeing ghost scared me. I was ashamed of her being overly medicated with pills. When my mom was crazy and not in her right state of mind, she spoke deliberately as though there were nothing wrong. It was then that she was in the right frame of mind. Her discipline usually included some sort of child abuse; fussing while whipping with tree branches and extension cords; the same as her mother. My mother had courage when she was insane, her rage blended within her courage.

I experienced embarrassing moments with her, as well. I recall my mother walking outside nude. She did manage to take her Epsom Salt and Salt Peter goddess baths through all the chaos. She made sure everything was extra clean and organized. My mother was always cleaning, washing clothes, and hanging them on the line to dry, every day. She even had the kids cleaning.

My grandmother stepped in to help the family when LaRosa was placed into the state mental institution. She wasn't sure what to do with the five children. Family mem-

bers agreed to take us, but we would have to be split up. My stepfather was not good for the family, so leaving the family was the best thing he could do. He left the family, and child support was never collected for his three children. My mother became unemployed, on welfare, collecting food stamps, and continued living in public housing.

I gathered so many golden nuggets from my mother's life. I can hear my mother's voice while I am on this bus.

"If a man is verbally and physically abusive before marriage, it's going to get worse"; "Study the men and know his history"; "A leopard doesn't change their spots"; "Get your education, make your own money and take care of yourself."

My college days were my best day away from home. Like an old movie playing, my mind wanders to the visits with my mother in the Psychiatric Hospital. Like a child playing, I remember it had been months since I'd seen my mother. She was having another episode, as my grandmother called it.

"I want to see mommy," I remember asking my grandmother.

"Your mother is not fully present in her mind and is in a long-term treatment care hospital. It might be best for you to see her when she comes home." My grandmother would try to explain.

"I want to see her." As a child, I didn't really understand anything other than my need to see my mother.

"D'Alise you're a big girl. I promise to take you to the hospital." Her answer didn't fill the void I had.

"When?" I asked, hoping it would be immediate.

"D'Alise, if you visit your mother now, you're not going to see her at her best. If you see her now, it will leave a negative impression on you."

My constant day in and day out nagging, I remember my grandmother giving in. A visit was scheduled to see my mother at the Alabama State Hospital for the insane. The facility houses fully committed patients. The main facility is part of the National Register of Historic Places. The Italianate building was designed using the Kirkbride plan and is surrounded by trees and woods. It is built on a slave plantation.

I recall the day of the visit; I was so excited. I picked red roses from my grandmother's flower garden for my mother. I drew a picture of a large sun-colored in bright yellow with a smiley face and green grass with flowers. The picture showed me standing in the middle of my grandmother and mother. My brother was on the other end, holding a ball in his hands. My cousin drove up to the front of the house to pick us up. He got out of the car and waited for us. He really supported the family throughout the years, picking us up taking us to and from the hospital. I remember him always looking very serious, but he has a good heart.

My grandmother packed lunch for each of us and had a special care package for my mother. I remember her saying, "Come on, kids let's get in the car." Off we went. My brother and I are sitting in the backseat giggling and playing. We arrive at our destination in less than thirty minutes. We enter the entrance gate, which contained two large white light towers, the security house. You can see the facility driving straight ahead; it's a huge white building. I have never seen anything like it in my life except on television. Once the car was parked, we got out and started running around. Our grandmother gave us the look, and we stood at attention. My brother and I began to whisper in each other's ear. We were really excited to see our mother.

We proceeded to follow my grandmother and cousin into the administration building and checked in. The ceilings were high. We walked down a long hallway. The walls were white. No pictures or decorations were on the walls. We passed doors with square portals to view patients. The nurse with a white uniform and a big white hat escorted us the private visitor's unit. We stood at the entry. I saw what appeared to be my mother in a wheelchair facing the window looking outside. I hid behind my grandmother and held the hem of her skirt. The roses and picture I held dropped to the floor.

My mother had one of her episodes and was heavily sedated. The nurse goes to the window to turn my mother towards us. She didn't recognize us. I picked up my roses and my picture from the floor. I ran over to give them to my mother and wrapped my arms around her. Her body was lifeless. One small tiny teardrop trailed down the right side of her face. I kissed the tear and tasted the salty liquid on her face. I let go, slowly gliding backward with my arms stretched out they fell limp. I moved to the back of the room and sat in the bolted-down chair. My brother stood behind me, waiting with my grandmother for his turn. They asked if I was okay and reached to console me.

"I am okay" My reply was barely audible. My cousin was sitting patiently waiting for us to enjoy the tender reunion with our mother.

"D'Alise would you like to sit with me." He asked without reason. I told him no as I looked around the visitation room into the open area and observed all the patients wearing long draping ponchos. The room sure had a lot of activity. One patient was crawling on the floor. Another was seated driving an imaginary car. I even noticed one person sitting alone, having a conversation with two invisible people. A female was laying on the couch, clutching herself in the fetal position.

I recall one visit when my grandmother requested to view the sleeping quarters. My mother's private room was all white. The walls were padded with a large secured window. There was a single bed and a hard mattress with no headboard. The bed was covered with white sheets and a pillow.

My mother was placed in psychiatric hospitals many times voluntarily, and in many other cases, involuntarily. The state wanted to permanently commit her, that's a death sentence without committing a crime. The only crime she committed was marrying and staying with an abusive man. My grandmother fought to keep her out the system.

My thoughts continue as the bus makes its way on the open road. I began to think of all the generations that have dealt with incest.

My mother let this man come into our home and left him alone with her innocent children. Our lives will never, never, ever, be the same. As a thief in the night steals the innocence, Willie Haywood is the monster. He proved that much in the night. He came for me each night, placing his hands over my mouth. No one heard my cries or screams in the house. He would lean into me to cover my mouth with his hands. I remember him towering over my four-year-old body. I can imagine he has done this a lot of times to someone else. One hand over the mouth to shield the screams and the other hand removing the tiny underwear. He took his hand to his mouth to wet his fingers. He inserts them in my vagina, massaging and stimulating me. He later inserts his long penis inside me. I remember my fear, where is the God in the house of darkness? Where is my mother? I recall this dark night with no soul coming for me repeatedly each night. He gets straight to his business. I was left in the bed after being stripped of my virginity. Leaving home, I realize the reasons I've left. Now grown I've given this some thought. Wasn't my mother enough for him? Maybe she wasn't present with all the abuse, maybe she was in denial. After all, she was blind to her abuse. Maybe she couldn't see me being hurt. Is he washing the sheets and pillowcases to hide his sins? I remember her telling us Willie Haywood beat her and my brother but never harmed me. I could only close my eyes and wonder, really?

I remember late at night I heard background noise, the sound of fussing and fighting. I heard my mother sobbing and questioning, "What are you doing to my child?"

I remember thinking, "Finally!" But as quickly as the thought passed through my young mind, I heard the demon's response.

"Stop it right now! Are you accusing me of something? You're crazy. I am a good man. I take care of you and your two children. Your mother kicked you out of her house because you had two children out of wedlock. You should be happy to have a man like me." I heard my mother crying in the background. "I am taking good care of you and your bastard children." If only he knew LaRosa was kicked out of her mother's home because she wasn't respecting her mother's house rules.

I felt as if I was the pawn. My mother gave me to my stepfather. I wish she would have stood up for my brother and me. We really needed to be protected. She didn't have the courage to leave. She stayed for security, but he treated her so badly. He had no respect for our family. I realize now when she was having her episodes of mental illness, she wasn't present. All these thoughts, as I sit on this bus. I chose this window seat.

I smile now. *"Thank you, God. Finally."* I get to leave the unpleasant neighbors in Kenzie Lane Apartments. That apartment was different than where my grandmother lived. The apartments were lined up in one single row, connected closely and had numbers like 1A, 1B, 1C, and 1D. The red brick complex had mixed finances for, public housing, Section 8 and low-income residents. The facility was located on the bus line, had an office, maintenance men, recreation center, auditorium, and a playground. The three-bedroom apartment had a living room, kitchen, one bathroom, closets, and a utility closet. The front porch, yard and back yard were small and contained a clothesline for hanging clothing. The compound was nice. Married working-class individuals lived there with their children. They even had cars. They didn't stay there long. They would later move out to purchase their own homes and land. You can't be angry with a person for wanting to better themselves. They moved on. That's what I am doing moving on.

I am thankful for those protected angels Yogi and Mary. I will miss the good neighbors and will forever cherish their friendship. They supported me through elementary, junior high, high school, and college. I hope LaRose is doing well and recovers from her episodes.

Just as I pause in thought, I can see that the passengers are finally settled in their seats. There is a man placing the last suitcase overhead for the lady sitting next to him. The driver is standing at his seat, looking down the aisle. He lifts the microphone as he takes his place in the driver's seat. The microphone sounds with his message before our departure.

"Good morning, ladies and gentlemen, my name is Greg, and I will be your bus driver for the duration of your trip. It's an eight hour and fifteen-minute ride to Louisiana. We will make a few stops on the way...ALL ABOARD; We're headed out now."

As we are departing, I take the time to notice the little things which I don't usually do. As I look out the window, I notice the restaurants, gas stations, trees, vehicles, dogs, and cats. I realize I have been taking these small things for granted every day. We're passing through small towns, rural construction, open fields and farms.

As we pass the farm, I think about the time my grandmother told me she and her husband owned a farm. The USDA trained them on procedures for farming. I am grateful for having the experience of eating organic food all my life. I didn't necessarily like getting up working the land, but it taught me discipline. We've been riding a while, and I am still focused on the view comparing the newness to what I've known over the years. The bus begins to slow down as we approach an exit on the highway. The click of the microphone silences the whispers throughout the bus.

"We're stopping in Biloxi, Mississippi. You can get something to eat, freshen up, and use the bathroom."

I place my pen and journal in my seat, hoping no one will move it or take my seat. I stand and wait as other passengers are making their way to the front of the bus. Just as I get closer to the front, a passenger gets out of their seat and blocks the aisle. Taking her time, she reaches into a bag in the overhead bin.

"Excuse me, I would like to pass." I sigh, waiting for her to move.

"Give me a minute to get my earplugs from my bag. You can pass now, lady."

Her response seems to suggest that I and the passengers behind me are annoying her. I realize this move will show me a lot of differences. I simply respond, "Thanks." The driver is standing at the door, assisting passengers off the stairs.

"Ma'am. Watch your step going down." He reaches for my hand to assist my steps. I get off the bus wide-eyed reading the sign on the building ahead.

Chapter 3

The Bus Ride

"Let me get that door for you." A passenger from behind hurries to the entrance of the bus terminal.

"Thank you," I replied, now thinking about the slight rumble in my stomach. I am thinking about my grandmother's packed lunch and decide I will get a sandwich at the deli where a small line has formed. I'm next in line, and I have finally made up my mind to call home and give a destination report.

"Hi, I would like to order a turkey sandwich and a glass of water with lemon. Can you cut that in half and give me change for the payphone?"

The man looks up from the receipt where he was writing the order. He gives an abrupt but courteous "Yes, next."

"Thanks for the change. I'll be back in a few minutes." I interrupt his concentration only for a moment. He gave me the change and returns to the next customer. I saw the phone when I entered the deli. I was glad I'd have a moment to give my grandmother my travel update. I dial the number. As the phone rings I turn so I can watch the counter for my order to be called. I recognize the "Hello" and spoke quickly.

"Hi, grandmother, I am in Biloxi, Mississippi." I waited for her to be as excited as I was.

"How is your bus ride going?" She asks. Her voice is filled with more concern than excitement.

"It's good. How are you and the family?" Everyone would know by now that I have left.

"We miss you already. I remember the first time I took you on the bus." I don't have the time to join her on memory lane. I want her to keep it short, so I won't miss home.

"The next time you see LaRosa tell her hello for me. I hope she is recovering well. I got to go. I need to call John and his wife." I know she'll understand my reason to hurry.

"Goodbye, baby. We love you." I hang up and pick up the receiver again, and there's the sound of the dial tone. I dialed John's number. I wait as the connection is made and the phone rings.

"Hi, John. I am checking in. I am in Biloxi, Mississippi. I should arrive in New Orleans Louisiana at 6:00 p.m."

"Okay, little cousin. We'll be at the bus station to pick you up." We say our goodbyes, and I hang up the phone. I go to the bathroom before returning to the counter.

"Your order is ready," I ask for it to be wrapped and packaged to go. I express my thanks and return to the bus.

I board the bus hoping my sandwich will be as good as it smells. A melodic male voice interrupts my thoughts. He is standing in the aisle right before my seat when he speaks to me.

"Ma am. You missed a couple of bus stops. I saw your head resting up against the window. I am watching out for you. If you sleep when we arrive in New Orleans Louisiana, I will wake you up. I promise."

I had a thought, mixed with questions, "Who are you; Why are you?" But I couldn't be rude. I answered, "You are so kind. Thank you for looking out for me."

"You have an exotic look." My face gives a response to which he instantly replied. "I mean that in a good way. You are beautiful. Did you model?"

I am a little shocked that he would know that by looking at me. I feel uplifted a bit as I answer proudly, "I've modeled in college and did a few commercials. Nothing professional. I have acquaintances, both male and female, that have professionally modeled with Ebony Fashion Fair. One of my best friends from college does the makeup for the models."

"What are you mixed with?" He brings my attention back to the immediate topic, me.

"Why do you assume I am mixed with something?" Again, I am curious about his questions. Never has anyone asked me about my background. His attention gives a reason for many details others just never cared about.

"Seriously, I just want to know. It's something about your facial features."

"Just my parent's DNA. A little of everything African, Spanish, French, Korean, Italian, and Indian. It's a big melting pot." I notice the aisle is filling quickly with passengers. "I need to get back to my seat. The passengers behind me are patiently waiting to board the bus."

Undisturbed by the line of passengers behind me, he formally introduces himself.

"By the way, my name is Greg." Greg extends his hand, and I extend mine. A proper greeting, I'm impressed by his ways.

"Nice to meet you, Greg. I'm Danielle Alise James. You can call me D'Alise. I'm going to take a seat now. Can I have my hand back?"

He smiles and releases the gentle hold. "Certainly."

"Wow, he was nice! I love his smile and those pearly whites. A little too old for me." At this time, I just want to eat my sandwich. No further thought is given to Greg or the attention he's given me.

I prop my head up against the window, take out my pen and journal. I begin to jot a few goals in life: Changing my Alabama identification over to Louisiana a driver's license; a job; apartment or house; a church; studying the Bible; save; purchase an economy car; look out for family; have a nice boyfriend; get married and have one or two children. I want to show my cousin and his spouse gratitude. I would like to get hired as a federal employee or work at a television station or even be a buyer for a major retail store. I want to obtain a real estate license and even write a book. I'll go back to school one day to get my master's degree. I can't let this opportunity pass me. The next announcement came over the intercom, and I recognize the voice immediately. All I can do is smile.

"Good Evening, this is Greg, we'll be arriving in the New Orleans bus terminal in ten minutes. Please gather your personal items and prepare to exit the bus."

The darkness of night is beginning to fall, and the bus was parked. I must have been tired. I dozed off between the announcement and our arrival.

"D'Alise, wake-up. You're in New Orleans and the last person on the bus. Welcome to the 'Big Easy.'"

"Hmm…uh, Greg." I was still adjusting myself, barely awake but thankful. "Thank you so much for looking out for me."

"I know I just met you. This might be a little forward, but I would love to get to know you better. When I first saw you, I felt something. You're probably about twenty-two. I'm older than you, but I'd like to make a connection with you. I know you think this guy is crazy. I must take this chance otherwise; I know I'll regret this the rest of my life. I'm an honest, hard-working guy. You're running away from something; why don't you run to me?"

"Greg, hold up stop. You're moving one hundred miles per hour. Can you take it down to fifteen miles per hour? You sure do have good intuition. You are correct with all your assumptions. My cousin invited me here to start a new life."

I can't help myself, why I don't know. I never met anyone that I felt as comfortable with as I do in this moment. If he is playing a game, I'll play along.

"Why don't you start your life with me? Give me two numbers for you. I don't ever want to lose contact with you."

"Greg, you're scary but okay. I like your smile and pearly whites." I gave him both my grandmother's and cousin's number.

I look him over. He wasn't a bad looking guy, and I didn't really know what I expected other than him being nice. Greg seemed to fill my concerns.

"I know I don't look like much driving this bus in this uniform." Once again, his intuition was correct.

"Greg, I never judge a book by its cover. It's what's in the heart. That's all that matters." His smile is warm. I have a good feeling about him.

"You feel this connection also. I promise not to disappoint you. I've never been married. I have no children. I don't drink, smoke, or do drugs. I'm just looking for a good, trustworthy woman to settle down with. D'Alise you are the one I've been waiting for all my life. I am a virgin."

"Greg. Too much information." This guy knows exactly what he wants. I respect his honesty. He's moving too fast for me, though.

"I finished medical school and completed my residency training. I have a career. I am driving this bus while I am on vacation to help me with my social skills. My grandmother lives in the garden district. We live in the same house. I help look after her. My parents live in California and are both doctors. I have an older sister who's a prosecutor in New York. She's married with two children."

"Well, I would have never thought you had a problem with social skills."

"Greg, since we are being honest, let me share a few things with you. I am the first-generation college graduate in my family. My family is dirt poor. I come from nothing. I don't drive or own a car. As a matter of fact, I don't have a driver's license. I paid my way through college. I worked two jobs and helped with supporting my family. I carried sixteen to eighteen class credits each semester. I have a student loan that's due to be paid off. I've had some bad childhood experiences. I sat on this bus today and wrote out my business plan for my life."

"Can you incorporate me in that plan? That's okay you had those experiences. I want to help you work it out. You're someone I can fall deeply in love with."

"He can't be for real."

"Oh, so you believe in the love at first sight? That stuff is an illusion. I see my cousin and his wife. I must go."

"Let me help you. Stop, running." He is pleading, and I'm not ready to figure him out."

"Goodbye, Greg. This is too much and fast for me."

I get off the bus and don't look back. Greg is still talking.

"Stop running."

Just across the parking lot are my cousin and his wife. They're looking in the other direction. I guess they thought I would be coming out of that terminal. John turns and greets me with a smile and a hug.

"Hey, cousin. We were looking for you."

"Yeah. I was on the bus. The bus driver was talking to me. How are you?"

"We are good. Is he the one you were talking to? Cousin, you spent all that time in college and didn't pull yourself a husband. You picked up a common bus driver."

His laughter is contagious and funnier than the joke he thought he has told.

"Oh, John, you got jokes. That's okay because I decided early in college, I wasn't going to be known for dating a lot of guys on campus. If I date someone on campus, I normally won't date anyone else. That was my rule."

"Look, he's coming over here. Cousin, have you ever considered dating outside your race?"

"I never thought about it." *"What is he thinking about?"*

"He looks like he might be biracial or mixed with something."

"I don't see that at all. I don't care. Why is Greg coming this way?"

"Ma'am you left your pin and journal on the bus." Greg stood, waiting to be introduced.

"Thank you. John and Linda, this is Greg."

"Nice to meet you. I'll be happy to help you get your luggage to your car. I am off now."

I open my mouth to speak only to be interrupted by Linda's shocking comment. I stand stunned, watching Linda's actions.

"Girl let that man help you get your luggage to the car. My husband needs to keep his back strong for tonight. Greg, yes dear, please be a darling and help the young lady get her luggage to the car. The white 1984 BMW 325E Sport-Coupe parked in the space belongs to us. D'Alise here are the keys walk over there with him to show him where to place your luggage."

I could hear my cousin and his wife in the background giggling. *Wow, Linda is something else.*

"Greg, I don't know how to use the remote," I admit I am totally embarrassed.

"Do you mind if I take the keys to show you how to open the trunk?" I hand him the keys trying to keep my composure. Greg adds to my embarrassment by giving me instructions. Me, the country girl. I hate being needy.

"Just press the button here, and the trunk will release." Greg pushes the button, and the trunk pops open. He looks at me with his pearly whites flashing.

"It's a lot I don't know."

Stick with me baby; I'll expose you to this melting pot of French, African, and American culture. The city has round-the-clock nightlife. The live jazz music is off the chain. If you love seafood, this is the place to be. It's seasoned well and spicy. I speak French and Spanish and will be your translator."

Just like that, he changes the mood. I feel at ease again and begin to rattle off what I knew. It wasn't much, but I am proud of the little I do know. Greg seems so worldly.

"Oh my God, really? I speak Spanish and a little French. I took Spanish in high school. I picked up on my French by listening to my mother around the house when she was there."

Greg is truly a gentleman. He listens to my shortlist of knowledge and then gives me what he hopes will be our next encounter.

"You've had a long bus ride. I am going to let you get back to your family and get some rest. I would like to call you and take you on a date tomorrow. My parents will be in town in a few days. I want you to meet them.”

“Greg, you move fast.”

“Baby, I’ve been by myself for a long time. All I’ve been doing is studying. I see you, and I want you to be mine before these vultures get hold of you. Will you go out with me tomorrow?”

I sighed, not wanting the opportunity to go out, slip away. “Ah. I don’t know what to say.”

Linda and John approach the car as Linda answers for me. They must have been listening as they got closer. I didn’t notice them getting near.

“Greg, Greg, Yes. She’ll go out with you. Here’s our address. What time will you be picking her up?”

The conversation is no longer between Greg and me. Linda sure has a way of stepping in.

“What about 5:00 p.m.?”

“Okay. I will have her ready for you.” I’m no longer shocked. I don’t know whether to be mad or not. Maybe not, I do want to check Mr. Greg out.

“Here’s my business card. I am going to write my parents and grandmothers contact number on the back of the card. I look forward to getting to know you. By the way, my last name is Thibodeaux. Goodbye. It was nice meeting you all.”

Linda starts in with the questions. She’s giving pointers, or so she thinks she is.

“What are you thinking? Yes. Yes. Yes, to everything. He likes you. Take the blinders off and open your eyes. Wow, D’Alise he is smiting over you. What did you do? What did you say?”

I hadn’t said much. Like Linda, Greg did all the talking. I answer her hoping she’ll let it go. “Nothing much.” John joins his wife, giving her a few of my past experiences.

“Cuz has always had the guys chasing her. She’s the honeybee, but she’s clueless. She didn’t start dating until she went off to college. Wifey, you’re going to have to school her to the game. I’m leaving in a few days for a little over 30 days. You can get her up to speed. Let's head out so we can get across the Westbank Bridge. We're not taking the ferry today."

I take notice of the BMW they own. It's beautiful. I feel up-lifted again. I'm really a big girl now.

"Let me get the door for you, ladies." John opens both the front and back door, waiting for us to get in.

"Thanks Hubby."

"Thanks Cousin."

He enters on the driver's side and puts the car in gear. The engine's silence impresses me. I've only been in cars where you have to speak up when you start the car. I can hear John clearly as he puts the car in drive, and we leave the terminal.

"Little cousin, this seems like a decent guy. Relax, and let go of all those rules and self-limiting beliefs you have. You've never had to try. You show up, and the men accommodate you. You've missed many opportunities. Show up and be present. Okay?"

"Yes, John." He is older and wiser about such things. I listen and hope they don't think I don't appreciate their help.

"My wife is going to hook you up. She's just a year older than you. She hooked me. I am close to ten years older than her. I wasn't thinking about getting married."

I haven't been in New Orleans an hour, and John has me pre-paring for marriage. That is on my list, but there are other things I've listed ahead of marriage. I change the topic hoping we can leave the matchmaking out for now.

"Cousin, this car is something. This car has everything. Black leather interior, a power sunroof, power-windows, power-locks, power mirrors, sport-seats, an on-board computer, air conditioning, leather steering wheel, AM/FM radio and alloy wheels. I've checked this model out. When I start working, I am going to get me a Toyota Corolla and work my way up to a luxury vehicle. Grandma's, old black antique has nothing on this car."

"Why is she still holding on to that car? I know she inherited the car from her husband. The car has been sitting in her driveway for years. She doesn't have a driver's license, nor does she drive.

She could get a lot of money for that car. She doesn't realize the value in the car."

John didn't understand the things our grandma valued. There were antiques within the home as well. She wouldn't part with any of them.

"Maybe, she does realize the value that's why she is holding on to it."

"She needs to let it go. Back to you, young lady. I want you to look classy tomorrow not trashy. Aunt LaRosa always had a classy Jackie O' look. You are the spitting image of her. I'll show my wife a few pictures of her, so she'll have an idea of how to present you."

The diversion is short-lived. I wonder if this is what he had in mind by inviting me. *Hook me up with a husband and take a bow?* I answer reluctantly, but I do want him to know I appreciate this opportunity.

Yes, Cousin. LaRosa always encouraged me to look natural. We can use minor enhancements such as face powder, mascara, and lipstick, that should be enough. I want to be presented as a real woman. I don't want to be presented as having any substance and only being an illusion with fake stuff. I have a little black dress that fits in all the right places.

My comment was ignored. *I hope this is going in the right direction.* Linda turns in her seat smiling as she speaks.

"I can't wait to hook you up. We're going to get your hair straighten and trimmed so it will flow when you walk."

I feel a little excited. A make-over that should have been on my list.

"Linda, I can't wait for you to work your magic. This is something I always imagined. Is auburn your natural hair color?"

"Yes."

"It goes well with your complexion."

We talk a bit about hair color, makeup, and fashion. The traffic on the bridge is slow, and John moves from lane to lane to get across the bridge as quick as he can. We make a few turns before pulling into a parking space at the apartment complex.

"Okay. Ladies we have finally made it across the bridge. This is my parking space. Let's get the luggage and head upstairs. We need to get rest and prepare for tomorrow."

Linda pitches in to help, and I do too. John can't carry it all and open the door.

"Baby give us some of those bags."

"Let me find my keys so I can open the door. D'Alise reach your hands in my side pocket and pass me my door keys."

The apartment complex is quiet. The lot is filled with other cars. I can only guess how many families live in the neighborhood. I reach in John's pocket and find the keys. He opens the door slowly.

"You guys have a lovely apartment."

"Thanks." Linda begins to explain the living arrangements.

"We're going to be moving to a two-bedroom apartment. You'll get to have your own room. You'll be sleeping on the sofa temporary until we move. When John is traveling, we can share the king-size bed. Whatever you decide. Let me show you around." I get the impression my cousin wasn't really prepared for me to stay a long time because I will be sleeping on their nice sofa.

We walk through the apartment, which is bigger than most one-bedroom apartments.

"This is the living room, the kitchen, here is the bedroom and this bathroom. You can store your luggage and clothing in this closet. Make yourself at home."

"Let me give you the money I made from the summer," I remembered what my grandmother said about paying my way. I didn't want them to think of me as a burden. I reach in my luggage to get the money.

"No. We just want to help you."

"Can I use the phone to let grandmother know I'm at your house?"

"Sure."

I saw the phone on the end table in the living room as Linda gave me the mini-tour. I know my grandmother will be waiting for my call. The phone rings and I am happy, and I want her to be happy for my arrival.

"Hello, Grandmother. I'm here with John and Linda. I made it safely. They were at the bus terminal waiting for me."

"Tell them, I say hello." I can't express my excitement.

"Grandmother says hello. Do you guys want to speak to her?" I extend the receiver to give it to John or Linda.

"No. We will speak to her another day." My excitement is not contagious, but I guess traveling long distance is a usual thing for my cousin and his wife.

"I love you, baby." My grandmother's voice is distant. I can't tell if she's surprised, I made it or upset I left. There was nothing left to say. I'll talk to her later.

"Goodbye, grandmother."

"If you're hungry there's pizza in the refrigerator otherwise, let's get ready for bed."

I notice Linda has put sheets and a blanket neatly folded on the couch for my use.

"Goodnight." There would be no further conversation to-night. They left for their bedroom and closed the door behind them.

Linda is one year older than me and running things like a boss. I've never lived on my own where I was the head of the household. I attended Upward Bound in the summertime and had college roommates my freshman and sophomore years. Those were all single-room dorms. I ran LaRosa James' house when she wasn't present much of the time. Some of my college friends had their own apartments. I moved back home after my sophomore year to help around the house. I am really a big girl now. Once I get a good job, I'll have my own apartment.

Chapter 4

A New Start

It's Saturday morning at about 8:00 a.m. everyone is still sleeping, it is quiet. You cannot hear a pin drop; unlike at grandmother house, you can smell the food cooking and hear the gospel music on the radio. I decide to get up to wash my face with the soap that smells like lemons. I brush my teeth with my favorite pink toothbrush, cinnamon toothpaste, and baking soda. The baking soda helps to keep the teeth white. I am attracted to men with good dental hygiene.

I turn the faucets on and fill the bathtub with the running water. I add a foaming bubble bath. I enjoyed playing in the bubbles. After I finish my bath, I dry off and place the used towels in the hamper. I'm making that conscious effort to take care of what is given to me for my use. I dress myself in the clothes I laid out the previous night. A habit from childhood, I never let go. Once dressed, I enter the kitchen to see what I could cook for the family. My grandmother would normally greet me with a warm smile in the morning "Good Morning Danielle Alise James" and give me a hug. I am a big girl now; I get to do this on my own. I am going to cook eggs, bacon, grits, and biscuits and serve Linda and John, a tall glass of orange juice.

It took only a moment to find the utensils and the pans I needed. All the food was in the refrigerator waiting for the cook to prepare the meal. I am more than content with the preparation and the completed cuisine. I wait to hear if anyone is stirring. I found the serving trays and set them up, each with a napkin, fork, and knife on their plates and glass of juice. I am proud of my first breakfast as I make my way to the bedroom door. I knock, balancing the trays, waiting for a response.

"Come in." They look at me as they raise on their elbows from their bed.

"Good Morning. I made breakfast for you. Here's some eggs, bacon, grits, biscuits and orange juice. Maybe, we can discuss the house rules today, so I will be clear of what you expect. Enjoy your breakfast. I'm going to sit at the table and eat my small plate of food. Bye."

I didn't think twice about the conversation the night before until Linda spoke.

"We must discuss your look for tonight."

I am unsure whether to be excited or worried. I allowed my thoughts to speak what I dared not say. *"I am new to the city and get to go on my first date fresh off the bus."*

I take my time, enjoying the meal and my new environment. Cousin John has given me a chance, and I won't ruin it. I prepare the dishwater to clean the dishes as I wait for their dishes from the bedroom. The phone rings, and I hear John say, 'hello.'

"Cousin, you have a phone call, can you pick the phone up in the living room?"

Excited, I think it's my grandmother checking on me or maybe another family member wanting to know how my travel has been.

"Good morning. Hello, this is D'Alise."

I hear his voice and can hardly believe that he's calling me this early. This is my sign that I am a big girl, and I can handle this without being giddy.

"Good morning, baby, this is Greg. I wanted to hear your sweet voice this morning. I hope you slept well last night. I can't stop thinking about you. Girl you on my mind. I'm calling to confirm our date for tonight. I have a nice dinner planned for us. I want you to wear something super sexy. Afterward, I want you to meet some of my colleagues. I want to show you off. They've never seen me on a date because all I do is study. I'll be picking you up at five. I can't wait to look into your brown eyes, gaze at your silky skin, and touch your bronze hands again."

"Greg, you sure do talk a mad game. Where do you find the words? You're a real flirt."

"D'Alise, baby, when you meet the one, the correct words fall in place. I want to stimulate your mind without ever being intimate with you. I want to stimulate you without ever touching your body. I just want to whisper sweet words in your ears. This is my gift to you baby. This is perfect timing."

"Greg, see you tonight." I can't say anything that wouldn't make me laugh. I giggle and tell him, 'goodbye."

I am feeling emotional right now. My hormones are raging. *Let me open the freezer door.* I should finish cleaning up the kitchen, so I can take my mind off this guy. About thirty minutes later, the doorbell rings followed by a knock at the door.

"John and Linda, someone is at the door. Is it ok for me to answer?" I really don't know if I should. They haven't come out of the room to see, and John casually answers.

"Sure, go ahead."

I open the door only wide enough to see flowers. I open it wider so the delivery person can speak.

"Hi, ma'am. I have a floral delivery for D'Alise James. Will you sign for it?"

"Yes. Let me place them on the table. The bouquet is beautiful." I return to the door and sign where there is an x. "Here's my signature."

John yells from the bedroom. "Cousin, who was that at the door?"

"Come see. I have a bouquet of stargazer lilies, red roses, red mini carnations, white freesias, white tuberoses, and accents of baby-breathe." I am so excited. This is too much for me before ten in the morning. Both Linda and John enter the living room. We stand together and stare. We are in awe.

"John, go back to bed. I need to work my magic on your cousin." He doesn't give her a second thought and leaves us with the floral arrangement. Linda is looking at me as though she is confused. I touch my face. I can't imagine what she's looking at.

"Your eye color has changed to hazel; they were brown yesterday."

I'm relieved. This has happened a few times in my life. "Yes. I have mood eyes just like my mother. They change colors depending on how I feel."

"Already? You are something special D'Alise. Let's see what you got in that footlocker. You have some nice clothes. That little black dress will work. I want you to wear the black open toe four-inch heels with the dress. Later, I'll have you purchase eight-inch heels for something else. You should wear thongs with the dress."

I'm looking at her the way she was looking at me a moment ago. "What is that?"

"D'Alise, a thong is a type of underwear you wear to eliminate panty lines and bulges under tight clothing. When you're wearing them under your clothes, you feel sexy. Have you ever been to Victoria Secrets?

"No."

She pauses for a moment in thought. "Let me get dressed, and we'll go to Victoria Secrets to purchase you a thong today."

She left me to finish the dishes John brought out the room. Linda is ready in about twenty minutes, plenty of time for me to finish cleaning the kitchen.

"John. We're headed out do you need me to pick anything up for you?" After his response, we head out the door. Linda seems relieved John didn't want anything. Once we get seated in the car, I remember my life's plans.

"Linda, thank you so much for helping me. I need to find a job, so I can get my own apartment." She didn't seem fazed by my remark.

"My relatives have stayed with us. Your cousin only comes home once a month. You won't be in our way. We'll give you a year to get yourself together. Greg is bringing it correctly. He's setting the standard for the men you will be dating." I just listened.

I didn't want her to think I didn't know what she was talking about. "I need to stop and get some gas. You go in to pay the cashier."

I've never pumped gas before, but I know how to pay for it. "Hi Sir, I need to pay for gas on pump #2."

"That will be $20.00. What's your name?"

"My name is D'Alise," I answer without giving his question a second thought.

"I'm David, and I manage this service station. Are you relative to the lady on pump #2?"

"She's married to my cousin." My answer is short. Just as I thought. *"Always a motive"* "Nice to meet you. Bye." The sun was reaching its height as it would soon be noon. Linda was at the pump.

"Linda, here's your change."

"I forgot to ask you to purchase some cigarettes. I'll go in and pay for them."

I watch from the car. I could tell the conversation is friendly; they're both smiling. Linda waves bye to the manager as she leaves. She's carrying a bag too big for just cigarettes. I sit back in the seat. Linda will definitely talk about his flirting, I'm sure.

"Hey, D'Alise the guy likes you. I didn't have to pay for the cigarettes. I picked up a few groceries while I was in the store. Girl, you are my lucky charm. I didn't have to pay for anything. He told me to bring you back the next time I need gas. He wants to take you out on a date."

"I am not attracted to him. I didn't even notice him."

"You're not open. You don't know what a man will do for you. You are the type of woman that doesn't have to do nothing a man just wants you on his arm. You need to date as many people as you can. Take whatever they want to give you. Your time is money.

"I wasn't raised that way." My grandmother's words are repeating in my head as she's talking.

"When you get old you need to have something to show for your time. When men get tired of you, they move on to the next thing. When I married your cousin, I gave up all my devious ways because he loves me. He is a traditional man. He likes his smokes, drink, and alcohol. I am down with him. I'm his ride or die. He chose me."

I can't believe she's telling me this. My mother and grandmother did briefly talk to me about this when I was young. She continues talking comfortably as though she had taught the topic in a class. I listen closely.

"The man is supposed to choose you. You never choose the man or call him. When he chooses you, he gets the prize? You see, Greg is choosing you. He doesn't have all that drama with him. He asked us if he could call you, that's respect. It's not about the sex either. A man can get and have sex with anybody; all us ladies got holes. At the end of the day, it's about personality. A man up and changes on women because he's tired of the personality.

"My mother said don't ask a man for nothing he already knows what he wants to do for you."

"True. Your cousin bought me a house down in the country. We're letting my sister live in the house because we like living in the city. These women are walking around demanding men pay their bills like gold diggers."

"My bother said if a woman can't pay her own house note and car note she shouldn't have those things. That's why I am on public transportation until I can pay my way."

I understood some things that my mother, grandmother, and brother told me. Linda was teaching me something different. I keep trying to put the lessons together as she talks.

"Sometimes, a man wants to bless you. Take the blessing and be thankful, especially if you didn't ask for nothing. Greg comes from good stock he wants to bless you."

"Some men use their money as control. They'll give you something in return for something. They will want to take it all back in the end."

"Always keep a stash and make purchases in your name. Pay the large bills with your money. Let men take you out for entertainment, buy you stuff. When they give you money, put it in the bank and make real investments that are going to add value to your life."

As she speaks, she's driving. I can tell she's really given this plan she has a try. We've passed houses, stores, and places that I can't pay attention to. I'm listening closely and watching the road. I wonder if she sees the lights changing. The car slows down and comes to a stop at the red light. She's still talking.

"You got to over-deliver. Date with no agenda, it indicates you have high standards. Don't be afraid to express your preferences. Show passion by keeping that body tight. Don't be the same way all the time, be spontaneous D'Alise. Bring unique positive experiences to the relationship and in your life. Mix it up in the bedroom in a classy way, not a nasty way. You got to be a good actress to walk away with the academy award when it comes to a man. Hey girl, then you'll get those guys that are proper trading like they got something to give. They'll be trying to get close to you."

I look out the window. Linda is talking as though I'm in training to be a call girl. My grandmother, mother, and even my brother didn't mean this type of attraction to men. I know they didn't. Linda's conversation was getting me ready for life.

"Listen, pay attention. These men are telling you what they're about upfront. I pray you, and Greg can be together. You're going to have pretty children. Let's run in Victoria Secrets so you can purchase your thong for your date."

She parked the car. We enter the store, and I try not to look shocked. There are all kind of panties, thongs, lingerie, and perfumes. They have a fitting room with a lady to help you pick whatever you want. I watch the other women filling their baskets with fancy selections. I could only imagine what Linda's dresser is filled with. She smiles and hands me a few pieces to try on.

The camisole is so soft. I love the feel of the material against my body. I try on a few of the items Linda selected. I love them all. Victoria Secrets is my new store for undergarments. I walk out of the dressing room and see Linda picking through the thongs displayed in the center of the store. All sizes, colors, and types. Some with sequins, feathers, and other decorations. Everything in the store is worth the purchase. *I am a big girl.*

"I am purchasing the strappy black thong, it's so feminine. What do you think about me wearing red lipstick to set off my dress?"

I smiled as I held up the thong for her approval. I loved shopping, and now I had a good reason.

Chapter 5

A New Start Continues

"Yes, you're going to be runway ready tonight. Let's hurry home so I can wash, blow and flat iron your hair. While you're out tonight, I have something romantic planned for John. I made a purchase when you were in the fitting room. Don't rush home."

I was sure Linda was totally in charge of John and me. There was nothing to say. She wanted me to be perfect for the evening. I didn't want her to think I wasn't grateful. Now I had another opportunity before me. After all, dating and getting married was on my list.

We made a few stops on the way. Nothing exciting but Linda showed me a few stores she shopped in. We were gone for a few hours, but it felt like the entire day had passed us by.

"John, we're back home. Are you ready for lunch?" Linda moves quickly putting down the bags from Victoria Secrets and walking toward the bedroom. She stops waiting for his answer through the closed bedroom door.

"No. Do what you need to do. I am resting."

"Okay baby." Linda turns and looks at me. "I'm glad your hair is relaxed. Otherwise, we would have needed to start early this morning. Trust me, you are in good hands. I am a licensed cosmetologist. This reminds me of the days when I had my own hair salon. I styled hair and rented chairs to hairstylists. Oh, by the way, thank you for preparing breakfast for us.

"It was my pleasure. Do you miss being in a salon?"

"I still have clients. I travel to them by car, and they pay me well. I have a package agreement set-up that covers my gas, mileage, a flat hourly rate of seventy-five dollars. The shampooing, cutting, styling is broken down into a separate fee. You see, I have all my professional supplies."

I follow her to the closet, where she pulls out a few plastic totes. They are filled with hair products and supplies. She puts the products that she needs on the kitchen table. She has all the items I've seen in the professional hair salons in the apartment.

"Your cousin is gone a lot because of his job. Styling hair occupies my time on the weekend. I have a regular nine to five with paid medical benefits and vacation time. I'm a sales agent for a tourist company plus, I get bonus checks. The business is good when all the tourist come to this city. It's always good to have different streams of income. You can't just depend on one job, one thing, a husband or any men. Your cousin and I are doing well. We don't need anything from you. He has helped me support my family. When family is having a hard time, we cover the expenses of our property in the country."

"I can't wait to start working and making my own money."

She gathers all the products and puts them in a smaller tote.

"I am going to set everything up in the bathroom. I'll call you when I am ready for you."

I sit down and then think about my journal. I need to put a few notes about my arrival and my hectic morning on the next few pages. It isn't long before Linda tells me she's ready.

"You can come on in now. Here, let me put this black shampoo cape around your body. I am going to wash your hair in the sink; I will be using a shampoo spray hose to rinse your hair. You can have a seat on the stool. Humm, I'll explain everything as I go along. I have a selection of shampoos, coconut, apple and pear, lavender rosemary, eucalyptus, and honey. How do you want your hair to smell for your date tonight?"

I pick them up one after the other and sniff.

"I can't decide between the coconut and the apple pear. They all smell too good to put on my hair. I want to eat the apple pear."

"Either one is good. When Greg, smells your hair he's going to want to eat you."

I can only laugh as I imagine this man going crazy over the smell of the shampoo.

"Stop! Linda put the apple pear on my hair."

"Let's get started. First, I'm going to rinse your hair thoroughly with warm water."

The warm water on my scalp feels good. It's relaxing after that long bus ride.

"You have long beautiful black hair, so I need to condition your hair before I shampoo."

Linda knew what she was doing. I have heard beauticians at the salons say the same thing.

"Linda, you are a professional."

"Yeah. Now, I am going to gently massage shampoo into the roots of your hair. I am not going to shampoo the ends of your hair. "D'Alise, are you comfortable?

"Yes." I am relaxing. This is just what I need. Linda's hands make a circular motion as she continues to massage the shampoo into my scalp. The fragrance eases me to another level of comfort.

"Now, I'm ready to rinse your hair and squeeze out the excess water and put a leave-in conditioner in your hair." She carefully rinses my hair again, being sure not to get any soap in my face. "Here's a towel. Come over here and sit under the hairdryer. I need to check on my husband."

We step right outside of the bathroom where she has set up the dryer and a chair. I take a seat, and she adjusts the dryer and the temperature. Before she lowers the hood, she smiles.

"I'll be back. That's a catchphrase used in the science fiction film The Terminator."

I saw the movie and remember the catchphrase. We both laugh as she makes sure my head and body are positioned correctly.

Linda enters the bedroom for the first time since we returned to the apartment. John smiles as she gets closer to him.

"Hi baby, come over here and give me a kiss."

"Hi, when I stopped to get gas today, I got cigarettes for us. I didn't have to pay for anything. The guy in the service station likes your cousin. I got the groceries for free too.

"What?"

"Oh, I forgot to bring the bags from the car. Can you go to the car and get the bags? Also, can you and put the groceries away?

"Yes. I'll put the cigarettes in the nightstand. How is your day going with my cousin?

"It's going well. She's green, though."

John listens, understanding what Linda means he explained my life or a part of it.

"She's had a lot of trauma in her life but manages to maintain a certain innocence about her. She can be very introverted at times. I don't want her to end up like LaRosa, her mother. She's my favorite aunt. I wonder if she will ever be cured of her episodes." Her ex-husband was a narcissist.

Linda listens and sits on the bed. She can see the worry in her husband's eyes.

"Greg called while you and D'Alise were out. He wants to show her a good time."

"Do you trust him?" Linda thought that may have been his worry.

"He's a good guy. I feel it. He's booked a hotel with double beds and promises he will respect her. He said he wants her to meet his friends and didn't want her coming in late to disturb us. She doesn't know about the hotel yet. It's going to be a surprise. I'm glad he's in communication with me. I'll be leaving in a few days. While she's out, it will give me a chance to have a romantic time with you."

"Let's go to early morning service tomorrow."

"Sounds like a plan."

"I'll finish her hair while you get the bags." We can start our quality time once she's gone.

Chapter 6

A New Start Resumes

John leaves Linda in the bedroom and sees me sitting under the dryer. He doesn't say anything about the conversation between him and Greg.

"Hey, cousin. How is your day going?"

"Good."

"I'm going downstairs to get bags out of the car and put the stuff away; then I'm going back to watching television. It looks like Linda is taking good care of you."

Linda had taken care of me. Between last night and this morning, I've learned more than what I knew in the four years I went to college. I responded with a simple "yes."

"Well, I'll leave you, two ladies."

Linda enters the living room as John goes out and closes the apartment door. She lifts the hood of the dryer and inspects my hair.

"D'Alise your hair should be well conditioned by now. Let's get you back to the stool so I can blow dry, flat iron and trim your ends."

"Linda, thank you." She is taking good care of me and my hair.

"Here hold these butterfly clamps in your hands. I am going to part your hair in sections. I'll be taking the clamps from your hands and clamping your hair to keep it out the way. Do you need another dry towel?"

"Yes."

"You can give me the used towel. I'll put it in the hamper now. Here's a new towel.

I have a hand dryer with a straightening pic attachment. I'm blowing out the wavy hair to make it mostly straight before flat ironing your hair. Are you tender-headed?"

"Yes." I couldn't think of a time when I wasn't tender-headed. I hated combing through my curly locs. I got a perm as soon as I could. My hair still gets tangled, and I still hate having it combed. I close my eyes and said, *"thank you."*

"I will be gentle with the heat and pulling your hair. I don't want you to look in the mirror until I'm finished. Your hair is jet black, full and thick. It looks like you're eating the proper nutrients.

"Yes." My mom and grandmother made sure I got three organic meals a day.

"Turn your head and hold your ear. This flat iron is going to help me achieve a silky-straight look."

I followed her instructions as I remember having the top of my ear burnt for moving or not holding it as a child.

"You can stop holding your ear now; hold your head up. Don't be alarmed I am only trimming the bottom ends of the hair. I am going to use the flat iron to add light curl to the ends of hair for body. I've accomplished what I've set out to do. Your hair is off the chain. Don't look in the mirror. I am going to pin roll your hair now and tie it up."

I sit patiently although I want to look in the mirror, I wait.

"I'm done. Wala! Help me clean up the bathroom and put everything away."

"Okay." This reminds me of helping my grandmother and being her assistant when I was growing up.

"Go to sleep, so you can be fresh. Your hair turned out nice. Set your alarm so you can get ready for your date later. The flowers are beautiful. Knock on the bedroom door if you need anything. I'll be resting with John."

Linda leaves me to follow her instructions. I can hear her talking to John as she enters the bedroom.

"John make room, so I can get in bed with you."

"Come on, let's cuddle baby; you want a puff of my cigarette?"

"Yes. Thanks for putting the bags away."

There's a pause in the conversation. Linda must be smoking because she's not talking, neither is John.

"You made out like a fat cat." John is talking about the groceries and our stop at the gas station.

"Yes. I did."

"Wifey, don't be pimping my cousin out now."

"Okay. Close your eyes and let me massage you."

I must have fallen to sleep the next sound I hear is my alarm clock. Greg will be here at five o'clock.

"It's time to get up." My heart begins to beat faster, my breath quickens. I start to feel butterflies in my stomach. I've had good dates and bad dates. I recall some of those experiences as I prepare for my date today.

I extended an invitation to a classmate to escort me to the Debutant Ball. He said yes but later declined once he found out about the out of pocket expenses to attend the ball. I understand it was a lot to ask of someone who wasn't my boyfriend.

A few days before the ball, I had to ask a platonic friend to escort me. He gracefully said yes. He didn't have time to reserve a tuxedo. He wore a very nice black suit, white shirt, tie with black shoes. He was the perfect gentlemen escorting me in my white chiffon dress. He purchased the pictures for the ball and even gave me a flower. He sat at my designated table with my family and was very attentive to everyone. He took me to the gathering, an after-party at a restaurant in the west end. He paid for our breakfast. When it was time to leave, he placed me in his car closed the door. He guarded me like a precious jewel. He got me home just before midnight. I told him, 'Thank you. I appreciate your kindness and will never forget you.' He walked me to the door, simply responding 'No, problem D'Alise.' There are kind, polite men in the world. One negative experience does have to remain in our mind.

I remember a crush I had during my freshman year of college. I met him in military science and interacted with him during my official hostess role for the campus. I wore a two-piece blue suit and white button-down shirt as we walked side by side around the campus. He was four years older and military bound. We were platonic friends, we hung out together. He took me everywhere with him in his car. I met his friends. He talked on various subjects and joked around. I told all my friends how nice he was to me. He never touched me or was aggressive. I received an invitation from him to be his date for the military ball. My entourage of friends got everything together, including my dress. I didn't have to think or worry about anything. He was dressed in his military uniform and me dressed in my floor-length gown. He showed up and was present; that alone was a fantastic feeling. As the night ended, he took me back to my dorm. In the front courtyard under trees, I was spinning around looking at the moonlit sky and stars. He grabbed me, pulled me close, and kissed me under the stars. I saw stars or eye floaters and felt dizzy…

Linda's voice startles me. I can't move, my nerves won't allow it.

"D'Alise what are you doing in here, daydreaming? The alarm clock is going off!"

"I feel a little nervous……" There is no other excuse.

"You have nothing to be nervous about it's only a date. Come on, start getting dressed."

Linda's voice is now normal. Just like that she changes her demeanor and sweetens her tone. She has some narcissist characteristics.

"The flowers are amazingly beautiful. I can't stop looking at the variety in the bouquet. I hope he doesn't cancel the date. Linda, you've spent so much time on my hair."

"You go shower and get dressed. I'll do your hair and make-up last. For goodness sake claim down. Go. Go now."

"Okay."

I will take a shower and get dressed. My nervousness has seemed to calm down. I'm ready for my first date.

"Here I am."

"Girl you are going to turn some heads tonight. The off-the-shoulder dress exposes your long neckline. The exposed back zipper will be easy for Greg to undress you. The sheath silhouette focuses on all your curves. The dress is hugging the body in all the right places. The knee-length dress is classy, not trashy. Greg is going to be jealous tonight. When I finish your hair and make-up. I'll call John, so he can add in his 'two cents.'"

I listen as she goes on excited by my look. I'm not sure I want the kind of attention she and my cousin think I need.

"Linda, maybe I'm moving too fast."

"Stop doubting the vibration and let it flow." She takes out the last pin and combs through my hair. She stands back to take the first look at her project. "I'm done go look at yourself."

I don't recognize myself looking in the mirror. I've changed in a good way. I don't feel like the ugly baby jokes that repeat in my head. They make me feel unattractive. Linda sees my expression. My feelings have made their way to my face.

"Oh, here we go negative thoughts. Think beautiful, and you will reflect beauty. The Law of Attraction. You are enough, you attracted Greg. John, can you come into the living room to add your opinion."

John comes into the room and stares for a minute. A slow but deliberate smile is coming to his face.

"Cousin you look exactly like LaRosa. She was classy and something beautiful back in the day. You are making me proud. It looks like your date should be arriving shortly."

"We're going to cover you up. When you get to your destination, let Greg help you take your jacket off. He'll get to see your backside and think about unzipping that dress. Oh, we almost forgot the red lipstick."

"Baby it's warm outside. She doesn't need a jacket. You're going to have a decent man lusting after my cousin."

"John, you told me to get her up to speed."

My cousin's thoughts have met mine. It was too much speed. I don't want to go as fast as Linda has in mind. John must be thinking the same thing. He gives the response I was thinking.

"Lord have mercy." The doorbell rings, and John quickly rushes us into the bedroom.

"Y'all go in the other room so I can meet Greg at the door."

Greg and John shake hands and exchange greetings.

"Greg, how you doing? The ladies are in the other room. I am trusting you will take good care of my cousin."

"I will, sir. I think I'm in love."

"Man, you infatuated with my cousin. You just met her yesterday."

"John, that's not what it is. When you know you know? I am not playing games with no one's heart."

"Have you ever loved anybody?"

"I love my family. She's like family."

"Your head has been in the books too long." John closes the door as they step into the living room.

"John, how long did it take you to know you wanted to be with your wife?"

John never answers the question. He calls us out of the bedroom.

"Cousin, Greg is here."

I stop just ahead of Linda as Greg smiles. He's pleased with me and my appearance. I'm still nervous.

"Well jeez, D'Alise and Greg, will the two of you stop staring each other down."

I didn't know what to say. I get a glimpse of the flowers on the table.

"Greg, thank you for the flowers they are beautiful." The moment is awkward. John attempts to make us feel better, I guess.

"D'Alise I forgot to give you a door key so you can get in the apartment. Linda and I plan on going to church and have brunch tomorrow. We'd love for you to attend church with us."

Linda interrupts him immediately adding sweetness to her voice.

"John, remember we have a date tonight. You're leaving in three days. D'Alise and Greg have an enjoyable responsible evening."

I then realize Linda and John's need to be alone. The thin walls between the bedroom and the living room would reveal their story. John stepped toward the door.

"Let me get the door for you." Greg looks back at John as we leave. I can hear Linda talking as he closes the door.

"John, you are suddenly acting like a father figure."

"Do you think it's too early for her to be going out on a date?"

Linda answers in a sultry tone. "John, let me give you a massage, relax."

I look at the window of my first home away from home. I see Linda and John peeping through the blinds.

Chapter 7

First Date – A Night to Remember

"Hey, baby, excuse me. Hey D'Alise, I'm talking to you like you already mine. I wanted to say; you look stunning."

"Thank you, handsome. Are we going to stand here for the duration of our date staring at each other?"

We are still standing in the parking lot, smiling at each other.

"Let me get the door for you and help you in the car."

"Thank you."

We walk to his Mercedes, and I admire his taste. I can't imagine how he got a top of the line vehicle.

"Greg, you seem to be doing well for yourself on a Greyhound bus drivers' salary."

As I get into the car, I notice Linda and John are still at the window. I can imagine their conversation as they look on to see what car we're riding in.

John would be excited and say, 'Damn, Linda, do you see that? He's in a black 1985 Mercedes-Benz 380SL 2 door convertible Roadster.' Linda would only be interested in one thing. 'John lets handle our business. Come on and let me massage you.'

Greg did most of the talking as we rode away from the apartment. I tried to keep my face from any expression that would lead him to think that I was stunned by the conversation.

"As I mentioned before I am working on my social skills. Driving the bus gives me an opportunity to communicate with a range of diverse people and to have empathy. I donate my check from Greyhound to my favorite charity. I've completed my medical residency. I have a career with benefits. I want to share my life with you. I told my parent's all about you. If you are available, I would like you to meet them on Tuesday they will be flying in from California for two days for a conference. My parents are semi-retired. My father's mother lives in the Garden District; she's elderly. I live in the guest house of that home. I can check on her when I am not working. I want you to meet all my family. We are very close; you can ask them anything about me. I have no secrets that you won't know about. I see your soul in everything you told me. My parents have a private investigator. Of course, they asked would your story check out. It doesn't matter to me where you come from. My parents and family want me to be happy."

"You waste no time." I didn't want to seem scared, but this was no coincidence. I began to think John or Linda knew more about Greg than I did.

"I hope you're not offended that I spoke to my parents about you. I hope you have good credit."

We both laugh. I'm at ease now as we ride through town. He's easy to talk with, I'm not sure why his parents are so in-volved. He's a grown man. Who are they? Why are they protecting him? A thought crosses my mind, *'Did he check my wallet on the bus while I was sleeping?'*

"That's perfectly fine with me. I'm glad we're getting this all out in the beginning."

"Baby, I am a brand, and you will be a part of that brand one day. I want you to sign a confidential disclosure agreement and get a complete physical. We can both go on the same day. As Maya Angelou would say, "Let nothing dim the light that shines within us." I am not saying we're in an official relationship try me out for two weeks. As I said when you know you know. I know you won't take advantage of me. We can go to the bank on Monday. I'll put a couple of thousand dollars in a safe deposit box and give you the key. You're going to need that money one day. Oh, on the other hand, your cousin's wife might be a bad influence on you. I don't want you to discuss any of our conversations with her. Do you hear me?"

"Yes." I hope my facial expression doesn't give away my fears. *"What is he asking? Where is this leading?"* I've never heard of this type of commitment, but there was a lot I didn't know. I want to like Greg, I like his intuition.

"You got something that she'll never have in many lifetimes. She'll keep coming back hoping to be the same as you."

"Greg, you have a lot of insight."

"D'Alise I have supernatural powers."

"Okay, Superman can you fly us across this bridge." I laugh as we approach the same bridge my cousin brought us across the night before.

"I can't fly you across this bridge. I can book a flight, and we travel to Europe. I'm leaving for a conference in two weeks overseas. I want you to travel with me. Is your passport ready?"

"Greg, you think fast on your feet. I don't have a passport. All of this is a bit much."

"We'll have to get you one. We have a lot of ground to cover in a short time. I will make all your dreams come true. I'm not just one of those fast-talking fellows that has nothing to back it up. I am your future. I am multi-dimensional. I want to bring you into my circle. Let this be a present precious. I have a wonderful day planned for us. Would you like to listen to music?"

It is the first time since we started this date that he asked what I want. I quickly respond, "Yes."

"What would you like to listen too?"

"I have an eclectic taste in music."

"Me too. I enjoy listening to jazz, opera, country, hip hop, gospel, and classical music. For this occasion, can I select our music selection?"

Here I thought I would have a say. *Of course, you would want to select the music.* "Sure. Greg."

"What about Boney James, his music from his album, Body Language? Then we'll move into some, "We have a lot in common." Girl, I can't wait for you to meet my mother. Are you okay over there in the passenger seat beautiful?"

"Yes. My wonderful man." I thought about the opportunity that Linda would think was more than I could ever want. A girl from Alabama with someone that she and my cousin John thought was just a bus driver, won't they be surprised.

"I was tempted to let the roof down, so I could watch that long black hair of yours blow in the wind. I'm going to save that for another day. Girl, I am alive; my heart is beating strong for you."

I listen without a response. I can honestly say with all Greg is saying I am just overwhelmed. I look around as we cross the bridge and turn into town. Small businesses and stores are still open. A few restaurants and people are walking along the side-walk. We're stopping at each traffic light, and I am pleased to take in the scenic view.

"We're almost at our destination sweetheart. We're going to Galatoires Restaurant, a family-owned business. You'll enjoy it; take it all in."

I am enjoying it. I like the look of the area. I turn to look at some of the places we passed.

"Do you feel like a short walk?"

"Yes."

"Okay, I'll park the car and we'll walk to the restaurant. If you didn't want to walk, maybe, I would have to carry you."

"Greg, you are so nice."

It's only a few blocks to the restaurant. I can see the awning and the sign adorning the front of the building. Most of the build-ings are two-story brick buildings. Small and quaint, I like the at-mosphere. I can smell the food as we step in the foyer.

"We're here, are you ready to take this in. Can you smell that good food? Breathe in. Sweetie do you like French doors?"

I never really thought about it. The main entrance of the res-taurant has a French door that leads into the first-floor dining room. The first-floor dining room is a mix of high ceilings, slow-moving paddle fans, and mirrored opposing walls, maintaining the look of a mid-19th-century restaurant. The second-floor dining room is where we will be seated, they have smaller rooms overlooking Bourbon Street.

"This is so nice, Greg. I appreciate you explaining everything to me."

We step up to the podium where a host meets us.

"Good evening. Mr. Thibodeaux will you be sitting in the balcony room overlooking Bourbon Street?"

"Yes. Thank you."

The host, a very young-looking man, leads the way to the balcony. The restaurant is not filled, but it has a few patrons on both levels. The conversations are light but engaging. Everyone seems to be enjoying the food and their company. The host points to the table, and Greg approaches my chair to help with my seating.

"So, what do you think?"

"I am impressed." I smile as he reaches from behind and wraps his arms around my shoulders. I feel like I have found Mr. Right.

"Let me help you with your jacket. I have died and gone to heaven. I can't wait to show you off to my colleagues. You're not wearing any jewelry."

A waiter has come to our table for our drink order.

"What will you be having to drink mama?"

"I'll have water with lemon."

"I'll have sparkling water, please. I left a package here earlier today can you bring it out to me please?"

"Yes. Sir." The waiter leaves, and Greg is silent. I dare not ask what the package is. I'm sure it is another surprise. I can't imagine what else he can add to this, our first date.

"Sir, here is your blue bag."

"D'Alise I purchased something for you from Tiffany and Company earlier today. I am going to show it to you. Tell me if you will accept this gift. This set of pearl clip on earrings and the floating pearl necklace in 18K white gold is for you. Sweetheart, what's wrong?"

I need to leave. I can't stop the tears from coming. I've never had anyone offer so much at one time.

"Why are you crying? Did I offend you? Is the gift not good enough for you? I can take it back and get you something else bigger and better."

Oh, my God. He just won't stop. "Greg, I need to excuse myself."

"No. I don't want you to leave. Can we talk about it? Is it ok if I touch you? Waiter. We are going to step away for a few minutes, okay."

"Yes. Sir." The waiter steps away, and as I get up to walk away, Greg guides me to a bench in the hall.

"D'Alise let's sit here in the corner on the bench. What's wrong baby? Why are you crying?"

"Greg. I needed to leave because I didn't want everyone in the dining area see me crying. I am so embarrassed." I feel foolish, I try to look through the tears to see if anyone is looking.

"It's okay love."

I can't tell him that this is the best day of my life. My tears are overflowing because they are tears of joy.

"D'Alise look at me." He suddenly leans forward. "Let me dry your eyes with this tissue." He whispers in my ear, "You are a beautiful lady, and you deserve beautiful things. Do you accept the earrings and necklace?"

"Yes." I am trying to pull myself together.

"Look at me I want to put the earrings on your ear lobes. Your hair smells like apples and peach. Girl, I want to eat you right here. I can barely resist you."

I smile in amusement. "It's apple and pear." His words arouse me.

"Your neck is so long. Lean into me baby, so I can place this necklace around your neck. Your natural body smell reflects strawberries, oranges, grapes, and cherries. I'm going to eat you right here."

All I can do is giggle.

"Are you ready for our romantic dinner?"

"Yes."

"Then let's go back into the dining area."

"Okay."

Greg watches me as I walk in the open toe high heel shoes. His eyes move toward my long bare strong legs as the motion of my hips sway back and forth.

"Greg, Greg Thibodeaux. Greg Thibodeaux."

Hypnotized by my presence, Greg doesn't acknowledge the person calling him until they call him again.

"Hi. Hey baby, can you come here." Greg pulls me close to him.

"Greg, I saw you when you came in. How are you doing?" Special emphasis on these words. "Who is this?"

"This is D'Alise James."

Special emphasis on these words. "Where have you been hiding her?"

"She's been studying in one of those Ivy League Schools."

"Man, I must say. You must be feeling lucky to have Ms. James as a date."

"We're going to finish our dinner, and I'll introduce her to everyone."

We return to our table without me knowing who he was talking to. There was no introduction.

"Baby, do you feel like meeting my friends and colleagues?"

"Greg anything for you. Who is that guy?

"Let me get your chair. I'll explain it to you another day. Remind me, and I'll tell you everything, ok. It's all about us tonight sit close to me. I want to smell the scent of your body."

We repeat the seating ritual as we had when we first arrived.

"You got that small waist. I was watching your hip action when you were walking. You got those long attractive legs. All I could think was, 'Walk, baby walk.' Did you see the expression on his face when you walked up?"

"Yes." I heard his words and couldn't stop smiling at the attention I was receiving. Maybe I was wrong, but for the moment I felt special.

"Greg, can I ask you a question?"

"Yes, anything."

"How did you manage to get this far and not be married?"

"I've been focused on my career. Honestly, I get lonely sometimes. I flirt with you a lot. Just for fun. I like to see the expression on your face. I wish I could take a picture. No real man has ever talked to you this way before. I want you, but I have self-control. If a man can't wait, he surely has no self-control in the marriage or relationship. Trust the words that are coming out of my mouth. He will cheat and never be faithful. I am not going to be with anyone or have sex with anyone because that blueprint will be with me for the rest of my life. I call it, 'The You in Me.' I am a medical doctor; Microchimerism is real. When you sleep with someone, you carry the imprint of them for the rest of your life. Baby, you can't wash it away. My mother talked to me a lot about women. That's how I know you are the one. I am ready for a real relationship. I want you in me for the rest of my life. I choose you. It's my choice. I am choosing this for me."

"Greg, can I share something with you."

"Yes, sexy."

"I get lonely too. I was sexually molested as a child. I am not having sex with anyone. I want something or someone inside me to fill me up inside. I squeeze my legs tight and hold onto my pillow. I am alright, though. I am good. I want to make healthy choices. I'm just so scared of being abused." I think to myself, God is filling me up on the inside.

"Baby, I see your inner child. I feel you. That's why I know how to handle you. You need patience and lots of love. I respect you and your body. Baby, my heart is bleeding for you."

"Are you ready to order now?" The waiter stands at our table, patiently waiting for us to place our order.

"D'Alise have you had a chance to look at the menu?"

"Yes. I will have the soufflé potatoes, seafood okra gumbo, salad Maison and lemon fish and asparagus with hollandaise sauce and for dessert black bottom pecan pie."

I hope I don't sound hungry, but I am starving for this kind of food. I've heard so much about New Orleans and their cuisine.

"I'll have my usual. Thank you." Greg leaned toward me to speak as though others were listening.

"Baby you ordered some things I never ordered before. I might have to taste some of your food. Tell me something good." He waited for me to speak with a sensuous grin. I play along, hoping it's the right thing to do.

"Baby, I'll feed you. I feel happy and safe, very safe. You've been so good to me. I want to be good to you for the rest of my life."

While waiting to be served, we play the teasing game. I've never had this treatment before, and though I find it stirring emotions, I still don't want to seem too forward. The waiter is standing at the table holding the tray that has our plates.

"Excuse me, sir, your food is ready." He takes his time placing the food in front of us. I can't wait to taste these dishes I have read so much about in magazines. I will not admit to Greg; this is a food tasting date for me.

"I see you made a good selection with your food choice. It's appealing to my senses."

I smile as I bow my head silently in prayer. I look up to see if Greg has done the same. He's placing his napkin in his lap; without prayer, he begins to eat. I notice the small things and often miss what is right in my face. I don't want to be negative, so I decide to give Greg something to think about.

"Greg, I have what I call an adult curfew. I always want to be at home before midnight. I never want to be remembered as being the last person to leave an event."

"I feel the same way as you baby." His reaction is not what I expect from a man his age. But then he adds something I never expected.

"I made reservations for a double room at Hotel Monte Leone. You can have the room to yourself. I'll stay in the room next to you alone. I was hoping you would go to church with me."

"I have nothing to wear." *This is a bit much.* My thoughts are running between the words of warning from my grandmother and the lecture from Linda about men and opportunities.

"You have nothing to worry about sweetheart. I purchased clothes for you today."

I want to ask him if he was just a little crazy, but I hold my tongue. I really don't understand his behavior.

"Greg, how do you find the time to do all this?"

"It's my little secret. The clothes are in the trunk of my car. Say you'll spend all day tomorrow with me. After church, we can really talk, and then you will understand my intentions."

"Humm…"

"I've already asked your cousin's permission and provided the addresses for all the places I have planned us to visit.

It sounds so exciting. I haven't been anywhere other than my home and college. I sound desperate I know but I throw caution to the wind.

"Okay, I do want to check in with them later."

"Absolutely." He doesn't give it a second thought. I watch him as he takes in more food. He's a different type of man. Linda did say that this was an opportunity I wouldn't want to pass up.

"Greg, you are so observant. You miss nothing."

Yes, I am, I noticed everything about you. Your eyes changed from brown to hazel today. When I first met you, I noticed you weren't wearing any jewelry. You had that footlocker with everything you owned in the world. This was not your first time on my bus, you know. I knew this time it was to be more permanent. I'll explain more tomorrow."

"Well, when I first met you, I noticed your smile and those beautiful teeth. I said to myself he so fine and athletically sculpted. You looked so refined with your mustache. I did think you were too old for me."

"Really? Age is only a number. I can make all your dreams come true. I'm not just one of the fast-talking guys that have nothing to back it up. I am your future. I am a multi-dimensional man. I want to bring you into my circle. Do you want children?"

"Only one or two, I had to help raise three siblings. It was hard even with a maternal mother and grandmother. I can't imagine being a single parent without any assistance or a husband."

"If we do decide to have children, I will be right there with you."

"I had to grow up fast. I didn't have a lot of time to play with the kids in the neighborhood. I had a lot of pinned up emotions inside of me, which resulted in sickness."

I don't want to share with him all of the sicknesses I've been through. I pray each day that I never have to return to that time in my life. I've done some reading on the conditions I've had to endure. I know that leaving home was a part of my healing. I really don't want pity from anyone. We all have our burdens to bare.

"That's why we are going to exercise every day to release stress."

"I purchased a book by Louise L. Hay years ago called "You Can Heal Your Life." She talks about the problem, cause, and an affirmation to release the problem."

"I am very familiar with the book and have a copy in my office."

"I got so much out of reading her book. I looked up a lot of the things I was going through, and a lot of it means I am refusing to release old ideas. I am stuck in the past."

"Baby I want you to say the affirmation that is mentioned in the book 'As I release the past, the new and fresh and vital enters. I allow life to flow through me.' I am a flexible man-baby. I don't have to share you with anyone. It's your call if you want children.

If you're finished eating, you can meet the gang. You're gorgeous D'Alise."

"Thank you, handsome."

"I notice you're gaining your confidence now. When you first got on the bus, your arms were folded, and you were holding yourself like you were extremely cold. You always ride alone. I often wondered what was on the mind of this beauty who travels alone. This time I wondered what you were running from, why you were leaving."

"As I traveled this time, it was different. I was revisiting some very traumatic experiences. I had eight hours of silence to reflect and think about my childhood and abuse."

"You even changed your name from **Danielle Alise' James to D'Alise.**"

"Greg, that's my alter ego, the multi-dimension me. I guess it's the risk-taker. I can be free and have no fear. I don't have to take life so seriously. I am choosing to leave my old life behind me, that's why I left my hometown. Simply to find me and be comfortable with who I can be without looking back."

"Alright. I'm going to keep D'Alise. She sounds like fun. D'Alise Thank you for taking this adventurous ride with me this evening."

His remark makes both of us laugh. I am at ease. Greg makes me comfortable. I am finally at ease. Greg has given me a lot to think about.

"Baby, why don't you call your cousin and his wife? I'll wait right here. I want to watch you walk."

Again, I find myself smiling. I know what he wants, another chance to watch my hips. I teasingly roll my eyes.

"Can you tell me where there's a payphone?"

I prepare for my walk, knowing that he will enjoy it. I smile, waiting for his direction.

"It's on the first level."

"Thanks."

I turn and walk knowing, I am a big girl. I find the phone in the corner near the cashier and host post. I quicken my steps, anxious to speak to John. The phone rings and I wait as I look over the dining area.

"Hi cousin, I am checking in…. Yes. I am having a good time. Is it ok if I come home late tomorrow? ...... I know you're leaving on Tuesday. I want you to have your quality time without me being in the way…… Yes, I will start looking for a job next week. Thanks, see you late tomorrow before 9:00 pm. Goodbye."

I hang up the receiver smiling. I am proud of myself. I stand and smooth my dress, preparing to return to my fantastic date. I turn to maneuver through the dining area to the stairs and almost bump into a well-dressed man. His smile gives me an uncomfortable feeling.

"D'Alise, James. How are you?"

"I am well. I don't recall being formally introduced. Do you know Greg?"

"Yes, it's okay he didn't but let me introduce myself. I am Donald LeBlanc. That old Greg has been keeping secrets from everyone. You are young and vibrant. You are something out of this world beautiful. You and old Greg must come over for dinner. I'll have the chef prepare a nice meal. Greg still drinking that sparkling water?"

I don't like his tone or his insensitive smile. He gives me a bad feeling.

"Excuse me. I need to get back to Greg."

I don't wait for him to move as I push past him in the direction of the stairs.

"Greg, can we meet your friends and leave?"

I am embarrassed to say I met Mr. LeBlanc. I just want to leave.

"Yes, baby, we can."

"I ran across the guy I saw earlier."

"He likes to play mind games."

He seems to be a metrosexual pretty man with issues. "He's also creepy."

Maybe I shouldn't have told Greg his friend was creepy, but if we are to be together, he needs to know what I think about his friends.

"Yeah, baby he is."

Although Greg agrees with me, he doesn't seem taken aback by what I've said.

"He told me his name."

"Did he tell you anything else about himself? I'll have to give you the 4-1-1. He and his wife are both medical doctors. You'll meet her tonight. They have a strange arrangement.

"Why do you say that?"

"Long story. Are you ready?"

We have left our table and are going through the tables on the same level. The crowd has grown since we entered earlier. It is a very popular restaurant where tourist and locals come to eat. I keep close to Greg, following his lead we approach his table of friends.

"Hi everyone, I would like to introduce you to D'Alise James."

I am shocked as they all stand and introduce themselves, in order, around the table. They each give me a smile and a courteous nod.

"Donald LeBlanc points to the lady standing next to him. This is Crissy LeBlanc, my wife. I formally met D'Alise downstairs and invited her and Greg to join us for dinner."

"It's nice to meet you all. We look forward to having dinner with you."

"She's beautiful. You've done well, Greg."

"Thanks, and thank you for the invitation. We have had dinner and will have to join you at another time."

Everyone takes their seats and begin to talk at the table. Greg says good-bye, and I simply compliment his words with a friendly nod. Donald LeBlanc is holding the creepy smile. I can feel his eyes upon me as we turn to leave their table.

"Baby let's stand on the balcony before we head out."

The doors to the balcony are open. It is a beautiful evening, and the night is proving to be perfect. There is no chill in the air, and I take a needed breath of the freshness that it holds.

"Greg, this evening has been the best. I love the view. You must be a regular here."

"Why do you say that?"

"I noticed everyone knows you. It's like you're a celebrity."

"I am. I told you I am protecting my brand. D'Alise, where are you seeking employment?"

"I would like to be a CEO of a large company or be a television personality. I am good at supervising, training, and mentoring."

"If you marry me, you wouldn't have to work."

I find it strange that he wouldn't want me to work. As a professional, I would want a job of my own. I can't visualize myself doing what I did as a child. Taking care of a home, children, and a husband without exploring my dreams.

"Your mother works," I say this as a statement but mean it as an indirect question.

"Yeah, my father met my mother in medical school. You've been taking care of people all your life. I want to take care of you. It's your turn to be taken care of now. I want you to go everywhere with me. Are you going to the conference with me?"

"Yes, but I need to look for a job."

"Well, do you mind if I take off to drive you around?"

"No, I don't mind. This will give me an opportunity to spend more time with you."

I smile to myself. I'm glad he volunteered his time. I didn't want to spend days with Linda giving me her lectures while I was seeking honest employment.

"You're new to the city. I don't want you taking the bus by yourself. Let's head out so we can walk and talk."

There was an exit from the second level balcony to the ground level. We didn't have to go through the tables again. Greg is careful to guide me down the stairs. When we get to the ground level, he chooses our direction.

"What do you think about my colleagues?"

I really don't know how to answer. What did I really know about them? The LeBlanc's seemed strange, but it could be the energy I felt from his friend Donald LeBlanc.

"They all seem nice. The LeBlanc couple stuck out to me."

"Explain why."

"Donald's wife has masculine energy." Greg laughs. "Why are you laughing?"

We approach the car. Greg felt as I did. It was a night for a nice walk. We continued our conversation, pass the parking lot.

"Donald is on the Down Low. Do you know what that means?"

Yes, Greg, I love being a feminine woman. I knew I was attracted to boys in elementary school.   I did witness a bathroom scene where I saw two 4th grade girls making out in the bathroom. They came for me. I told them no and told everyone in our class. They never came for me again. We remained friends and never discussed the incident again. The two girls married men and had children. I heard rumors of people talking about the two being lesbians. So, I do know there are some on the down low, both male and female." I am not casting any stones because I am not perfect.

"Good I don't have to explain that to you. I don't think his wife cares. Hey, their relationship agreement could be set up like that. They both want children. They have a hefty combined income."

"You sure do know a lot about them." I thought it was a bit much as my grandmother would say, *"It ain't good for everyone to know your personal business."*

"It's good to understand your associates. I'm not judging any of them. I just know all their stories. When people drink, they spill the tea. Do you know what that means?"

"No, I never heard that before, explain."

"They start talking a lot. You get all the backstories of their lives and relationship. In this, the medical profession, you need to be sober. People are trusting you with their lives."

"Ah, I see now."

"What?"

"My grandmother is a bootlegger. She once told me you had to be sober at all time. You have to keep your eyes on your money."

For the first time, since I was small, I was able to put the words Clara Rosa told me in a content I could understand.

"D'Alise you have people standing around in these public places waiting for an opportunity. They want to get the slightest bit of information to take to the news media. Some of the women hanging at the bar are looking for an opportunity to get paid. If I leave my drink unattended, I never drink from that glass again. I'm always out and about. It's important to socialize, that's how you get connected. You connect and get placed in the right positions. Do you understand you need people? You need them to like you. I am likable and loyal. I saw you working my colleagues, you gave them just enough, and we moved on. Thanks."

Once again, I am confused. How did I give them anything? Especially the creep, I shouldn't call him that, but I didn't mean to give him anything. I'm listening to Greg like I did Linda. I'm learning so much in such a short time.

"Donald and his wife might have an agreement in place where their marriage is of convenience. Baby, I don't want a marriage of convenience. I want to marry for love. I know you're going to fall in love with me."

"Greg, I am falling in love with every tick of the clock." I smile, teasing him again. I don't know if it is truly love, but I do like him.

"Yes. Do you know how that makes me feel?"

"Tell me."

"I am in the clouds right now." Greg looks up to the sky and extends his hands. We laugh like old lovers. The feeling, the date, and the company is just right."

"Come on silly let's get to the car." We take the short walk back to the car.

"Let me get the car door for you. I'm going to change the music to Doc Powell – Life Changes." Greg pushes the button, and the music begins. He taps the steering wheel, keeping in rhythm with the music. What do you think about that bass in the song?"

He pulls out of the lot and onto the street. He is still tapping the beat on the wheel. I can tell this is one of his favorite songs.

"I love the beat. It makes you want to move."

"Baby I want to kiss those red-hot lips so badly. Come here, lean over here. Brush your hair back so I can see your long neck."

"Greg, keep your eyes on the road."

"Do you want to work my stick?"

I hope he's not saying what I think he's saying.

"I want us to make it to the hotel."

"D'Alise girl, you are driving me crazy."

"I haven't done anything to you yet."

He looks at me, and I can see the sincerity in his eyes.

"You feel this, too don't you? Baby, you are my soulmate."

I don't want to admit it, but maybe I am feeling this. The sign for the Hotel Monte Leone is ahead. The lights on the front give it a picturesque view.

"Hey look there's the hotel. It's not on the line of a Hyatt. It's a traditional hotel. The property is registered as a national literary landmark. The lobby has crown molding, crystal chandeliers, and grandfather clock and traditional rooms the hotel is the only high-rise building in the French Quarter and is well known for its Carousel Piano Bar & Lounge, a rotating bar. I'm going to let the valet park the car. Let me grab our bags from the trunk. Let's take the elevator up."

"We don't have to check-in?" I wonder if he has done this too. It's more than I would have expected if he did. Then I was shocked by his reply.

"I know the owners. I thought about everything."

"Press the hold button baby. We're on our floor." We walk down the hall, and I notice Greg has fallen back a bit to watch me walk again. I stop not knowing where I am going.

"We're going to the Penthouse suite."

I can't control my facial expression. He said he made reservations for two rooms, not a Penthouse suite. With his eyebrows raised, he answers the obvious question.

"It's a two-bedroom. You'll have your privacy. I'm going to let you open the door."

I've never been in such a beautiful room. I am struck by everything in the room. Greg has noticed my expression. I can't move.

"Let me put the bags down. Look out the window and check out the skyline."

Greg is standing back, watching me view the skyline. I can feel his eyes watching my body language. The black dress is working. Just as Linda said, I know he can't see any panty lines and is curious if I'm wearing any panties. He's proud of himself. I am on his imaginary pedestal.

I turn to see if I am right. He's standing there watching me with his hand under his chin. I put a big smile on his face. I run to him and give him a big hug. I hold him tightly. I can't withhold what I feel. I know he doesn't know how to react. He takes my hands and holds them and looks deeply into my eyes. My emotions are on high. Of course, he can tell by my dreamy eyes he has won me over. He takes his index finger and rubs it across my plump red lips. His touch is soft as he makes his own path with his fingertip down to my neck. The smudge of the red lipstick has made a line from my lips to my neck. He leans in to smell me.

He whispers, "Baby, will you be all mine?"

"Yes, Greg Thibodeaux." His manner and voice is intoxicating. I feel like I'm floating.

"Come on sexy. Let me give you a tour of the penthouse."

We enter each room, and in my amazement, I am speaking gibberish pointing to the décor and colors that excite my creativity. Greg follows me as I take his hand as I would a toddler. He doesn't resist my hold and smiles from room to room, admiring my reactions. We approach another pre-set surprise. On a table in the sitting room, there are two eleven-inch-tall Waterford Champagne flutes with snacks.

"Love, I have six bottles of champagne here. Take your pick."

"They are so nicely packaged." Again, my creative senses are touched and pleased.

"Yeah, The Weibel Vineyards in California make the sparkling non-alcoholic champagne. They make a variety of flavors."

"I'll take the apple and peach."

"We might be able to locate that apple and pear the smell of your hair one day. Let's sit and enjoy. I'll give you half a glass to start.

"Greg you have shrimp, pasta, nuts, popcorn and to top it off pound cake and beignets. Everything is so pretty. How did you have time to do all this?"

"Stop thinking so much. Relax, here let me take your shoes off. Your legs are so long. I like watching you. Wow. Come here, sit here in front of me and lean back. Rest your head on my shoulder and look at the skyline."

"Wow, this feels like a dream." My voice has a softened tone. I recognize it immediately. I am comfortable and finally relaxed.

"This is my reality. I am here with you. Do you have any questions for me, baby?"

"I can't think of anything right now. Do you have any questions for me?"

"Sure, tell me about your parents? How did they meet?"

"My mother's name is LaRosa James, and my father is Artie Dives. They met in Alabama. She met my father through her brother, who worked at restaurant as the head chef. Her brother consented to the relationship. My father is ten years older than my mother and is from Louisiana.

"Baby age is just a number. I said that to you earlier. Does it bother you that I am about twelve years older than you?"

"No, my mother was about the same age I am when she met my father. Now I am meeting a man in about that same age group. That is interesting."

"D'Alise that does not matter. What matters to me is you. How does your mother look?

"My mother is very feminine; she loves to wear her hair in a bun. She has curves in all the right places, and all her clothing is tight-fitting, in perfect alignment with her body. My mother is 5 6' and has a caramel complexion and hazel sometimes brown eyes. Some people called her eyes mood eyes because they change colors."

"Baby it sounds like you are the spitting image of your mother."

"My mother doesn't think so. She says, I look just like my father."

"Tell me about your father."

"I met my father when I turned eighteen. He is a reserved and peaceful man, but he can hold his own. He is very handsome and fashion-conscious. He likes to dance and have fun. He is six feet tall with a honey bronze complexion, brown eyes, and curly hair."

"So, both of your parents are attractive. Did they divorce?"

"No. My mother was never married to my father. She got pregnant and later found out she was the third party in third party situation. My father was married to a woman who lived in another state. The company that employed my father hadn't relocated his spouse to Alabama."

"Does your father have children with his wife?"

"No. My father doesn't have any children with his wife. She's not able to have children." He has two older children with different women. As you can see, he's determined to keep his legacy going. Greg, do you want to keep your legacy going?"

"I'm going to leave that up to you baby if you want children. I don't really have to share you with anyone."

"I am told my father was a lady's man. He wanted to be adored. I think he loved attention."

"What was your parent's communication like?"

"He asked my mother to give me to him. He wanted me to be raised by him and his wife. My mother was young. I think he knew she was going to have more children. My father broke it off with my mother because all he wanted was a baby to bring home to his wife.

"Did he ever offer your mother any financial support?"

"No. He relocated to Louisiana and never returned to Alabama. There were no phone contacts or visits to see me."

"What about court-mandated child-support order or something?"

"He provided none. My mother felt my father should not be forced to take care of his child through the court and felt whatever he wanted to do should be voluntary."

"That's an amazing back story and the consequences of love. You survived love. You are still here. Is it ok if I hug you? I want to offer you, healing love."

We hug nothing really romantic, more like a caring hug. As he said a healing love hug. I think in the moment I wanted more.

"Let's sip on our champagne and enjoy these snacks."

We walk over to the table. It is a beautiful set up I can't get over the arrangement. I can see all the details and cuts in the crystal flutes. "Greg, you have exquisite taste."

"I sure do." He says this with a smile, and again, his head is slightly tilted to the side. "I have you with me. We have a full day planned for tomorrow. I want to get your approval on the things I purchased for you today."

Greg steps away from the table. He retrieves the bags he brought up from the car when they arrived.

"Here, I hope you like everything, and they fit. I picked what I thought you would like. I like them. As I said, I've seen you a few times traveling. So, I imagined what I wanted you to have."

"Baby thank you. I am grateful and appreciate the gifts that you have purchased for me. This is just beautiful. You've made perfect selections for all the clothing. You are spoiling me. I cherished all my childhood gifts and took very good care of them. I will take care of everything you give to me. I held on too many of my childhood toys until I graduated from college. I packed all the toys to include my bike and gave it to the next-door neighbor once I decided to move to Louisiana. I guess its time for new clothes as well.

"That's good you released your childhood toys. Now you're getting adult toys."

We laugh, I guess we both thought of the difference between the two. I couldn't stop smiling.

"Greg, sweetheart."

"Yes, baby."

I don't want him to know I really don't know why I feel so giddy. "I'm filled with so many foreign emotions."

"Ah, you need a hug. Looks like you're getting emotional again. I'm going to start carrying handkerchiefs. Baby, it's safe to love, open your heart."

"Greg, I'm starting to feel like a child again. I don't want to be vulnerable."

"Your secrets are safe with me. When you shower and change for bed, place the clothing in the laundry bag by the chair."

"I will be in the bedroom next door, okay. I'll be up writing and planning for my conference. Call me, and I will tuck you in."

He smiled at me and put his arm around my shoulder. I felt his comfort and knew in that moment all would be okay. I follow his instructions without hesitating. He remains seated in the chair. I allow my thoughts to reflect on my day. It has truly been an eye-opening experience.

God, this has been the best day. I am thankful to be found finally happiness. I am really feeling Greg. He's a wonderful man.

I thought I heard Greg at the door. Maybe he picked up the clothing bag where I put my clothes. He said it was for the clothes I take off. Maybe he will be placing his clothes in the same bag. Curiosity got the best of me. I peek out the door to see where he went. I don't understand what I'm seeing. Is this a fetish? It has to be. Greg Thibodeaux is seated in the wingback chair, holding my thong and allowing it to touch his face. He is holding on to my clothing as he fondles the thong as if his touch would tear the skimpy material. I'm about to bust in on his moment. I decided not to if it will satisfy him, I'll let him have the moment. I hold back my laughter and step away from the door to giggle. I contain myself ready to call him to the bedroom door.

"Greg baby."

"Hey, baby I thought you were going to call me. I'm really turned on by you. I am touching the small delicate fabric that I know has been touching your most intimate places on your body. I'm imprinting you, and the experience on my memory. I'm sitting here taking all of you in. I was curious if you were wearing underwear. Now I get to touch and smell the black strappy thong. The night is over. I am reliving our time together. Baby, I'm caught. You see, I am aroused by your scent. I'm not embarrassed. I'm just a real man trying to maintain his control and respect for a very special lady."

"Thank you, Greg. I accept the compliment."

"Sexy you D'Alise. The Scarlett lace teddy is fitting you in all the right places."

As he speaks, I feel sexy. I saw this same teddy at Victoria Secrets. I feel the need to model as I thank him again for the gift.

"You have perky breasts. What happened to the robe I purchased for you?"

"Oh, my God. I didn't even think about the robe after seeing him please himself with the thong." I am embarrassed and cover

my mouth, as I explain. I don't want him to think I am being forward.

"It's on the bed. I forgot it when I saw you in the chair. I didn't realize I didn't have it on." I retrieve the robe and cover my body.

He seemed to ignore my excuse. Still aroused, he asked, "Baby, is it okay if I take your thong to bed with me tonight?"

What was I going to say?

"Yes. It's okay."

"I see your perky nipples." He said, flashing his pearly whites.

"You and I both are horny."

Before I could object, not that I would, Greg swept me up and took me to the bedroom.

The surprise was he took me to my room. He sits me on the bed.

"I love it, you have so much respect for me. I feel safe. I trust you."

Greg falls to both knees at the foot of the bed and beckons for me to join him in prayer. *This is truly too much.* We pray silently. We each have our own words to say to the God we serve. We stand, and Greg pulls back the covers. I follow his gesture and get in the bed.

He whispers, "Goodnight."

As he leaves the room, he cuts off the light. I can hear the door lock as he exits the room.

As I lay in the bed, I feel exceptionally safe tonight. I realize for the first time in my life, good men do exist. Throughout my life, my sleep has been interrupted by nightmares. I must have dozed off I see faces. I don't know who they are. Suddenly I see the familiar figures that taunted me as a child. I still fear the scary faces of the lions, tigers, and bears. I am the four-year-old child praying that the thief of the night will not invade my room. The rape is real, and again, he has come back in the middle of the night. I only know one person to call. I begin screaming.

"Mother, Mother, where are you?"

I didn't hear the banging on the door or Greg calling from the hall.

"Baby, D'Alise are you ok in there? Open the door. Open the door."

He breaks the door down and comes running in.

"Baby, baby, baby."

Greg rushes over to the bed in his briefs. He lifts and holds me firmly in his arms. He comforts me. I press my face against his hairless chest.

"Baby are you okay?"

"I sometimes have nightmares from the rape," I answer trying to calm myself while in his embrace.

"I understand and feel your pain." Greg holds me closer and begins to cry.

"Greg, I don't understand why you are crying?"

He whispers as he holds me. "Baby I'm never going to let you go. You're safe. I am here for you. I got you. Let's get under the cover."

It's the end of our first date, and my past has caused us to fall asleep in each other's arms all night long. We cuddle, and his arms overlap mine. I feel his tears as they fall on my shoulder. I've never seen a strong man cry before or even felt his tears. I only know how many of my own tears I have shed. Tonight, I don't have to wipe them away by myself.

Chapter 8

A New Day

The next morning Greg rose to the sound of our hearts beating as one as we laid together in the bed. A hint of the sun was beaming on the floor. He silently removed himself from the bed, and I can only imagine him looking at his amazing treasure he found on the bus. I believe and so does he believe, we must look at the world with different eyes and a new perception. Nothing is what it seemingly is. The thought of the damaged door frame had to remind him of my call for help the night before. I believe in him. I believe he really loves me.

Greg has a past that I am unaware of. I guess we all have lived through things. He too has reason to look into his past. This has become a morning ritual for him. One I learn about later. As I think about it. I am imaging him the morning after our first day placing his hand across his face and covering his eyes. He begins to cry as he looks in the mirror, he remembers a scene from his childhood. His childhood has left him a little bruised. I can hear the shower running. I know he does as I do. We shower as the mist of memories hangs on. The water rinses them away. Greg's memory of a man and him staying one night with the person passes through his mind. He does that as I do. Shakes it off, showers it off, we rid ourselves of the thoughts that haunt us. I know he shakes it off. I hear the water stop. Greg must be getting dressed for church.

"Good morning, beautiful."

"Good morning. Did I oversleep?"

"No, here's some breakfast for you baby."

"Wow, my wonderful man brings me breakfast. Thank you, baby."

"I laid your clothes out for church." Greg turns to leave me to eat my meal and prepare myself for church.

"Wait, Greg don't leave. Come here, I apologize about last night. The door frame is damaged. I feel so bad about everything."

"No, worries. Beautiful. I will get you some professional help when I return from my conference. I mean, that's if you want some help."

"Yes. I do. Thank you." I reach for his hand. "Greg your hands are so warm."

"That's my warmblood burning for you, girl."

I could only giggle. I felt better seeing he was not angry. He was okay.

"I'm glad I could put a smile on your face."

I pull him close to me and give him a huge hug. We look at each other's wide eyes. They engage in a long hug, which seems to last forever. I know Greg's kiss of comfort on my forehead was meant to be a passionate kiss on my lips.

"Greg, you have so much internal wisdom and inner beauty."

"Thanks, baby. I've had to struggle with my inner demons. We all have them."

"Not you, Greg."

"I am a wonderful man, but I am not perfect, remember that okay."

I am a little puzzled, but I'll take it. *He can't possibly have the demons I've had to face.*

"You go ahead, and finish eating and get ready for church. I'm going to check my office's answering service, make a few phone calls, and make sure our flights are lined up for the conference. Hopefully, we can make the nine-thirty service. Don't forget to check in with your cousin and his wife before we leave. We'll talk more in the car. I promise."

I enjoy my breakfast before it gets cold. I felt a little rushed, knowing he was already dressed and wanted to go to the early service. I wondered if I could get my hair and makeup to look as perfect as Linda made it look. I took a deep breath before looking in the mirror. I picked a dress from the clothes Greg picked for me. I thought about asking him where the sniffing bag was. I wasn't sure if he wanted to have the red teddy to start a collection. I smiled. Yes, sometimes I could be naughty. I was complete. Yes, I am a big girl.

The valet brought the car to the front door. Greg thanked him and gave him a tip. We left the hotel to create new memories.

"Hey, baby, you look smashing. Let me get the door for you and help those long legs get in the car. The chiffon long sleeve-fitting dress and shoes make you look like royalty. I thank God for your parent's DNA."

"Baby you are so organized. This dress matches perfectly with the shoes. I would have thought you knew what I was wearing last night."

"I don't have a lot of distractions in my life; that's why I managed to be successful. Anything or anyone that causes me to lose my focus is eliminated."

"Greg that's a strong work ethic. I'm learning a lot from you."

"I am working on some deals where I'll be able to retire before retirement age. I have a lot of generational wealth in my family, but I want to make my own money for you and me. You are in my plan."

"The earrings and necklace go well with the outfit. Thank you, my wonderful man."

"I like the way you're talking to me this Sunday morning praise God. Hey, let me pop this track in by William McDowell – Withholding Nothing, I Surrender All."

"I like your music selections."

"Baby this is perfect timing for us. You are my soulmate. I hope this encounter with me changes you for the rest of your life."

We ride listening to the music. Content with each other and content with the blessing for the day. I called my cousin and told them I would be attending church with Greg. John didn't sound disappointed that we wouldn't be joining them. I was pleased I wouldn't have to give Linda any details.

We arrive at the Cathedral after riding for thirty minutes. Greg smiles as he finds a parking space.

"Oh, I never asked what your religion is. Are you open to being exposed to something different?"

"Yes, I am."

"Great, baby I'm exposed to a lot of cultures. In this profession, you must be open and go where you're invited. I'm glad to hear you are open. I want you to see this beautiful Cathedral that has a lot of history in this city. Are you open?"

"Yes."

"Let's do this."

Greg comes around to help me out of the car. We walk hand in hand as we walk from the parking lot. Greg gives me brief details about the service as we approach the entrance. I am amazed at the size of the building. The edifice is grand.

"Greg, this is my first time visiting a cathedral."

"I want you to experience many first times with me."

"The exterior has a gothic look."

"Let's go inside, let me get the door for you."

We are greeted at the door. There are other parishioners entering. Each being greeted and welcomed.

"Good Morning Mr. Thibodeaux"

"Good Morning, this is D'Alise James. Sir, Here's a check donation."

"Thank you, Mr. Thibodeaux, the Cathedral, will use it wisely."

The service was beautiful. It was the first time I was in another church. My family went to my grandmother's church; there was no other choice. We left the church feeling refreshed. We bid everyone a good day. We walked to the parking lot hand in hand.

"So, what do you think?

"I have never seen anything like this in my entire life. The interior and exterior are mesmerizing."

Greg continued to amaze me. As he opened the car door, I noticed a newspaper on the passenger seat.

"I picked up a newspaper for you this morning. I placed it in your seat when you got out.   You can start your job search while I am driving. Baby let me adjust the seat for you, it looks like you're cramped. I don't want your legs to be cramped.

"Greg, Thank you. I appreciate you so much."

"Okay, now we'll listen to this track by Tash Cobbs - Fill Me up- Overflow. God is everything. I want us to pray and attend church together. God is going to provide everything for us. Do you believe that?"

"Yes. I believe it baby. I feel we're going to be alright."

"Don't say I feel, say, you know. Say it with me, baby."

We said it together. "We are going to be alright."

"Yes. That's what I want to hear. Listen to this track by Israel and New Breed it's called, To Worship You I live."

"Baby you have high energy. Stay focused"

He was driving, talking, and singing. I was watching the road. I am sure he's a good driver, but I am learning the folds in New Orleans are high strung.

"I am focused on you. Wait, check this out baby we're going to Brennan's Restaurant. I'm going to park on the street you won't have far to walk. Is that okay with you?"

"Yes."

"Baby did you locate any interesting jobs?"

I was looking through the paper as we listened to music. I found a few jobs I was interested in.

"One at a hotel, radio and television station."

"Great! Let me take that newspaper and place it in the back. Let me look at you."

He kissed me again on the forehead before he gets out of the car. We walk down the street to the restaurant. There is a long line waiting. There is a host taking names for the tables as they become vacant. He approaches us as someone in a suit is pointing our way.

"Good Morning Mr. Thibodeaux. I didn't realize that was you waiting in line. Your regular table is available if you would like to be seated."

"Yes. Thank you. Come on, baby." He gives the host a tip as we pass him and the line of customers waiting to be seated.

"Thanks for the tip, Sir."

"Baby this Creole restaurant is known for its creation of Bananas Foster and breakfast."

A waitress came to our table with water, coffee, and the menus. I am a little hungry and smile over at Greg as I look over the menu.

"D'Alise you can have whatever you want. I'll let you look over the menu. Oh, baby, do you have a resume?"

"Yes."

"Do you mind if I review it when I take you home tonight?"

"No, I don't mine."

"I checked my messages and calendar this morning; I have a surgery scheduled for Monday. I forgot baby. I apologize I can't take you around. I need to be in bed by seven this evening. Why the sad face? Come sit closer to me."

I didn't realize my emotions were showing on my face. I was looking forward to our day as strange as it seemed. I want to get to know him. My appetite is beginning to fade.

"Greg baby, I understand. I don't want to be a distraction."

"I am going to have my driver pick you up and take you to my office. I'll have my secretary make any noted changes to your resume that I make tonight. The driver will take you to the locations you found. You don't have to worry your little head. I got you. Also, my secretary will contact vital statistics, help with your passport pictures and passport."

"Love, thanks for everything." It's still a little fast for me, but his push is what I need.

"My secretary is going to love you. She keeps the cougars off me."

"What's a cougar?"

Greg laughs and pretends he's looking over the menu.

"I must explain it to you another day."

The waitress returns. "Excuse me, are you ready to order now?"

"Yes. Baby, you go ahead and order."

"Everything on the menu looks so good. Hmm. I would like to order the crispy chicken & waffles with water and lemon."

"What about you, sir?"

"I am ordering the same thing. Thank you."

"Greg, you're ordering the same thing as me?" The waitress paused just in case there was a change in the order. Greg hands her the menu, and she leaves to put our orders in.

"Baby, I am flexible. I haven't had chicken & waffles in a long time. I normally eat a plant-based diet."

"I eat one good meal a day. I try not to eat anything after 6:00 pm. Will your parents still be here next week?"

"Yes, as a matter of fact, on Tuesday, you'll get to meet my parents and grandmother. You get to see where I live. I'm not sure if my sister will be flying in. She and her husband are working on a big court case in New York. Are you still willing to get a physical exam, credit check, and sign a non-disclosure agreement?

"Greg, I consent to everything." I think this would be the best thing for both of us. A signed agreement is always the best to outline what can and cannot be done while in the relationship. He is a man with money and a brand. I think I understand his reasoning.

"I like the fact you don't smoke, drink or do drugs."

"I've been around all that stuff, but I never had a desire to indulge in those types of activities. When I was six, my oldest brother gave me a cigarette to puff once. I drank grape wine around that same age and got intoxicated. The wine tastes like grape Kool-Aid. I never drank again. As I talk about it, the memories make my head hurt. I don't need anything to alter my mental state."

"Do you have any tattoos or body piercings?"

"I have no tattoos. I had plans to get my ears pierced just before I moved here. I have sensitive skin and can't wear cheap jewelry. I'm allergic to nickel."

"Baby I'm only going to purchase the best quality jewelry for you."

The conversation is small talk filled with questions. The waitress returns with our plates. The food looks great, and there is more than enough to fill us for the rest of the day.

"Baby everything you're telling me is so attractive. I would like to add that in the temporary relationship agreement. You are already packaged perfectly for me. I don't want you to change. I only want you to get better."

"All the things that attract you attract me. Hopefully, you feel the same and will be willing to sign the same type of agreement."

I want the same thing. An agreement to protect me in the relationship can't hurt. I watch as he eats and listens to me as I talk. Linda was right. He may be just what I need, but I have so much to learn about him. Also, I still want my own job and to be able to have my own apartment.

"Yes, baby anything for those long legs."

"You are such a flirt." I know he's teasing me. I like it.

"Only with you. Do you agree we are a match?"

"Yes. I'm not always going to be young and beautiful."

"I know. You are beautiful on the inside. You're easy on the eyes. I think you mentioned your cousin said you had to move in a year."

"Yes."

"I hate you're sleeping on their sofa."

"It's not bad." I forgot I told him the living arrangements in our talk last night. I contain my thoughts, hoping my expression doesn't show my embarrassment.

"I want you to get proper rest. You don't have a lot of miles on you."

"I will."

"I'm going to give them enough rent money to cover you for a year. "Greg, I can't accept that. That's too much, it's too early in our relationship for that."

"It's a gift. We'll be married by this time next year. I have it all planned out in my mind.

Oh, don't worry, you will have an opinion in all of this. I see your expression is changing again."

Yes, my expression was changing. I changed the topic. I couldn't change my emotions.

"Baby you made a good selection for breakfast."

"Greg Thibodeaux" A woman has walked over to our table. She is looking at me as she speaks to Greg.

"Hey, hello." Greg is caught off guard, but he responds. It is obvious to me that they know each other.

"How are you doing darling?"

"We are doing well." He puts an emphasis on "we." I can only imagine why.

"Who is this?"

"This is my companion." I am not as slow as many may think. I notice he didn't bother to introduce me or tell the woman my name. I look her over as she has done me. I can see she's closer to his age than mine. She is refined and sculpted, well dressed and obviously on the prowl.

"Hmm… She's a lovely model type. Hmm"

There is a waiter passing by, and Greg summons him for the check. He seems a bit on edge. The woman gets the hint and moves on. Outside of the restaurant, I notice Greg is not as talkative.

"Baby who is that lady?"

"She's a cougar, no more like a stalker. An old rich woman looking for a young man."

"I see now. You got the goods. The witch is trying to get them." I said what I felt. She had checked him out and wanted what he had. She made it so obvious. I learned something new…. Now I know what cougars are about.

"Baby, you got jokes," Greg smirks. I can tell he's still embarrassed about the older woman.

"I saw you last night. Your boxer briefs were covering your jewels when you came to my rescue. You have low body fat and high muscle; those abs are made of steel. Baby, you are ripped. What woman wouldn't want you?" I have never talked to a man the way I am talking to Greg.

"D'Alise, I like the way you're talking to me right now."

"You want me to take you. I know you want me to seduce you, baby."

We get to the car. Greg opens my door and quickly secures me in my seat. I reach for the stick shift in the console. I love the feel of it in my hands. Greg gets in the car and smiles.

"Baby, you want me to work your stick?"

I am surprised when he replies, "Yes, baby."

"Show me how to do it. This is my first time." I'm excited. Another new thing I've learned. I love his car and hope if I learn, he'll let me drive it.

"Give me your hand baby, here let me guide you. Put it right there, no right there. Relax baby, breathe."

He is right; I need to relax. It's a first, and I am so nervous. Greg is driving, and I am, with his help, shifting the gears. This is so exciting for me. My body is tingling. We're sitting at the light, and he gives new directions.

"It's not going to work if you're tense. We're going to start over. Relax. Look down, let your eyes follow my hands."

An aggravated driver blows the horn. It startles me because I am so focused on learning to shift the gears. The light has changed colors.

"Baby we're holding traffic up. I'm going to take over now. I really enjoyed that moment. I am going to let you work my stick more often."

"Alrighty, Mr. Happy." We both laugh. I feel so good with Greg. It is so different from being free to learn without worrying about who is watching.

"Baby lets go back to the penthouse, relax, and collect your clothing. I want you to check in with your cousins to let them know you'll be home around four, that will give me an opportunity to review your resume."

As we ride back to the hotel, I remember Linda saying not to let an opportunity pass me by. I really enjoy Greg and the attention he has given me. I want to be sure that he doesn't think I don't appreciate the gifts, affection, and attention. I want him to want me more. We arrive at the entrance to the suite, and I open the door. Greg is standing behind me, holding and massaging my waist. He's looking downward admiring my hips giving me an eye over. I turn around and make eye contact with him. It was then I finally kiss him on the corner of his cheek and follow it with a hug. He brushes up against the door and as he leans in the keys drop to the floor. I bend over to get the keys and open the door. Greg follows me into the suite like a little puppy wanting to be feed. I know he's enticed by my natural aroma. Especially since he claims the scent from my thong is embedded in his brain. Yes, he is intoxicated by my scent. I want to put this to the test.

"Greg, come here."

"Yes, baby."

"The door is repaired, and the penthouse is clean. It's as if we never stayed here last night."

"Baby I told you not to worry your pretty head."

I turn and face Greg. I am so happy; I give him another hug. He runs his fingers through my long black silky hair. I move my face close to Greg. We are so close our eyes are almost touching. I deliberately flutter my eyelids rapidly on his lips. I want him to feel as though he is being kissed. I'm teasing his senses with my butterfly eyelashes.

"Greg baby."

"Yes."

"I am really feeling you. You got me caught up with mixed emotions."

"Let's go to the sitting area and sit."

I want to talk about this and understand how this relationship is going. I understand my feelings, and I hope I am not leading him on. I keep hearing *"Don't miss the opportunity"* in my head. I followed Greg into the sitting room and sat in the winged chair.

"D'Alise are you ashamed of what you are feeling?"

"I can't explain how I'm feeling."

"It's going to be alright. Just let go and relax. Remember what I told you when you were working the stick."

"Yes, baby."

Greg takes both of his hands and gently touches my shoulders. He pulls me close to him. He looks into my eyes and begins to sing "The Flow of Love," which is written by a close friend.

It's the flow of love. The flow of love. I keep feeling. I keep feeling these feelings inside of me.

It's the flow of love. It's the flow of me. Feeling each day. Feeling each moment.

It's the flow of love. It's the flow of me. Feeling the vibrations of me, of you, can't you see.

It's the feeling of love. It's the feeling of love. It's a feeling of me. Can't you see each day? I love you each day. I love you more. I feel you more.

It's the flow of love. It's the flow of me. Can't you see? It's meant to be.

It's the flow of love. It's the flow of me. Feeling these feelings, Feelings of me.

It's the flow of love. It's the flow of me. Feeling the vibrations.

It's the flow of love. It's the flow of me. I keep feeling. I keep feeling these feelings. It's the flow of love. It's the flow of me.

"Greg, your baritone voice, is resonating in my heart. Wow, I'm getting serenaded today. This is nothing like the music you play me in the car. I can hear it all in the lyric's gentleness, kindness, and love. The artist is in tune with the spirit. She must have been in love."

"As a matter of fact, I know the artist."

"You do?"

"She lives in North Georgia."

"How did you meet her?"

"We are distant cousins. She was trained in classical music. The next time she's here singing at an event, I'll purchase tickets. We can go, and you can meet her."

"Great. I sing opera myself. I will sing '*Summer Time*' for you one day."

"I would love to hear you. Maybe we can go to New York and catch Porgy and Bess. That's one of the old operas that was performed in 1935 by all African American singers who were classically trained."

"Greg, I have to admit, I secretly wanted to be an opera singer."

"What happened?"

"My mother didn't want me to leave home. She was afraid I would get pregnant."

"That would have been a great opportunity for you to experience being away from home."

I told Greg about my mother's episodes and my responsibilities at home. It was simple. I had to be home for my family. My mother's condition was a priority all my life, and I gave up a lot of chances for me to be involved in extra curriculum activities.

"Baby you've been sacrificing all your life. No one should be envious of you because they don't know your story. You're still beautiful inside despite all you've been through."

"Greg, baby I like the way you look at me. Over the past couple of days, I have felt so pretty. I've never felt like this in all my years growing up. I was always teased about my dark skin and curly locs. The weight teasing never bothers me because I decided in elementary school, I wasn't going to be overweight. I've always liked my mother and grandmothers body type. I recall them never having any weight problems."

We talked until we both were a little tired. I enjoy talking with Greg. He's giving me a new way to think about my situation, my past and my future. He suggests we take a nap. Rather than dozing off in the chairs, we go to the bedroom where the door had just been repaired. I am comfortable and content laying by his side.

I can feel Greg shaking me, but I am paralyzed. This has happened before. I can't tell him at this moment what is going on. He is shaking me, telling me it is time to get up. I can feel him touching my face. I grunt to give him some sign that I am not dead.

"Baby what's wrong?" I can hear the panic in his voice, but I can only blink my eyes. He is checking my pulse. He won't find anything wrong. I just can't move. I know he will think I have sleep paralysis. I can hear him saying "breathe, breathe" as the paralysis is lifting.

"Greg…" I feel a little groggy, but I am coming around.

"Do I need to contact the paramedics?"

"No." I am sorry he looks so worried.

"Has this happen before?"

"Yes."

"Explain this to me, what has happened? He sits on the bed with his arm around my shoulder as I explain my condition.

Greg, sometimes I wake up and don't have the ability to move or speak. I am paralyzed. I can be laying in the bed wide awake, and it feels like someone is laying on top of my body weighing me down. I have never shared this with anyone. This happened a lot when I was a child.

"Have you been diagnosed?"

"I have sleep paralysis; it's not dangerous."

"That was scary seeing you like that. I am not a sleep specialist but will be happy to help you find someone to help you."

"You are the best. I've laid a lot on you the past couple of days. Do you still want to be with me?"

"That's a silly question. Yes."

"I want to get you back home; we both have a lot of ground to cover tomorrow."

Chapter 9

Things Aren't Always What They Seem

We made our way across the bridge and relax on the sofa in my cousin's apartment. I gave my resume to Greg to review.

"I only had to make a few changes to your resume. My driver will pick you up in the morning as I said my secretary will have instructions to help you with everything.

When your cousin and his wife return tonight, make sure you give them this check to cover your stay with them for the year. I'm going to leave an envelope with a key to a safe deposit box with the driver, so you'll have some emergency cash money."

Once again, I felt it was too much. While Greg was handling his business during the balance of the day, I had time to think of the things he had done for me. In just two days, our relationship was similar to couples who had been together for more than a year.

"I'm not going to use it."

"Trust me, baby. I see something that you don't see. You're going to need the money one day. It's a gift. Don't be too proud to use the money for an emergency. I want you to set your alarm clock and get some rest when I leave."

"Okay."

Greg's intuition had been right since I met him. I didn't want him to think I would need everything that he was giving me. It was good to know if I needed money I didn't have to work. Greg kissed my forehead, we hug, and he leaves. I stand watching what a man who could have been in one of my dreams drive off.

I woke up the next morning feeling refreshed. I needed the rest and made up the couch early. John nor Linda were home making my evening easy. I didn't have to talk about my date and the experience I had with Greg. John's voice was the first thing I heard. He walked into the living room as I was folding the blanket and the sheets.

"Good Morning, Cousin, you must have been exhausted. You didn't hear us when we came in last night."

"What time was that?"

 "Around eight o'clock. Did you have a good time?"

"It was amazing. He's the perfect guy."

"That's good. He provided all the details to me. I'm leaving Tuesday to go overseas for work. I should be back within thirty to sixty days."

"Check this out, cousin. He told me to give this check to you and your wife. Open it."

I'm excited. I want to see his expression.

"What? We can't take this. We really can use it."

"He said it should cover my living with you for the year."

"That's awfully kind of old Greg."

"You're the second person I've heard call him that."

"It's a joke, nothing serious. Thanks for the check. I don't' know if I should share this with Linda. I'm going to tell her later. I will be putting it in our savings for the move."

"Okay."

"I am taking Linda to work this morning. Help yourself to breakfast on the stove."

"Thanks. I'll clean up for you."

Linda came into the living room. We both look at her. I guess she thought we were talking about her.

"John, what are you two talking about?"

I cut in before John speaks.

"My date. Oh, I'm going job hunting today. I expect to have a job within two weeks. My student loans payments will start soon."

"Greg might help you." Linda is prepared to give instructions without knowing about anything that Greg has done. One date and he's paid an expense for my living.

"I wouldn't dare ask him he's already done enough. If anything, I could get a deferment.

Linda starts in again. Although she doesn't have the age, she has the ways of what Greg described as a cougar.

"Girl he's paying his way. Take everything he is giving you; I mean everything. Do you hear me?"

I answer, hoping she won't ask anything about the date. I simply answer, yes. I see why John won't tell her about a check reading four thousand eight hundred dollars. I don't want her to know.

Greg's driver arrives in time for me to go to the office to meet his secretary. As promised, Greg has made the corrections on my resume. I also have to get everything together for my passport. After taking care of those details, the driver is prepared to take me to fill out applications and leave my paperwork for the jobs I have selected.

"Ms. James we're glad you're able to interview for the position. You did well in your interview."

The manager shows me the paperwork he wants me to fill out. I take it and review it as he's talking.

"Thank you."

"We're tentatively able to offer you the entry-level Assistant Hotel Manager position. The hours are from nine to five. We'll check your references, and you'll be required to take a drug test. Our employee is being transferred to another location. If everything is okay, we call you in for orientation in less than two weeks to sign your offer letter."

"Thank you so much. I will be on public transportation."

"That isn't a problem. We look forward to having you on our team."

I am so excited. I hurry to the car and tell the driver. He's been with me most of the day, and I just have to tell someone.

"I received a job offer."

"Congratulations Ms. James."

"Thanks," I say a silent prayer of thanks.

"Where will I be taking you now?"

"Did Mr. Thibodeaux say when he would be available?"

"No, ma'am."

"Please take me back to the apartment."

"Yes, Ms. James."

We return to the apartment, and I thank the driver. His manners are the best. I feel special. Once again, Greg has my emotions on high. I can't wait to tell him I got a job offer. I change my clothes from the black two-piece suit into T-shirt and sweatpants and since I am alone. I go to sleep on the sofa.

Two hours or more pass and the ringing of the phone awakens me.

"Hello, sexy. How was your day?"

"Ah…. Hey baby."

"There you go again with the baby talk. Slow down, you know I'm missing you."

"Your secretary and driver were so nice."

"They are happy to finally see me with someone. They both like you a lot.

Tell me about your day?"

"Well, the best part is I was offered a job at Hotel U."

"I am familiar with the hotel."

"It's an entry-level Assistant Hotel Manager position. The hours are from nine to five."

"Congratulations, baby. I knew someone was going to hire you on the spot."

"Greg, I want to show you how grateful I am for you helping me."

"Baby, I like the way you are talking to me."

"You're so attentive. You didn't have to review my resume, but you did."

"I have a lot of responsibilities. I must make time for you. I want to see you so bad. Do you want me to drive over the bridge tonight, so you can show me how grateful you are?"

"I would like to see you but…."

"But what?"

"We both need our rest. Your parents will be in town tomorrow."

"Yeah, I want you to be well-rested."

"What day will I be getting the physical and signing the relationship agreement papers?"

I don't want to miss any opportunities. If this is what God has for me, I'm ready.

"On Wednesday. Is it okay if my parents are present for both? Our family attorney will also be present."

He's really serious about this agreement. I begin to wonder about his worth. It seems to be more than just a normal doctor's request to protect his 'brand.' It's not like we will be married, but I don't mind and tell him so.

"I don't mind. Your family is really in our business."

"Baby I told you that we are a brand. We have medical patents."

"So, you're big like that?"

"Yes. My family is big like that."

"What exactly is that you do?" It was time to get some truthful answers.

"I am an Orthopedic Surgeon."

"What?" I can't believe it. Patents and a Surgeon? I am sure I'm dreaming, and I don't want to wake up.

"Let's not talk about me. I want to talk about you. Is this position something that will make you happy?" Greg is always concerned about the things that make me happy.

"Yes. I have student loans to pay off."

"Oh, I know about that. It's a good feeling to have them paid off. I can pay your student loans off."

"Thank you, but no thank you. You have done enough to get your angel wings this week."

"D'Alise, it's important that you be loyal to me."

"I understand baby."

"I want you at the house early tomorrow. I'll have the driver pick you up in the morning. I can't wait to see you."

Greg is amazing, and I am in total disbelief. It is true, everything he has said has been proven, but I need a moment to stop spinning. Linda will not believe this, and I don't know if I should tell her everything. I was glad John and Linda were out again. I turned on the television and nodded between the programs.

John and Linda came home, and by then, I had made up the couch and laid down for the night. They came in teasing me. I sat up groggy. I looked at the television and realized it was off. They must have shut it off when they came in. I don't know what time it was when I went to sleep.

"Cousin, you've been getting that beauty sleep. Every time we come home, you are asleep on the sofa".

"You sure Greg is not on another date?" Linda teased.

"Linda Greg's not that type of a man."

"What do you know BAMA?"

I always hated that expression in college. It gave others the impression that a person from Alabama didn't know what others knew. I knew more about Greg than Linda. I was sure of that.

"Linda trust me he's not that type of a guy."

"I'm just teasing. I know I'm a jealous girl."

John interjected. I guess he knew I wasn't happy with the way the conversation was going.

"Okay, y'all talking like I don't hear you."

I had a chance to rub my good fortune in, and I do.

"I'm going to be hanging out with Greg today. I have a job offer at Hotel U. I start in a few weeks if all of my paperwork is okay."

"You are on the straight and narrow. You got the job, especially if it was a man who interviewed you. He probably hired you on the spot. Look at you, we don't have any ugly people in our family. Your, mama, made sure she was going to have some pretty babies."

I don't think Linda liked John complimenting me. She is suddenly in a hurry to take him to the airport. It's the first time that I can tell she is right. She's jealous.

"Well, I am taking John to the airport and heading off to work. We'll start looking for an apartment in a few weeks, so you can have your own room."

"Linda, I put that check in the bank that Greg gave me for little cousin."

"You ladies be good to each other. I will see you cousin in about sixty days. Come on, Linda, let's head out."

"I'll see you later tonight."

"Don't rush home. Girl, enjoy this time with your man."

I didn't plan on coming in early. I didn't want Linda to know or ask. The driver picks me up to go to Greg's home. I take the time to catch a nap. I can't wait for me to get off the emotional rollercoaster. Too much excitement is draining. The ride isn't long. Forty minutes later, the driver parks in front of the home.

"Ms. James, we're at the residence. Mr. Thibodeaux has asked me to give you the details of the Garden District property."

I step out of the car as he begins to point to the home and the land surrounding it.

"The Regency Style home is a 7,465 square foot living quarters constructed over three years ago. The interior has a three-story open stairwell with an atrium. The property has four bedrooms, seven baths, and a master suite with two master baths. A large professionally equipped kitchen with separate silver & china walk-in closets. There's a large grand formal space for dining that seats twenty-five. It has one open and one private walled garden. The property has an elevator and gated parking for six vehicles."

The driver steps back to the car to close the door as I step to the rear of the car and take in the sight that he has described. The home is beautiful. I can't believe how large it is. I'm sure I'll get a more thorough tour walking the insides of the home. Greg comes out to meet us, and I am truly happy to see him.

"Sir, do you need anything else?"

"No, thank you."

Greg is all smiles, and I am just as happy to see him.

"Come on in sexy."

The home is decorated with French and Victorian style furniture.

"Show me how much you appreciate me."

Greg grabs for my waist but is interrupted by a sweet voice. I imagine his grandmother before the small-framed lady approaches us.

"Greg, Greg, Greg, where are you?"

"I am in the hallway, grandmother. I thought you were sleeping." He laughs lightly.

"Who was that at the door? Her voice is getting closer.

"My girlfriend has arrived. Come on in the grand room so you can meet her."

Greg greets his grandmother with a loving hug and a kiss on her cheek. He guides her with his hand toward me.

"D'Alise this is Grandmother Thibodeaux."

"Oh, my she's gorgeous." Grandmother Thibodeaux gives me my first compliment of the day. I smile admiring her. She too is beautiful.

"Grandmother let me help you."

"Oh, don't fuss now. This old lady wants to sit right here next to your little doll. My grandson won't stop talking about you. I see why."

"Ladies I am going to let you get acquainted. I'll come back and check in on you."

"Greg has sacrificed fun for a life of study. I was beginning to worry about old Greg. His parents had him in the hospital before he could walk. Crawling around on floors and playing with medical equipment and that stethoscope. He was destined to be a doctor. Greg told the whole family how he met you. We know everything about you."

"You do?"

"I think Greg is in love with you. Can I share something with you?"

"Yes. Sure."

"He had puppy love when he was young. He still has the little girl's hair bows in his room next to his bed. The little girl was his best friend. Let me share the pictures with you."

She stands prepared to go to the curio when Greg calls out from another room. He enters the room, talking.

"Hey, grandmother. You don't need to pull that old photo album out. I brought Moringa and Ginger Tea for you ladies." He sets the tea on the table.

While they talk, I think about the scrappy black thong. I wonder if the hair bows were embedded in is memories. *When I told him, I gave my childhood toys away, he thought that was a good thing. He's still holding on to something in his childhood memory. He's stuck in some way.* I realize at this moment this man is for real. He's not playing with my emotions; he really has a desire to be with me for life. I'm thankful to be meeting his family early. This is giving me an opportunity to get the intimate details of his life, somethings he will never share with love. I thought he had planned a fiesta. I think I should just listen and not ask questions because everything is going to come out. Greg has problems from his childhood, just like me. He is strong and confident, but he still has problems. I am determined to find out as much as I can today before I leave this house.

"Grandmother, don't be in here spilling the tea on me old woman. I might have to help you back to your room and have the nurse watch you." Greg laughs, and I remember that spilling the tea means that she is disclosing too much about him. I smile and giggle a bit.

"Greg, I am enjoying your grandmother."

"My grandmother has studied the healing arts and is a licensed clinical psychologist. She's been studying me for years. I'm not crazy. Am I, grandmother?"

"No, son. Go upstairs and get my pink robe."

Greg doesn't hesitate to obey her request. I realized she sent him out of the room so she could finish spilling the tea.

"Greg is correct; I have been studying him since he was a little boy. He is a good man. I'm not saying that because he is my grandson."

"He has been very good to me."

"I can tell you haven't dated around a lot. I don't want to stereotype men by implying they are all bad. Beware of the narcissist, sociopath, and psychopath. All men are not the same; they come in different packages. They experience the world differently through their environment and five senses. If you ever have doubts about your relationship with Greg. Always ask your self, is that true? How do I know it's true? You will be guided in the correct direction. Your gut feelings will never steer you wrong. Pay close attention to your intuition."

"I feel so blessed that I attracted Greg in my life. He is so loving."

"I'm glad you found each other."

"You really know a lot about human behavior."

"Yes. I could take all day to discuss the three behavioral characteristics I have mentioned. I just want to focus on the narcissist for now."

"I am not familiar with that trait." I am not sure why I didn't fest up to knowing a little. I just wanted to hear a subject matter experts' opinion.

"Everyone knows a narcissist they show up in families, friendships, work, and close intimate relationships. About ten out of every fifteen people can be a narcissist. This is just a number I'm throwing out. I don't have any statistical data at hand."

"I studied psychology in college. I have an interest in human behavior because of my adverse childhood experiences." I am enjoying this talk. Greg's grandmother is as interesting as he is.

"You need to study Greg just like he's been studying you from the first day you met."

"Oh, I see," I remember he said he had seen me a few times on the bus. He knew about my clothing and the fact that I didn't wear jewelry. She was right. He had studied me for a while without my knowing it.

"He's figured you out and knows you better than you know yourself."

"You think so?"

"Yes. Trust and believe I know this."

I am taking all this in. I don't know what to say or to ask. Greg's intuition comes from his grandmother. This is not something you learn in books.

"Now you need to determine what behavior traits you're dealing with."

"Can you explain the narcissist behavior traits? Maybe we can discuss the sociopath and psychopath another day?"

"Sure. There is no blanket term for a narcissist and the many traits. I would not put them in the category of all being openly grandiose and outwardly intrusive. Basically, the narcissist is insecure and needs lots of validation. They need to prove they are winners. It's all about them. A narcissist has no empathy. They are in love with themselves. Their emotions are not regulated. They demonstrate openly their leadership authority, superiority, arrogance, self-absorption or self-admiration, and exploitative entitlement."

"I'm glad Greg has his emotions under control."

"Okay, a few more traits of a narcissist are being grandiose, covert, malignant or communal. I'll explain all of them to you or might even add Greg in on our discussion later today."

"Okay."

"Woman to woman we got to look out for each other. You need to know what you are getting yourself into so have all the information to make an educated choice about the men you date."

"Grandmother, here you go." Greg returned with the long robe. His grandmother smiles and places the robe over the arm of the chair.

"Thank you for bringing me my robe."

"You are welcome. So, what have you been telling D'Alise about me?"

"We just started a discussion on narcissist behavior traits."

"Hopefully you explained them all so she can determine I am a good guy."

"As a matter of fact, I haven't gotten around to explaining them yet."

"Why don't you sit right here, and I do some counseling right now?"

"Really, grandmother?"

"Yes, son. You're in the early stages of the relationship."

"I brought her here to meet the family, not a counseling session. What do you think, baby?"

"I'm ok with it if you are Greg."

Greg sighs and sits with us before reluctantly saying, "Yes, baby sure."

"It's going to be a while before your parents are released from the conference. This is going to give us plenty of time for our discussion and get to know each other."

"Grandma…" I want to laugh at Greg's whining like a little boy.

I respond eagerly to learn more about this man who must be in love. "I'm ready."

"D'Alise how do you see Greg?"

I look at Greg sitting on the opposite side of the room. I haven't known him long enough to give a definitive description of my emotions or what I feel. I give her my first impression thoughts.

"I see him as being educated, ambitious, and influential. Anytime we are out people know him. He strikes me as a celebrity type."

"My achievement matches my ambition. If you're fully confident the attention will be drawn to you."

"A grandiose narcissist has an ego, is arrogant, and seeks attention."

"I don't see that being either one of us. What about you baby."

"I agree with Greg."

"That's good to know let's move on. Greg, what do you think about D'Alise's life?"

"Wow, over the past couple days while talking with her, I get the impression she's had a hard life. Of course, everyone has a story. I embrace her story and life. She might need some counseling. I haven't seen any passive-aggressiveness behavior."

"D'Alise would you like to make any comments?"

"Greg is correct with his observations. I admit I've had a hard life. Being raped as a child has impacted my life and relationships. I might have suffered from trauma in the past, but it's made me a better person. I have compassion and sensitive to others emotions at times."

Let me briefly describe the covert narcissist. The Jeckle and Hyde secret, life has issued them a bad hand. They are passive-aggressive. Normally they are treated for depression. Do have any question thus far?"

"No." I'm surprised Greg, and I answer simultaneously. This seems like a mini counseling session.

"Excuse me." I interrupt his grandmother's next statement. "I have a comment. My mother married a covert narcissist. I promised myself I never want to appear to have a perfect life, and behind closed doors, it is different."

"This is why we are having this conversation so we can familiarize ourselves with the behavioral traits of a narcissist. I am going to ask a few sensitive questions for both of you. Please answer honestly Greg and D'Alise."

"Okay," I reply immediately, and Greg nods his head in agreement.

"We are trying to build a strong foundation. Please be honest. Since you started dating has either of you lied, cheated, stolen anything, or done bad things?"

"No. I have no reason to do those things to Greg. I've seen a lot in my childhood. For instance, I soon learned I was able to feel much deeper than most individuals. I have empathy. I could read the mood and emotions in any room I entered. I could decode through non-verbal language. I realized I processed information differently from most people. They say animals can sense emotions. I am intuitive. I understand what's going on around me. I am able to pick up on a person's emotions to include joy, surprise, fear, anger, sadness, disgust, and some illnesses in the human body. I gained this knowledge from my childhood environment.

This meeting is insightful and confirms I need to stop ignoring the red flags. I am fully aware of what I need to do but, on many occasions, have given up my power.

"What about you, Greg?" Saved by the ringing of the phone.

"Son. Please answer the phone."

Greg answers the phone, and soon we know who is on the line. I take the time to look over this older woman who holds so much wisdom.

"I love you too, mom and dad. See you this evening."

A child can become so much when they are encouraged,
get hugs and hear the words "I love you" from their parents
in the early stages of life. I admire the man Greg has be-
come; he has been nurtured from birth. It appears to me
that Greg's family has strong family values.

"That was mom and dad; they will arrive around five."

"Grandmother, I've never told D'Alise my exact age. I told her I was older than her."

"Is it important you know his age?"

"I…When we first met, I knew he was older than me." *Strange it didn't bother me until now. I didn't know his age.*

"Greg." His grandmother says his name waiting for his response. He doesn't say anything. He raises his eyebrow and glances at me.

"I've tried to do the calculations in my head."

"What did you calculate?"

"Well, four years of undergraduate, four years of medical school, residency four-six years. He said he lives with you."

"He lives with me." His grandmother looks at him again and calls his name for a response. Again, he has no reply.

"He's accomplished, I guess he's 36." I have no idea if I am right. I hope I'm close. So, I call on him.

"Greg."

"Baby, I'm forty-two years old. I am close to your mother's age group. I recall you telling me your father was much older than your mother."

"Greg, oh my God!" *He's close to my mother's age group.* I wonder if there are male cougars. I don't have anything to offer, though. I guess he's not a cougar.

"I never lied to you. I just never told you my age."

"Greg, do you want to tell her something else?"

"Yes. I told you I lived with my grandmother. We live together. This house belongs to me. My grandmother's Victorian style home has been donated and is displayed a historical site in the Garden District."

"Let me say something here. The malignant narcissist lies, cheat, steals, and do does very bad things. Do you think Greg falls into this category?"

Greg never disclosed any of this information. He has this don't ask don't tell thing about him. I don't know how to feel. I blame myself because I should have could have asked more questions to clarify his age and living arrangements.

"Let's take a break we're almost finished."

His grandmother takes her time to go and check with the chef about the upcoming meals. Lunch and dinner are being prepared, and she excuses herself to check the kitchen. Greg moves closer to talk to me, but my mind won't let go of the questions I should have asked.

"Baby, look at me."

"Greg, you are about the same age as my mother. I could be your daughter."

"I've been studying all my life. I am exhausted being by myself. Tell me, does it matter? Look at me."

"Greg. No, it doesn't matter, but it's something I should have asked. I should have known although I want to take this opportunity for love."

"Can I get a hug?"

"Yes. Of course." His embrace comforts me as it has since we met. I can't be mad about not knowing. I can only be mad at myself.

"Let me give you a tour of the house."

"Okay, the house is out of this world much different than the public housing and farm I grew up on."

"If you don't like this house, I'll let you select another house."

We hadn't walked through the entire first floor before his grandmother beckoned for us to return to the grand room.

"Son, I can't believe you didn't tell her your age, and that this house belongs to you."

"Thank you for breaking the ice with this conversation. I chose to take this opportunity for love and to be open with everything."

"The last behavior trait is the communal narcissist who needs recognition. Well put together and has no empathy for people. I'll leave this open for you two to discuss. It looks like we got everything out in the open."

"D'Alise please promise me you will not be a negative distraction for my grandson. If this relationship is not what you want, you should say so now."

"I promise to be positive. Oh, I've been seeking employment and received a job offer for an entry-level Assistant Hotel Manager position. I'd be working days full time from nine to five. I don't plan on being a burden or negative person in his life."

"That's good congratulations. The family is about protecting the Thibodeaux brand by any means necessary. I look forward to you being a part of the family. Get the physical examination and, sign the relationship agreement."

This was more than a mere conversation. It was an interview. Greg didn't give me a warning. Another thing I should have asked more about. I'm learning.

"Greg told me he made the arrangements."

"Very well, my dear. Son, help me get to my room."

His grandmother stands slowly stabilizing herself before taking a step.

"Grandma, are you going to have lunch?"

"No."

Greg returns and sits next to me. I've been allowing my thoughts to run free. I don't know what I was thinking at that moment. But when he sat down, I wondered about his attention to detail. Especially since he was so attentive to her needs.

"You're so attentive it didn't take long to get your grandmother to her room."

"I want her to be rested so she can give the report on you to my parents. I also wanted to get back so I would have more time to spend with you before my parents arrive. Baby your lips look so juicy."

I giggle. He's such a corny romantic. "I know you want to kiss me."

"I do, but I have self-control. My grandma likes you a lot."

"She got straight to the point on our informal relationship counseling. Greg, this home is something beautiful."

"If you want it, I'll sign it over to you."

"That would be very generous, but no. I noticed on the mini-tour you didn't show me your room. Is it off-limits?"

"No." I thought he would say more, but he didn't.

"Do you feel like sharing that private part with me?"

"I'll share but let's wait until later or another day."

I notice there's something more to that than his response. His room and the photo album holds a part of him that he is not yet willing to share.

"I noticed something about you."

"What?"

"You always tend to push things to the side with me when you don't want to deal with it."

"Why do you say that?"

"I can give you plenty of examples, but I am not. I really need to start calling things out when they happen."

"Baby I didn't realize I was doing that."

"We're gathered here today so let's deal with this now. I want to see your room, and I want to look in the family photo album. What is it you don't want me to see?"

"Hmm." He grins. It is a different type of look. I believe he is turned on by my aggressiveness. I don't want to be surprised again about something I can ask openly.

"You know everything about me because you've been studying me. You even hired a private investigator. Tell me, what are you hiding?"

"Honestly. I have nothing to hide."

"I'm stronger than you think I am. I've shown myself to you. I'm feeling as if you were in love with someone else. You buried yourself in your studies because you didn't want to face yourself."

"Do you want to see or hear the dark side?"

"Greg, yes, I want to be as nurturing to you as you have been towards me. You have been sensitive to my needs as well as to hearing and understanding my past. Please let me show you I can be that way with you."

"I want a family. I want what my mother and father have in their marriage. You are so beautiful. I don't just want to sleep with you. I want to have a relationship with you. I can have anyone, but I chose you. My love is flowing for you."

"Greg." He's changing the topic again. I pout and smirk knowing he's deliberately hiding what I want to know.

"Baby you look so beautiful. Stop pouting. Let's get lunch from the kitchen. We can eat in my room."

We go to the large kitchen where the chef has prepared an area for us to eat. We grab our plates and drinks and head to the second level. Greg's bedroom door is locked. He uses a key to enter. He allows me to enter first. The room his huge nothing like I imagined. Once again, I am stunned.

There is a large window that overlooks the garden. The view is breathtaking. Greg is unusually quiet as though he is in deep thought. I can only hope that it means he will reveal some of his secrets. I am here to be interviewed for an important place in his life and in his family. I'm sure Greg is thinking of a short engagement. He's ready to get married and have a happy family. If this conference and the patents go through, he can retire early and spend all his waking days with me. He has been turned on by my passive-aggressive behavior. I've decided to accept his way of thinking. I may not get an opportunity to be in love like this again.

"Your bedroom is bigger than my family's apartment back home in Alabama. You have a mini apartment up here."

"Come here, baby, let's sit in the sitting area in the bedroom."

I had no idea there was another room. His bedroom alone was large enough.

"No, please give me a tour of this impressive and somewhat intimidating space."

"Come here, girl. Let me look at you." Greg pulls me into him, and I simply push back only to be pulled close again. "I've been fantasying about you baby."

I pull away again. "Tour, please." I see he's teased by me taking charge.

"You're feisty."

"Now."

"Demanding too. I like this side of you. Come on let me share my formal bedroom with you lovely. Its décor is quite masculine, as you can see." Greg takes my hand, and we walk hand in hand through the bedroom. "I hope you like the colonial-style interior."

"I do."

"Will you marry me? I'm joking." His emotions are speaking. I know he's serious and I choose to pretend I didn't hear him.

"Your bedroom feels so lavish and luxurious."

"Come touch the wooden wall panels, wooden columns, door and window frames. The wooden furniture is solid mahogany. The large custom area rug helps frame the area. It helps the furniture pop out. Do you see that? It sets off the mahogany flooring."

"Everything you do is with style."

"Thanks, baby."

"You can look at anything you like." That's what I wanted, a chance to explore. I look in the bathroom, the walk-in closet, and the dresser. The closet is huge and filled with suits and expensive clothing. I pull open one of the drawers slowly hoping he can't hear me rummaging through his things.

"Baby, what are you doing?"

"You said I could look at anything." I pushed the drawer closed quickly. Greg enters the closet to distract me. He pulls me to him. He obviously has something he doesn't want me to see.

"Stop, you said I could look at anything." He grabs my hands. I have managed to open a hidden drawer in the dresser. Greg appears to be withdrawn. *"Spilling the tea" is what he said to his grandmother. "Don't spill the tea." He fears she has told me something.* He doesn't move to allow me to look through the drawers. I leave him standing there and walk toward the nightstand. I look back at the closet. Greg comes to me as I open the top drawer.

He grabs my hand again, and I push his hand away. I've found his secret. His grandmother's words come to mind. *"He had a puppy love…. he kept her hair bows."*

"Greg, why do you have a little girls hair bows in your nightstand?"

Greg falls to the hardwood floor and begins to cry like a baby in the fetal position. I rush over to him and kneel by his side.

He whispers, "She is gone."

"Baby who? No, you don't have to talk."

I help him from the floor to his bed. I sit on his lap to give him a closer embrace. I feel terrible. Something has traumatized Greg in his childhood. I wish now I never opened that drawer. I hold him as a mother would hold her child. I hold him as he held me when my fears met me in the night. I can feel his spirit settling. I touch him softly as he calms down. I take his hands and rub them slowly across my breast. I'm doing this for me as well as him. I am turned on by his vulnerability. Greg begins to respond by touching me all over. His manhood responds too. I can feel its hardened shaft against my leg. I begin to open his shirt. So, I can touch his chest and his washboard abs.

"D'Alise," he whispers my name in a sultry tone.

"Greg, I am so sorry."

"Baby keep touching me." Greg opens the front of my blouse to expose my tangerine size breasts. His eyes widen, and his manhood responds as it begins to have its own pulse. He takes both of his hands to fondle my breasts. I lean in to kiss him.

"Greg and D'Alise, where are you? His grandmother is closer than either of us knew. We remain seated and close. My blouse is open, and my breasts are seated on his bare chest.

"Your parents are here." His grandmother walks closer toward the bed. "Oh, my Greg praise God. You are finally coming out of your slump. Did I walk in on something?"

"Grandmother, do you ever knock?"

"This old lady just checking on the two of you. I see you haven't touched your food. I see D'Alise is feeding you, but it's not food."

She's filled with laughter as she turns to exit the room. Greg sighs and shakes his head. I am so embarrassed I can't look her way, even as she leaves.

"Tell them we'll be right down."

"Okay." She waves her hand over her head.

"Close the door behind you, please. Baby I apologize for my grandmother."

"Greg." I turn his face toward me gently as I rub my breast across his chest. I watch his expression. I know we are good for each other. I begin to caress his back.

"Baby you are so passionate."

I lean back to look at his shirt. A few of the buttons have popped off.

"I damaged your shirt."

"It's just a shirt. Baby, I feel like a weight has been lifted off my shoulder. You are the best medicine for me. Sometimes, I get angry about not being able to save my childhood girlfriend. Before I could walk, I remember us always being side by side. Before I was five, she was gone. The only thing I have is the bows. I believe if we had grown up together, I would have married her."

"Oh! She's the other girl."

"I felt something for her at a young age. I have been carrying her with me all my life. Then you came along on the bus and sparked something inside me. I felt I needed to approach you. I was attracted to you. Something about you was familiar and felt like home. It seemed easy. As I said when you know you know. It doesn't take months or years to be in a relationship with someone. I've seen colleagues' string women along for years, not to mention it is often without offering anything. Just empty promises and unspoken words. Then they go off and marry someone else. I believe if she had lived, she would have resembled you. You are the adult version of her. It's like God reincarnated her in you. There haven't been any other women in my life."

"Handsome man you've made up for it in less than three days. It feels like we have been together a lot longer."

"Yes, I am present in this moment right here with you. I wouldn't trade this for anything in this world. Let's make ourselves presentable for my parents. My grandmother probably has already filled my parents in on what's been going on up here."

Now I am embarrassed. His grandmother's 'spilling the tea' must be normal within their family. I watch as Greg changes his shirt. Again, his sculpted upper body is teasing me. He takes good care of himself. He has the body of a twenty-year-old man. I am thirsty for his touch. I wonder how his lips would feel. *That first kiss.*

"Baby." Greg snaps me out of my trance as he kisses me on my forehead.

"Yes."

"Are you ready?"

"Yes."

"Let's do this, my queen."

The day has arrived, and I am walking down the stairs holding Greg's hands preparing to meet his parents. I suddenly begin to feel a little nervous because I want to make a good impression. My heart is pounding, and I am thinking I should relax. I'm saying to myself; finally, I get to meet the people that are an extension of who he is. We enter the sitting room. They stand. It's time for me to swallow the panic. I meet and greet his parents with confidence. The parents go in for a hug and a kiss on the cheek. His parents are influential and sophisticated, just like him. The family already knows everything about me. I want this nervousness to be gone. I notice how Greg has transformed himself from being vulnerable to a highly confident man again. He is very loving towards his mother and father. I notice a strong resemblance. Greg is the spitting image of his father. Greg is just a younger version of who his father is. I think his father is in the late sixties. His mother is very sophisticated and appears to be friendly.

"Mom and dad meet Danielle Alise James. She prefers to be called D'Alise. D'Alise meet my parents, Mr. and Mrs. Greg Thibodeaux."

His father reaches to shake my hand, "D'Alise, you can call my wife Margaret and call me Greg."

I smile as I shake their hands. "I'm sure Grandmother has filled you in."

"Yes." They reply together smiling. They seem to be impressed by my appearance. His mother gently pats my back as we walk toward the sitting area.

"It's so nice to meet you." I'm preparing myself for the small talk. I seem to meet their approval so far.

"Let's have a seat. Greg, she is lovely. I pray this relationship can evolve into a partnership."

"What do you mean mother?"

His father leans forward in his seat. "Margaret, do you mind if I explain this?"

She nods her head and smiles. "Sure."

"Do the two of you understand a partnership isn't about feelings?"

"Dad, will you please explain."

"I hope you are working on establishing and solidifying those feelings. If you come together in partnership, it's about taking those feelings and proving them every day."

"We're listening."

His mother holds her husband's hand as she begins to explain.

"Greg Sr. and I have been married over forty years. It wasn't easy with both of us being in medical school having two children. We had a lot of family support. We chose to stay together because we truly love one another. I know you probably feel a bit rushed by my son."

"Yes." I give a sheepish grin.

"Greg's father always says when you know you know."

"I recall him saying something like that." Greg is beaming as he looks from his mother to me.

"Greg has made many sacrifices. He has studied long and hard. A lot of patients put their lives in his hands every day. He needs to be focused and have good concentration. Sometimes he stands on his feet for hours."

"Greg has never really discussed his job with me." I am beginning to see how serious being his wife could be. The marriage will have to be stronger than those I have known about.

"You need to know what you're getting yourself into. Greg's father has had a big influence on his life. They have a good relationship. We have been talking to our son ever since he was a child explaining and telling him about traditions. Greg called and told me he wanted to purchase you a nice piece of jewelry. I told him Tiffany's was the best place. I see he made a nice selection the pearl earring and necklace look beautiful on you."

I put my hand to my neck. I have found comfort in wearing the jewelry. "I love the selection he made." I realize Greg has on-going communication with his family.

"My son has exceptional taste, just like his father. We have given Greg an opportunity to have diverse experiences. He is very disciplined. He's been training in martial arts ever since he was five years old. He and his father both have a black belt in Taekwondo. My son has self-control. I know him very well. He will never disrespect you. He is a surgeon and doesn't need a lot of stress in his life. I hope you're not one of those night creatures."

"Mother, we've already discussed that." Greg pats my hand. I guess he thought I would say something about her comment. I understand what and why she is saying all of this.

"We must protect our brand and medical patents." His father states. Ladies, Greg and I have been talking about medical terminology for years. My wife understands, and we really don't want to bore you D'Alise. My son can't stop talking about you."

"It looks like dinner is ready. I took your grandmother up-stairs so she could take a nap. Son will you go upstairs and ask your grandmother will she be joining us."

I am left in the sitting room with Greg's parents as he goes to check on his grandmother. He returns before another conversation can begin. Greg laughs as he explains.

"She doesn't want to join the family for dinner; she will get something later. She was snacking on the food she took from my room."

We walk into the dining room to be properly seated. The table is dressed with china dishware. Everything is beautiful. The chef comes out with platters of food. After he places the last sterling silver platter on the table, he nods to Greg's father. A sign that he was finished serving us.

"Let's have a seat. Greg Jr., will you lead us in prayer."

"Yes, father. Heavenly, Father, we thank you for the food that we are about to receive. I am filled with much gratitude to have family present for this joyous occasion and my addition to the family, D'Alise. Thank you, God, for blessing me with her. May we continue to grow in our faith forever amen."

The table conversation is good. We talk about family values. His parent's talk about traditions and to my surprise, there are many things that are the same between our cultures.

"Greg it would have been nice if you would have invited some of your colleagues over. How is Donald LeBlanc? We have not seen or talked to him in a while."

"Mom, he is the same obnoxious Donald. I just wanted close family here today."

"D'Alise I am so glad you have good intentions for my son and agree to sign the written agreement. We will have the driver get you home. The driver will pick you up tomorrow morning. Greg has an early appointment with a patient tomorrow. He will meet you at your scheduled doctor's appointment. Then we'll proceed to the attorney's office for signatures."

Greg's mother speaks as we finish our dinner. "It was a pleasure meeting you D'Alise. You have brought so much joy to my son's life in the past few days."

We walk to the door together. His father and mother give me a tender hug as we say our good-byes. Greg takes my hand as we walk to the car. It is parked in front of the house. The driver is standing at the passenger door.

"Baby, thank you for coming to my house today.

"Greg, I had a lovely time. I have never experienced anything like this in my life. Your family is so loving."

"I wish my sister's family could have joined us. I get along well with her two children. They would have loved to meet you. Goodnight baby, I will see you tomorrow. I will send the driver to pick you up."

The driver takes me to the apartment as I sit in the rear seat and reflect on the day I've had. As I get close to the apartment door, I can hear voices, laughter, and loud music. I turn the key and enter the apartment.

"Hi, Linda. Did John get off okay."

"Yes, girl. Look at you, looking all delicious. Did you and Greg have a good time?"

"Linda, you can't imagine my day. It was something out of this world."

"D'Alise you got yourself a good man don't mess this up. Oh, this is my half-sister."

"Hello." I feel uncomfortable. Her so-called sister is staring at me. Looking at me thoroughly from head to toe. The music, the drinking, and smoking is not new to me, but I'm wondering how John would feel. I thought I had gotten away from all of that. It's a different environment, but it's the same thing as back home. I wish Greg had invited me to stay at his place. I understand though, it would have been inappropriate since his parents were in town.

"Hey, sister it's a weeknight. I'll check you on the weekend."

Her sister never said a word to me. She walked out the door telling Linda, "Bye girl." I guess I was intruding.

"Hey, Linda, I hope I didn't break any of your bonding time with your sister."

"No, she was just passing through." Linda turns down the music and begins to clean up the mess they made.

"Do you two have the same mother?"

"Oh, no, we have the same father. I know it's a difference."

"What do you mean?"

"She tends to be a little masculine, you know? She a lesbian D'Alise. I saw her checking you out."

"Linda, I want to be clear. I've been through a lot in my lifetime. I am only into men. I'm not judging her for her lifestyle that's her choice. I don't want her to try to come on to me. I experienced this in elementary school, and I knew what I was attracted to." I told her about my past experience. I didn't want to be her sister's love interest. "Your sister can be herself. Just tell her never cross the line or test me."

Linda cut off the kitchen light without a comment. She moved around a few things in the living room and cut off the stereo.

"Alright well, I guess we'll go to bed on that note."

I simply replied, "See you in the morning." I guess she was put off by my story. I wanted her to know I did have a line that I wouldn't allow anyone to cross, and that was it. I can respect another's choice but don't push me.

We're sitting in the waiting room for the scheduled physical examination. The paperwork has been completed, and we are waiting for the nurse to tell us what to do next.

"Baby, I am here for our physical examination. I know we are in good health and I'm ready to move forward in our happy life. This physical is also a preventive step to catch up on vaccinations or detect a serious condition, like cancer or diabetes, before it causes problems. The doctor is going to check your vitals, including your weight, heart rate, and blood pressure. The doctor will complete a full blood panel evaluation. They'll also test your blood for HIV and STD's."

I hadn't been to a doctor's office since I graduated from college. I have always been healthy. I'm not worried.

"I'm glad we are doing this from the very start."

"I told you it is not about the sex for me. I want something long term. This is not a fly by night intimate encounter. My mother will be in the room when you get your mammogram, PAP smear, and a vaginal exam. I didn't want you to be by yourself. Are you ok with her being with you?"

"Yes." I thought about it for a moment. I guess her being a doctor, it shouldn't matter. I put the thought of asking, 'why,' behind me. "This is an all-day process." Greg didn't respond to my statement.

"I could never consent to being with anyone without them having a physical exam. You must protect yourself and those you care for. If you had not consented to this. I would have walked away. It's best to get everything out in the open fast. I don't need to be wasting my time on something that's not going anywhere."

"Greg, you are direct and to the point. I like that about you. I am learning so many lessons." *And so much about men. I can't imagine his father being this forward. There's got to be more to this.*

"Baby, do you take birth control pills?"

"How do you feel about taking birth control?"

"Why do you ask?"

"When we get married, we'll enjoy each other totally the first couple of years. Just you and I and if you decide you want to have children we can."

"No more than one or two." I've had my share of changing diapers.

"I am glad we're able to speak openly and be honest about this subject. Baby, I am really feeling you. I was walking on clouds today. I feel like a new man all because of you coming into my life."

The nurse beckons for me to follow her into an examination room. Greg's mother gives me a hug when I enter the room. There's not much to be said as we go through the various test. During the pelvic examination, I experience discomfort. The doctor requests an ultrasound of my pelvis. Greg's mother is right there with me holding my hand. The pelvic examination reminds me of the pain when I was taken to the doctor as a teen. The physician completed a pelvic exam and told my mother, "Your daughter's hymen is broken. She is not a virgin." This would have been an ideal time to have a discussion to find out why the hymen was broken. No mention or discussion was made of this doctor appointment. Once again, the rape is swept under the rug.

The non-disclosure agreement, the paperwork that Greg has said must be signed, is signed in the presence of the family and the attorney.

"Mom and dad, can I have a moment with D'Alise. We walk away from where we were standing ear shy of his parents. Baby, you did well today. How are you holding up?"

"I feel tired." I was annoyed. The exam reminded me of my mother's neglect to talk about the rape. The rape she knew was going on. Even if she feared her husband and his abuse, she could have asked the doctor or me how my hymen possibly got broken. I would have told everyone what went on. Yes, I was tired.

"I'm going to get you back to the house. We both can get in the bed and get some rest. My parents are leaving today. Our test results will be mailed to my attorney's office. We will open them in his presence."

"I can't wait to lay next to you again."

His parents come over and join us. I dare not complete my thoughts aloud.

"Greg."

"Father thanks for coming down."

"D'Alise, I really enjoyed meeting you. I look forward to you being a part of our family."

"Yes, thank you. It has been my pleasure. Safe travels back to California."

We leave the doctor's office and head to Greg's house. We make small talk in the car. The driver pulls up to the front door, and both he and Greg get out to assist me.

"Hey, baby, let's be quiet. I know my grandmother is snooping around looking for unlocked doors. Make yourself compatible, we have food and everything up in my room, there's a small hidden refrigerator where you can get anything you want to eat. I have some lingerie for you. I want you to get some rest. I really hate you're sleeping on that sofa at the apartment. I'll let you use the bathroom first. I have a closet for you filled lingerie and clothing. I need to check my schedule and make some notes. I'll be up soon."

I follow his instructions. I enter the bathroom and notice the bathroom color matches the bedroom. What a life! We are alone now, except how can I forget, his grandmother walking in   on us. Greg and I can enjoy this moment. To finally cuddle and be in bed in Greg's arms. *He'll embrace me with his strong biceps. I love his arms. I love the way he smells. I am a big girl now.* As Greg sits at his desk writing, I walk behind him and give him a playful kiss on his ear lobe.

"Baby I've finished in the bathroom. It's your turn now."
Greg turns around and smiles.
"I like the way that looks on you sexy."
"You really know how to dress me, baby." This is all new to me, a man purchasing my clothing. Is this what grown men do?
"You look good in any garment you wear baby. It's all about you. I'm going to shower. I'll be in bed shortly. Rest up pretty. Yes, I am feeling that on you girl."
Greg retreats to the bathroom. I can hear the water running. I relax. The smell of the linen is intoxicating. I don't want to be too sleazy when he comes to the bed, so I keep my thoughts on the past few days. I begin to wonder about John and Linda. Strangely I don't think John knows how Linda is when he's away. The water stops. I'm excited and anticipating Greg's body next to mine. He comes out of the bathroom with a towel around his waist. He seems stunned to see me lying in the bed. I giggle, he has bumped into the wall. The towel falls to the floor. I dare not turn my face. I am enjoying the view. His chiseled body continues below his waist on there is a clear definition of his muscles. Especially the muscle that is hanging in plain sight. My familiar spot is now pulsating. I can't control this feeling.

"Baby I'm sorry I woke you." He reaches for his towel to cover himself and go back into the bathroom.
"No, Greg come here please," I call him to the bed using my sexiest voice.
"Baby, you need me to get something for you?"
His feet are planted in the floor. He's motionless. This is the first time I've seen him somewhat afraid. I guess he's afraid of what he might do. I'm scared of what I might do. We're both afraid knowing our passion is on the rise.
"Yes. I want you to come to me right now."
"Wait a minute."

"Now."

I use that same demanding tone that he said he enjoyed earlier. He slowly walks over to me. I take his hand and guide him onto the bed. I slowly wrap my arms around his strong body. I love foreplay. The heavy petting turns us on. The touching, the kissing on my neck. The caressing feels good to us. We are totally aroused.

"Greg, Greg, Greg!"

"Yes, Grandma." Greg jumps up and races to the bathroom to get his pants. He rushes to the door as I roll over in the bed, pretending to be asleep.

"Greg open this door. I left my glasses on the table in your room." His grandmother begins to bang on the door.

"Baby, my grandmother is blocking us."

"It's okay. Give her the glasses. They are on the table." The moment is spoiled.

"Hi, Grandmother. How are you?"

"Son, I am good. I left my glasses on the table." She pushes her way past him to the table where she knew they were. She turns back to Greg, who is holding her glasses. "Hmm, you in here playing doctor I see. Hi D'Alise."

I dare not answer as I giggle softly into the sheets. Greg hands her the glasses and walks with her to the door.

"It's innocent."

"Yeah, that's what they all say until they get pregnant." Grandmother takes her glasses and leaves.

"Baby, I am enjoying you. The interruptions with my grandmother are insane."

"Greg it might be a blessing in disguise. We don't want to move fast."

"I agree but…."

"I appreciate you being gentle with me. Foreplay is important to me. The intimacy of just being held fills me up inside. I don't feel empty when I am being held by you. I feel safe and secure with you. It's not about having your penis inside me."

"Our relationship is not going to be based on sex. It's going to be rooted in something much deeper."

"Greg, when I had my vaginal examination, it hurt badly. Sex is somewhat painful for me."

"Baby you won't experience that with me. I am making love to your mind. You and I both need total love."

"I agree my wonderful man."

"Baby, I am so excited about taking you to the conference in Europe. My colleagues are going to be green with envy. We will probably leave on Thursday, so we'll have time to relax and enjoy some of the sights before the conference. I am working some major deals for the Thibodeaux legacy and you my queen. You and I will be set for life. I know you want to work, and you'll eventually get your master's degree. Did you get a confirmed date when you'll be starting your employment at the Hotel U."

"Sweetie, thanks for reminding me I need to check in with them or see if my cousin's wife received any messages."

We laid in the bed side by side enjoying the moment and the oneness of each other. We agreed to wait before we have sex.

Greg extended the invitation for me to stay the night, but he thinks it best that we sleep in separate beds. We've continued to feel, touch, and explore some heavy petting several times. The hormones have been racing out of control. I told him about Linda's sister and assured him I can handle myself. He was concerned about my living arrangement. He offered to put me up in an apartment if I was uncomfortable. I decided it's okay and I'll return to John and Linda's apartment.

The driver picks me up at the door later that evening. He takes me back across the bridge to the Westbank apartment. As we drove along the streets, I realize Linda has the better of two worlds. When her husband is away traveling, she has a single life and does exactly what she wants to do. When her husband is living at home, she is the good wife. The energy in the house doesn't feel like a place where I belong. It won't be long before I've started my job and can get my own apartment.

The days past with Greg working with his patients. Even though my job is confirmed, I continue to review the newspaper and follow-up on the other jobs I have applied for. I managed to talk on the phone to Greg between his breaks. He speaks sweet words to keep me engaged. I understand the fact I can't see him. Greg called today to say the test results have arrived at the attorney's office.

The driver arrives at the apartment to take me to the attorney's office. Greg is in the waiting room when I arrive.

"Hi, beautiful." He looks at me, and I can tell he's totally pleased. I don't think he's dealt with any honest women. With his personality and good looks, many women will be bold enough to approach the sexy doctor. Once they find out he has more to offer in finances and in the bed, I'm sure he's had to fight them off. I wonder how many couldn't pass this test.

The receptionist calls us into the office. The physician gives the results to the attorney, and he presents them to us. The attorney opens the results in front of us. The physician explains the test results. I knew I had a few allergies and high cholesterol. The doctor continued reading, saying I am nearsighted, and I have a cyst on my right breast. None of this was news to me. Greg has no discrepancies with his health. We review each other's test results and agree to sign the relationship agreement and the non-disclosures documents. His parents are phoned to confirm the signing of the documents.

"Welcome to the family D'Alise. This was an easy initial step to start a relationship. Sometimes it not easy when people are thinking in lust and not long term. Often, I wonder about things not discussed or the questions gone unasked, for example, are you a Christian? Have you been tested for HIV or STD's? Do have a good relationship with your family? How is your credit? We sign the contract without getting the pre-approval letter. Later to find the negative things and it all goes into a downward spiral."

The attorney explained it as though he was speaking to another attorney. His monotone statement caught me off-guard, but I understood his position. He was hired to protect Greg's personal and professional interest.

"My amazing woman welcome to the family. Please tell me you will be all mine for the time period we discuss once the time expires you decide what you want to do. I am already in and have no reservations about you. I trust you with my life."

"Yes."

I was intoxicated by the finer things in life over the past few days. I realize after signing the papers, Greg needs me more than I need him. His grandmother has exposed his inner spirit. It is clear that he wants to share his life with me. This is a family business, and the family will be in our relationship. I guess I can be okay with that. I won't marry him because of his family or the business. I want to marry for love. Unlike my mother, who once said, "I got married because I was having a hard time. I needed help."

After signing all the documents, he shows me his love once again. He surprised me with a nice pair of walking shoes. We walk Canal Street and explore the antique shops in the French Quarter. We share a vanilla ice cream cone. He teases me as he licks the melted liquid from my fingers. We laugh and giggle like little kids. We treasure the moment.

"Greg, I used to help my grandmother make homemade ice cream. Ours was better than this. It's so good to make ice cream. My grandmother taught me so much."

"Baby you have so many hidden talents. Thanks for sharing that with me. Maybe we can make ice cream in our kitchen one day."

"That would really be nice. I can perfect my skills. That might be something we might be able to market one day."

"Girl you're not just beautiful you have brains. It's so easy to communicate with you. We've ironed out relationship logistics that couples' take months and years to work out. I can't wait to meet your mother and father."

I don't know if I want him to meet my parents right away. I keep silent and let him talk.

"Do you want to share another ice cream cone?"

"Only if you lick my fingers." I giggle as he wiggles his tongue at me. "I'm joking."

"Baby, I feel so good about us."

"Greg picks me up and spins me around right in the middle of the French Quarter. I slide down his arms only to meet him face to face. We are burning with the desire to kiss one another. Greg looks away and begins to walk forward, and I follow him. He's determined not to mess this up by moving too fast. We go in a shop to view souvenirs. He purchases the ones I like. He tells me to ship them to my family. I love that he is so thoughtful. Maybe I was thinking wrong about his spirit.

My beautiful day ends on a good note the driver takes me back across the river. The apartment is quiet. There is a note on the coffee table. Linda is gone to her hometown for a few days. The note also says for me to go to Hotel U to finalize her paperwork for employment and schedule my training tomorrow. I call the hotel to confirm I will be in tomorrow. Greg calls to make sure everything is going well at the apartment, and I give him the happy details. He offers to send clothes from the closet, and he'll arrange for the car to pick me up.

I went to bed and included my thanks in my prayers. I wouldn't have to worry about the next few days. I could relax as I start my new job.

Chapter 11

I was picked up the next day by the driver, and there is a brown envelope on the back seat. I open the envelope to find my identification, birth certificate, and passport enclosed. I am excited about traveling on a plane for the very first time. Prior to graduating from college, I interviewed with Eastern and Delta Airlines for a flight attendant position. That was the perfect opportunity to travel the world. My mother discouraged me not to pursue that type of career because of the unforgettable aviation disasters with plane crashes. Everything is working out in perfect timing.

The feelings of love are flourishing in my heart for my amazing man. I'm falling in love with this man and wish I could control the feelings. I can finally separate myself from my past. Love is real. I am finally getting the much-needed support to pursue my dreams. *In my heart, I know Greg would prefer me not to work; he's so willing to support me. That fills me up inside.*

The driver helps me out of the car after he parks. I thank him and discuss the time he should return to pick me up. I did my research and noticed the hotel is only a ten-minute walk to the bus stop off canal street. I don't want Greg to ever think I would take advantage of his generosity. I head toward the entrance of the hotel. As I enter Hotel U, I notice things I hadn't originally noticed. This upscale hotel fits my personality. The glamorous hotel décor reminds me of the magazines I would flip through on the floor of my bedroom fantasizing about furniture, travel, and hotels. I would cut the pictures out and place them in my scrapbooks of all the things I wanted when I grew up. The visualizations that I had as a child is coming to life. I am going to be working in a beautiful hotel.

I go to Human Resources to finalize the offer of employment the background check and drug test are within guidelines. This service-oriented position is in line with what I have been doing all my life. The negotiation to start after I returns from Europe with the exception, I must start my training prior to leaving. The management team of men shake hands with me and acknowledge I will be an asset to the company. They give me a tour of the modern chic hotel.

I have never seen so many black, blue, and gray suits in all my life. My man looks better than any of these men in their stylish suits. The men are very accommodating towards me. As I leave the office, I think of a strategic plan to move up the ladder. The hotel is nothing short of the multi-tasking I did when I was cooking, cleaning, and servicing alcohol for my grandmother. This job will be effortless for I am going to move up the ladder fast. The management staff and employees seem to like me. This hotel is totally different than the traditional hotel, Greg, and I shared fun times viewing the skyline in the penthouse.

I am finally reaping the benefits of my hard work and community support. Who would have thought I would be the first woman in my family to graduate from college? My own Southern Baptist preacher uncle had negative predictions for me. A community of mentors saw my potential and didn't want me to be a statistic by getting pregnant or addicted to drugs. My aunt Crystal, John's mother, made sure I attended church regularly on Sundays.

The church and pastor supported me. They gave me a few monetary stipends out of the church funds. *When I receive my first paycheck, I plan on making a monetary donation to the church to support their efforts in the community.*

Upon my departure from the hotel the driver is parked outside like clockwork. To my surprise, Greg is posed as the driver.

"Congratulations, baby. Welcome to Corporate America." He pulls out a large bouquet of flowers from the back seat and hands them to me.

"The red roses are beautiful. Thank you". I was not expecting this. I pull Greg close to me looking him directly in his eyes. I kiss his cheek, although I really wanted to give him a French kiss.

As Greg makes sure, I am comfortably seated in the back seat of the car. I can feel the hotel staff's eyes on me. I am proud to have someone greet me when I get off work.

Chapter 12

Celebration

Greg decides to take me to Snug Harbor Jazz Bistro to celebrate my new employment. This was an amazing romantic date on Frenchmen Street.

"Hi, baby." Greg is holding a small box in his hands.

"Hi, handsome" I am curious what could it be in the pink box.

"Baby, my grandmother wanted me to give you this gift." Greg looks so handsome as he holds the small box in his hands.

"Greg," I paused, not sure what to say. "I'm not sure if I should take a gift from your grandmother."

"Okay, suit yourself, she is going to be offended if you don't take it." He shrugs his shoulders. "Do you want me to give you a little history of some other things my grandmother did before she retired."

"Hmmm." This family has been so loving towards me. "Sure, go ahead."

"I asked you once before, were you open when you went to church with me. I ask you again, are you open?"

"Yes," I respond, thinking he's only brought positive additions to my life.

"My grandmother owned a store in the French Quarter called 'Thibodeaux's Good Vibes.' She sold items to help clear negative energy. We don't get sick. Why do you think I am always drinking that H2O? Water keeps you alive."

"Silly, you should see how your eyes light up when you talk about your grandmother's store. Anyway, keep going." This conversation is a little boring and is of no interest to me.

"My grandmother sold books about eating a plant-based diet, meditation, yoga, and Feng Shui. She even sold essential oils, house plants, incense, herb, and crystals. High frequency sounds singing bowls. The Himalayan salt lamps were her best sellers."

I began to giggle. "Greg is your grandmother a Bruja. New Orleans is known for certain things." I notice his expression has changed. I think I just offended Greg. "I was joking. I hope I didn't offend you. I am open, please share the gift with me."

I think I just silenced Greg. I must find a way to get myself out of the hole I just dug for myself. I turned up my feminine energy to excuse myself to walk to the bathroom. I know he's watching me, so I turn up my sexy walk to the next level. When I come back, I walk behind him and nipple on his ear lobe. He responds. I got him back.

I lend into Greg and talk to him in my sexy voice. "Baby, would you like to share with me. I am open. The pink box is so pretty."

"Okay, baby, here it is."

I take the box from Greg's hands, and in a slow and seductive motion, I brush my hair back as I open the box. The charm necklace is beautiful.

"Baby, it's called a Lapis Lazuli the information card explains everything about the charm. You can also do your own research the stone has a lot of healing properties."

"Greg, I am going to drop a thank you note to your grandmother." This is a lesson for me not to joke about some of his family's rituals and practices.

"Baby, are you enjoying the jazz?"

"Yes, to be honest, my attention was focused on you talking to me." I've been studying him, and I know he likes it when I talk to him that way. I'm glad we could end the night on a good note.

Chapter 13

Unexpected information

Throughout the days, we make exchanges and tell each other how our day went. The chemistry in this relationship is no comparison to any other person I've dated. We can't keep our hands off each other through the days. We manage to date outside the confines of his house. The driver picks me up each day and takes me back to the apartment. Linda is still away. I'm glad she extended the bed to me while she was gone. My days are easy, considering what I do as a manager. Managing the hotel comes naturally for me.

"D'Alise, James." I hear a familiar voice calling my name. Only three people know I am employed at this hotel.

"Yes. You're Donald LeBlanc." It's the creepy man I met at the restaurant on my first date with Greg.

"Well, well, I see you're climbing the employment ladder. How is Mr. Greg?"

"He's well." I don't quite understand why his colleague has a concern.

A handsome metrosexual man walks up next to Donald they display public affection sealed with a kiss on the lips. He gives the man the ticket so the valet can retrieve the car. I'm in a state of confusion. *What about his wife?*

"I hear you got old Greg whipped." He turns to me and continues to speak as if I wasn't a witness to his actions. "He's a good loving man. I tell you he's got depth. What does he do? Wrap you in those big masculine arms and make everything all right. He knows how to make me feel safe. Old Greg stayed the night with me once. He held me so close. I didn't realize he cared so much. Lord Have Mercy." He waves me off with his hand.

"What? Wait?" I need him to tell me more.

"Old Greg stayed the night with me once. You can ask him to tell you the details. I felt his heart beating. He's been acting weird towards me. I think that was his first time……. Oh, I got to go. The car is here."

"Wait!" What did I just hear? My amazing man stayed the night with another man. That's why he knows so much about Donald. Even his parents know. They brought his name up when I was at the house.

I call Greg to tell him I'm going to have the driver take me back to the apartment because I wasn't feeling well. I explain I want to figure out how to ride public transportation. He called to check on me, but I wouldn't answer or return his calls.

I walked out of the hotel at the end of the day, and Greg was waiting outside. I turned around to go back into the hotel door. He jumps out the car and runs to grabs me.

"Hi, beautiful." He grabs my arm gently. "I'm trying to figure out why you're not returning my calls. I had fun celebrating your new employment."

"Hi, Greg." I know he could tell I was a little dry toward him. My mind kept repeating the conversation I had with Donald. *It can't be true that he held another man in his arms. I've been wanting him and not sure why he's keeping me at bay.*

"I was worried about you. I've been calling you. What's wrong? I wanted you to come by the house to see your new luggage and clothes I picked up from Canal Place. If you want to take your blue foot locker you can. I understand it has sentimental value." He paused and stared directly at me. "Baby, you look sad, are they not treating you right on this job? You can quit, and I'll take really good care of you."

I heard him speaking **as I remembered the words that came out of Donald LeBlanc's mouth.**

"You're really not talking much today. I can't wait to get you to the house. I want to show you something. I got a new jam I want to play while I'm driving."

"Can we just drive in silence?" *I am in a state of confusion.*

"Okay, baby, whatever you want. I am so happy. I never spent so much time in the women's department in one day. You would think I didn't have a career."

We arrive at the house where the chef has prepared a nice dinner. Greg is the only one talking. I am withdrawn and barely talking. As I look at him, I'm thinking he is so amazing. I know I am falling in love with him. I just can't believe; no, I don't want to believe the conversation I had with Donald. What was said is taking over that I believe to be true about Greg. My thoughts are making me feel exhausted. I sat back, almost slouching on the couch. Greg is concerned because my energy is so low. He stops trying to force a conversation and offers to carry me upstairs. I nod in agreement, and I close my eyes, wishing my feelings would settle on an understanding. There was nothing in what was said that I could hold on to. Greg left me alone in the bed and went to sit in the sitting area of the bedroom. I know he had to be wondering about the importance of the upcoming trip. *How could I travel with him now?* I know it's important to him and his family. The patents and the hospital partnership is to be set up in Europe. I know he's concerned about me and why I've been distant with him. I know it's bothering him that I won't communicate.

"Greg." I can't relax with this confusion stirring in my head. I'm trying to wrap my feelings around all of this. I need to talk.

"Hi, beautiful."

"I see you been sleeping with my black thong." It was folded on the nightstand next to the bed.

"Yes. It makes me feel close to you. Come, come look in the closet." I couldn't move. Greg turned to see my tears falling. "Why are you crying?"

I used my hands to cup my face. "Greg," I don't know where to start."

"Come here, beautiful." I got out of the bed and walked into his arms. His hug touched my emotions. This is an amazing man. "Greg, Donald was at the hotel with a man."

"What?" He seemed shocked, but in a way, I knew he knew about Donald.

"Yes. He…. He told me you once stayed all night with him and held him in your arms." I allowed myself to step away from his embrace.

"Is that why you've been behaving strangely?" Greg laughs.

"Greg, I've been trying to collect myself."

"What else did Donald tell?"

"You stayed the night with him."

"Did you ask him to explain or ask for any details….?

"No, the valet brought the car around, and he walked away. He told me to ask you about the details."

"I'm a little confused. Why didn't you call me immediately? Oh, you think?

"Greg, are you into men? I don't want to be a front for you."

"What?"

"You heard me."

"I am into you baby. I only have a desire for you."

"Greg, you never tried……" I couldn't say it, but it was true. He never took the initiative or allowed us to get further. Nothing ever happened, yet he said he was so attracted to me. I never had to tell him not yet, or I'm not ready. He never seemed to get so involved in our foreplay that he'd take it further. What was I to think?

"Wow, are we really having this conversation? You already drew your own conclusion. That's why you wouldn't return my calls. This is bad timing. Do these eyes look like lying eyes? Baby tell me you trust me with your life and we're going to be together forever."

"Greg, I am so confused right now."

"About what? D'Alise, I trust you with my life. Baby tell me you trust me. I told you when you know you know."

"Really?"

"I'm not going to get upset because I know the truth. Baby, let's go downstairs. I am going to have the driver take you home. Your judgment is not clear. You're not thinking clearly in this moment. I need you to tell me you trust me now."

As we left the bedroom, I look back, and Greg is walking on the black thong, which is now laying on the floor in the room. I felt a kick in my stomach. The one thing that was a part of me, what he said he needed to breathe in, he was now walking on without a care.

"Greg." I could only whisper his name. I didn't know what to think.

The driver parked in the front of the house patiently waiting prepared to take me back to the apartment. Greg opened the car door. His expression tells me his heart is broken, but the fact is I can't tell him I trust him. I made my decision about him, now he must decide about me. He leans in close and gives me a long loving hug. He rubs his fingers across my red lips and then places them on his. His fingers trace the veins in my long neck and leads to my breast. He touches them passionately. His touch is soft, and I know he is deliberately teasing himself and me. He stops and guides me in the back seat of the car. He has always been fascinated with my long alluring legs. He gently takes one leg at a time kissing my muscular calves, putting them in the car. He stoops down to look into my mood eyes.

"Baby tell me you trust me with your life."

"Greg." I paused for a long time without saying a word. My feelings held my tongue.

"I love you, D'Alise. I know you love me too. Tell me you trust me, and nothing will ever come between us. "

"Greg." I couldn't say anything else. Just his name. He had not settled the chaos that mixed with my emotions. Questions came and went unanswered. I could only say his name.

"It's clear I'm dealing with Danielle Alise James today, not D'Alise. This planned trip is important for us and our family legacy. My cup is already full. I can support myself. I chose you to join me and want to make sure you are compatible. I am not going to keep chasing you. You are dealing with a grown man, not a little boy. I have made you a priority in my life I am invested in you. I have been vulnerable to you. If I have ever messed up, I will apologize. I've let you know when I was busy and what I am building with the family. I will not lower my standards. You are testing me right now. You are becoming a distraction for me. I know my worth. I want you to have everything I gave you. I will have the driver deliver the wardrobe from the closet. I see you are a good person. I value you. You must work somethings out internally. You don't know how to appreciate me. You can't understand the love I am giving to you. It's unfamiliar. One day you will wake up. It's going to get worse before it gets better for you. I am leaving without you. I did nothing wrong. I value myself more and will not allow you to treat me this way. Someone is going to love me.

I looked at him, and I felt his pain. He had a burning desire to kiss me. The thought of this possibly being the only time he has desired to romantically kiss a woman made me queasy. He leaned tenderly meets the red glossy target. I think he knows it's now or never for this will be the last time he will see his love. Bang! The chemistry is there for both of us. The thirty-second kiss will forever be my mind.

"Baby, tell me you trust me."

"Greg, I can't give you an answer." I couldn't do it.

Out of nowhere, the following words hit me. "Do not contact me or any of my family members. I am sending you back across the bridge to be with your family. Goodbye."

The car door slammed shut, and the driver pulled away. I wonder if Greg is all messed up. I know I would have been the one to replace his childhood love. I needed clarity, and he had to let me go and hope I'll return to him one day. In that moment I know he thought I was being immature. He is a proud man, and he won't chase me. If our love is meant to be, I'll have to find him.

As the car leaves the garden district, I look through the rear-view window. I can see Greg's frustration and tears. He's pacing the front entry of the property with his fist charged towards the sky. For the first time in my life, I realize no one has ever shed so many tears for me. *I hear Just Once by James Ingram playing on the radio, and I remember the frustration of the guys in college that wanted to sleep with me for popcorn and a movie. Greg wanted to give me more than just a sexual encounter.* I now question my judgment, maybe I should have asked more questions. Maybe I should have called Greg as Donald requested. My future is slipping through my fingers like sand. *My mother and grandmother always said never chase a man, let him choose you.* I must trust their advice for it's the only thing I have right now. I sink into the back seat of the car, sobbing profusely. I really want to stop the car get out and run to him. I'll respect his wishes, and I won't contact him.

Chapter 14

As I step in the empty apartment, I reflect and want to kick myself for not being able to think faster. I could have offered Greg a response. We could have talked about it, or could we? Do I trust him? I admit I have trust issues that stem from childhood. I wish I had explained that to him and asked him could we take one day at a time. People have always taken me for granted. I've never really had anyone to give me anything. I am blessed to have cross paths with an amazing man. I don't blame him for cutting me out of his life, or did I do that to myself? I admit I was distracting him in a negative way. *My grandmother would always say to me get rid of negative distractions when I was in college.* Every day this man is performing surgeries on people that are trusting their lives in his hands. *His grandmother tried to warn me about distractions.* He was calling me, worrying about me. I didn't have the respect or the decency to return his calls. *What was wrong with me?*

I really want to call Greg, but my grandmother and mother's opinions are keeping me stuck. I am a big girl now? Really? A big girl who is not able to fight for the one man that is a fit for me. I am responsible for the break-up. I want to call him and tell him I love him. I want to call him and tell him I was foolish.

Chapter 15

Trying to Maintain Normalcy

As the days go by, I began commuting back and forth on public transportation. It's nothing like having a personal driver. I wear the flat shoes Greg purchased for me to walk from the bus stop to the hotel. It's a ten-minute walk. I change daily into my high heels in the bathroom. I really appreciate Greg for having his personal driver taking me around the city. It's been a week, and there's no call from Greg, no roses sent to the hotel. I am finally coming to the realization it's over. I'm still feeling some kind of way. I'm confused. I go into work every day faking, pretending to be happy. I'm sad on the inside. It's taking everything to get up in the morning to face my new reality.

I pour myself into my work and make my mark at Hotel U. This whole set-up is familiar to me, similar to the set-up in my grandmother's house. I am not above any of this work because I have done it all before. I am using all the skills I learned as a child. When a restaurant staff member was running late, I jump in to assist. *I helped my grandmother set the dining table for breakfast based on her instruction and her vision. I gathered the placement, plates, napkins, forks, knives, spoons, and glasses and proceeded each day to set the table.* My childhood lessons and skills came in handy in the restaurant.

When the mixologist needed help mixing the drinks in the bar or night club, I helped.

I remember my grandmother had a few clients that would drive by during the weekday to get a shot of alcohol. I learned to pour drinks in a shot glass and bring them to the client in the designated room. I hated the way alcohol smelled it made me sick to my stomach, and it does to this day. I also recall my grandmother's clients coming by the house on a Friday and Saturday around five in the afternoon like clockwork with their lady friends. This was the party time when everybody would let their hair down and eat the food my grandmother prepared for a few hours. I could hear the music and laughter and was drawn into the closed door. I would peep through the door. I saw the ladies bumping and grinding on their fellows. What a mess! Strangely enough, my grandmother would shut everything down by seven because she believed in getting up early.

The patron's behavior in the hotel bar is not offensive to me.

When the maid service didn't show up, I help clean the rooms. I did the laundry and starched the patron's clothes.

This reminds me of how I helped to keep our home clean and organized. I remember our home was never messy. My mother was always cleaning and washing clothes. I had to mop and polish the dark tile floors every weekend. I think starch was one of my mother's favorite things to use. The more starch she used, the stiffer our clothes would become after pressing the clothes. I recall her soaking our clothes in starch. I've even tasted the white floury flavor in the square brown box. My mother said she learned a lot from being a domestic worker. She said that experience trained her on how to take care of her family. My mother trained me on how to take care of the family.

I thought my college education was helping me with this job. It's really the experience I gained as a child back at home. The very thing I thought I was leaving behind is still with me, helping me excel in my career.

Chapter 16

Questions and No Answers

Linda finally came back. It seems as if she was gone longer than she expressed. I have not been able to explain or answer some of the simplest questions lately, especially when someone asks me about Greg.

"The driver brought all your stuff from Greg's house. Damn girl how in the hell did you mess that up with Greg?" Linda had been home long enough for me to explain the stack of clothes and bags that were in the living room.

"I can't talk about it. Thanks for letting me sleep in the bed while you were gone. I needed a few good nights of sleep."

"I'm gone for a week, and everything falls apart. Why you didn't call me to talk?"

"I don't know." I am trying to figure out what kind of advice she would have given me.

"The man was looking out for you and your family. Just like John is doing for me. I feel sick, I can imagine how you feel."

"Linda, I can't explain." I really wish she would stop talking.

"Well, you can't set around in this house. Girl, you are on the market. Let's ride by the gas station. I need to get some gas."

A lot of times, I felt like Linda is pimping me out. She never paid for anything in the gas station when the manager saw me in the passenger's seat. The guy would come out to talk to me and told us to get whatever we wanted. I would often tell Linda I couldn't go out with a guy I didn't like and wasn't going to go out with him.

Still, no phone calls or letters from Greg. We started looking for two-bedroom apartments and found a nice roommate set-up and placed a deposit with Greg's money. Now I'll be getting my own room.

Linda and I are becoming friends. It's like we're having girl sleepovers, she insists that I sleep on the opposite side of the bed. One night I heard her say John and she grabbed for me. I kicked her off me and fell on the floor. I never returned to the room again. I moved back to the sofa. I started to question if she was living a double life. Could she be a lesbian? I discussed the incident with her. I told her how it made me feel. She explained she thought it was John in the bed with her and brushed it off like nothing had happened. I got the impression she was testing me. I told my grandmother and mother. They pleaded me to come home. I told them I'd be okay. I believe this will pass. In order to keep the peace, I followed my family's instructions of not telling my cousin what happened.

I wouldn't normally be friends with a woman like Linda. Our core values are different. Since she is married to my cousin, I am forced to deal with her. Once I leave, I don't ever plan on communicating with her again. I don't think she has ever been checked. She keeps testing me. I listen to her in social settings smiling in people's faces and then talking about them behind their backs. I can imagine what she's saying about me.

John finally came back from work; he never asked me how I was getting along with his wife, and he didn't ask what happen to Greg. I'm sure his wife filled him in with what happened. They smoked, drank, and listened to music when he was in town. The apartment would be alive with their friends filling the small space. I try to stay out the way and find myself writing in my journal, praying and walking to relieve stress.

Chapter 17

Getting to The Bottom of Things

The traffic wasn't bad coming across the bridge today. I feel successful since getting the ratings up for the hotel. The company gave me a bonus. I placed the check in the bank so I would have a reasonable down payment for the brass bed I plan on purchasing. I managed to find a store in the French Quarter that would let me put the bed on layaway for a year. On the lunch hour, I heard someone call my name.

"D'Alise, James." It sounds like Donald. Today I feel happy to hear his voice.

"How are you doing Donald." I remained professional. I was trying to figure out his angle since he's always throwing shade toward Greg.

"I am doing good. Having a snack before I meet with the board at the hospital. You are looking more vibrant every time I see you. You broke old Greg's heart."

"Really." *What does he know about our business?*

"Why you didn't travel with him?" *How does he know I was going to be traveling?*

"Miscommunication or I should say a lack of on my part."

"Oh, Greg was crazy about you. Our family was ready to take you in."

"What do you mean our family?"

"Greg is my first cousin. Girl, you didn't know that? You are young."

"He never talked about you."

"He wouldn't. That's the loyalty he has for me. I put him in an uncomfortable situation. I attempted suicide. He saved my life when I wanted to jump. Oh, Greg stayed with me all night. He held me in his arms and would not leave the room. I realized he loved me. I was conflicted with my sexuality. I wasn't sure if I should marry Crissy. I have a beautiful wife. She loves me very much; we are best friends. I am her first, and she's my first. I even love her. I have never cheated on her with another woman. I am attracted to men. I have this sickness inside my brain. I knew ever since I was a little boy. I finally had to tell her the truth. She had a breakdown and was treated for depression. I hate I lied to her. She loves me unconditionally and doesn't want to leave me. She believes in till death do us part. She is praying for God to release the desires I have. She is a good woman. I'm putting her through hell. I can't believe she's putting up with all my drama. We have an arrangement. We live together, share everything, but we don't sleep together. She wants a baby, and I want a baby. Don't you remember me inviting you over for dinner?"

I am taking a moment to take all this in. *How can a woman stay with a man under such conditions?* I would not allow myself to stand for such a mess. When I was in college, I dated a guy that was drafted for a professional football team. He told me he could not promise he wasn't going to cheat on me. He was too young to be in a serious relationship. He told me he had many women chasing him. We had deep conversations. I decided it was best for us not to remain in a relationship. I respected him for his honesty in giving me an opportunity to decide. No lies.

"Hmm. Greg's mother asked about you. He didn't comment."

"The whole family knows about the suicide incident. We have no family secrets."

"How is Greg?"

"He's thrown himself into his work."

"It seems he's staying longer than he planned."

"Yes."

"When is he coming back?"

"Greg isn't coming back. He has a nice set-up over there. Old, Greg was in love with you! The paparazzi took a picture of the two of you the night we first met he got the photographer to give him a picture. I am sure he took it with him. He's sentimental like that."

"He never told me. I don't have a picture of him." In that moment I finally found the words to describe my pain. "Donald, I thought Greg was gay."

"What? Greg is a real man; he doesn't play that shit! He'll hang out with anybody as long as they don't try to put their values on him."

"I messed up."

"You need to contact him and make this right. Considering you failed the loyalty test I put you through."

"What"

"I told you to talk to him. The loyalty test was communication. I hear some woman over there is trying to lock him down. Seriously, you need to get your man before he gets snagged up. Hey, I got to go."

"Bye."

"Ms. James, what's wrong?" The manager looked at me, knowing I wasn't myself.

"I am not feeling well."

"Come in the office." I followed him without him saying another word.

"Okay, yes, I need a moment in the office."

I really messed up; the love of my life is gone. Greg isn't gay. I wonder what Greg would think about me if he found out I wanted to sleep my life away my senior year in high school. I had many responsibilities, school, college prep examines, chores, helping with my siblings, work, and remembering the rape.

Chapter 18

Tension

As the weeks and the days passed, I heard nothing from Greg. We finally moved into our roommate sized apartment. I have my own room. Linda is being persistent about getting me to go out. The management staff invited me to hang out with them. Linda encouraged me to go hang with them, she even offered to pick me up. Linda loved this because it gave her an opportunity to unwind and be socially outgoing. She liked to mingle, drink, and smoke.

The job was going well, and I had to admit, I was satisfied. The Director at the executive level for the hotel asked me to meet in his office for a meeting. The meeting went well; he complimented me on how I was managing the operation of the hotel. He started to ask personal questions and inquired if I was in a relationship. Throughout the weeks that followed, it continued. He finally came clean and asked if I would marry one of his relatives so they could obtain their citizenship. I was offered a hefty sum of money, which I declined. I couldn't see myself marrying someone at first sight, let alone someone I didn't love.

I discussed the proposal with Linda, who became instantly disgusted. She had a get over mentality. She claimed I let my second opportunity to come into wealth pass. Now we're not talking. I'm glad my cousin is traveling for work. He's unaware of the tension in our new apartment. I wouldn't want him to have to choose between his wife's idea of happiness and mine.

There is no problem at work, and everything is still going well at the hotel. I received another bonus. I was asked if I would reconsider the proposal to marry the relative. For the second time, I again declined. During our weekly staff meeting, the staff was provided with new work schedules. My hours were changed to the night shift eleven at night until seven in the morning. I looked over the schedule again, as if I would find a misprint. I thought about my dilemma. *This is crazy. I don't have a car and by no means am I asking Linda to take me to work that time of night. The crime at that time of night holds no safety for a woman.* I resigned, and now I'll have to find a new job.

Linda is trying to find a way to talk. She's talking again after weeks of silence as though we are best of friends. I know she wants or needs something from me. I've read her correctly, *Ms. Bossy and Moody. I'm standing my ground, so she'll have to meet me where I stand.*

"D'Alise you don't know how I feel."

"What are you talking about?" Suddenly I'm supposed to understand her misplaced feelings? "How do you feel about what?"

"I wish I had your opportunities. I would ride each and every one of them until the wheels fall off. How do you get men to want to give you all the stuff you get?"

"Linda, when you demand nothing, you gain everything. I apologize if I have offended you in any way. Are we friends again?"

"Yes." Who would have thought? I am learning something from D'Alise.

"I am glad." God supplies all our needs; he positions the right people at the right time to help us.

"D'Alise I will never forget the money Greg gave to help out with the apartment. You won with him, so did the family."

"If you keep talking about Greg, you're going to make me feel tense. I've done enough crying." I still think about Greg often. I know what I lost and pray that my future will relieve me of my loss.

"You got a message for a radio internship at WDAH Radio station. D'Alise you are the job slayer. Please say you will take it."

After filling out applications practically every day. I was glad to get the responses.

"I met the owner of the station when I was filling out my application for employment. I told him I would take a post-college intern position to gain experience. He's from Mobile, Alabama. Linda interns typically are not paid. I might get a small stipend. If anything.

"Girl say yes. We got to get in where we can fit in. I'll attend the events with you."

"Linda, I will give them a call to get the details." I realize it's good to have many irons in the fire. When one door closes, you can walk into another door. Linda blurts out her thoughts. She's making plans again.

"We're going to Hollywood."

"Linda, it was only a phone message." *How did this become we?* She is truly pathetic, but she has no choice.

Chapter 19

Radio Station

The jingle announced WDAH Radio. The station's favorite D.J. came across the airwaves. A familiar voice that I heard every day at the same time.

"Hello and welcome to WDAH Radio Station! We've got news, community events and gossip for you today, but first, let's check out the new song by Whitney Houston. "Saving All My Love for You."

I am fortunate to get a call from the radio station. I can't believe Hotel U gave me an excellent evaluation. I am sure I could have filed a complaint and got paid big bucks. What they are doing will eventually catch up with them. Even if I don't file a complaint, someone else will.

I am sitting with the owner of the station, focusing on my new post-college internship. The owner is from Alabama and showing a lot of love for me. His staff is teaching me everything I need to be a success at the radio station. My paperwork says I'll have a twenty-hour workweek. They let me know I am required to attend weekend and after-hour station events. I'll also be traveling without reimbursements, that's okay with me.

Over the course of days, I enjoy the internship. I enjoy the production and the News Department. I did a few voice-over commercials. It reminded me of when I was in college, one of my classmates asked me to be in a Green Track commercial for dog racing. The station played an array of lovely music. I remember some of the songs because Greg played the same music in his car. The station had celebrities on the first floor of the station every day. The staff members had many opportunities to get free tickets for events in the city. Linda was right there with me, encouraging me to get anything free they were giving away. She offered to take me to the events. Everyone at the station was so friendly we exchanged telephone numbers and hung out after work. This camaraderie reminded me of my entourage days in college.

"Good Morning Ms. James." One of the supervisors greeted me as I walked in.

"How is everything going?"

"Great! Everyone is very nice." I couldn't contain the pleasure I had working with everyone. It is a pleasant environment, and the employees were more than just co-workers.

"The staff loves your energy. You have that star quality. One of our on-air personalities is going on maternity leave. I want you to fill in while she's gone."

"Am I hearing you correctly?" I love good news in the morning. I need to contain my thoughts.

"Yes! Of course, we will compensate you for the time you work in her position."

"Can I think about it?" I pray I didn't say anything wrong. I see the change in his expression.

"What is it to think about?" He couldn't understand my reasoning. I've learned not to hold my tongue, so I'll explain.

"Well, it's a little hard for me right now because I commute on public transportation daily. My cousin's wife has been taking me around to the events."

"I really want this for you! Don't you want it for yourself?"

"It's a lot to think about. I only have classroom experience from college and did a few commercials. I'm trained to work a teleprompter. One of my relatives is an on-air personality for the gospel drive time in my hometown. Honestly, I have no experience."

There! I said it. I began to cringe as he pauses looked at me as though he was confused.

"I want to help you! Can't I help you?"

"Hmm." I've learned about help since leaving home. This could be a problem, for sure.

"Okay, think about it overnight."

"Yes, sir, I will. It's getting a little late I need to be checking in."

Chapter 20

WDAH Offer

There will always be that family member who perceives another's opportunity as a good offer. They don't realize the opportunity needs to be evaluated by the person who received the offer. They have to make their decision based on what is best for them through self-examination and values. I was at that point. I knew Linda wasn't the best person to help me make a decision about my offer but who else could I talk to about it?

"Linda."

"What, girl?"

"I was offered a temporary slot to be an on-air personality." I told her as soon as I got home. I was truly excited. My emotions were on an all-time high.

"Girl take it we're going to Hollywood. We're going to Hollywood."

"I must work out the logistics. Linda to be honest, this is something I secretly wanted to happen in my life."

"Girl that's the law of attraction."

"Yeah, I guess it is, I am always creating jingles in my mind."

"Take every opportunity God is blessing you with. I still don't understand how in the world you let Greg get away. Greg was on a whole other level. He was a real Alpha male. When you were dating him, you leveled up. I don't think you will ever meet another Greg. You need to make it right. You were wrong girl. Get your man. Someone is going to swipe him up with a quickness. He's overseas, he might find him one of those real exotic women that might just blow his mind, and you will be a thing of the past. If you choose not to contact Greg, you better ride this new wave to Hollywood. This man at the station is pushing you up the ladder. You're not just going to be an arm piece for a man. You're going to have the power to network with some heavyweights. You are being set-up to carry your own bags of money. We're in a nice two-bedroom apartment. Girl, if you work this right, you can get your own apartment and have your own stuff. You won't have to share living space with anyone."

"I need to think about it." Linda was talking so fast that when she mentioned Greg, my emotions went another way. I didn't want to make any more mistakes. Not with men, not with my job and not with her. I needed to think about it.

"And yes, you will take it. You need a driver. Better yet, when are you going to get your driver's license so you can get a car? In case you can't get across the river, they need to have a ho-tel or an apartment set-up for you. Some of those concerts and events go on past midnight. I know how you like to go to bed ear-ly. You need a clothing allowance. You can have them pay me for styling your hair. You know my fees and contract are already writ-ten up."

"What would John say?" She finally paused. I could almost see her thoughts slow down. Just like that. Then, suddenly she held her head up as though she were of some royalty.

"He's only home one weekend out of the month. I'm looking out for his cousin's best interest. You can only stay with us for so long. Okay?"

"Yes. I understand. I'm only an intern. You're jumping to conclusions on this assignment."

"D'Alise opportunities don't come around every day. You keep letting them pass you by. You got to get all you can while you're young. You don't want to get old reflecting on, 'I wish I could have done things differently.' That's why people are on you. You need to open your eyes and ears. Stop hiding; let the world know who you really are."

"I hear you girl." When I win everyone around me wins. She's looking for a win. She was making it clear. When I win, Linda and John win.

"I wish I could trade places with you sometimes. You don't know how I feel."

"What do you mean?" *Here she goes again. I guess what I eat fills her stomach too.*

"Forget it."

"Linda, you got me curious now."

"Let's table it. Your cousin always said you were going to marry someone older with money or another race."

"He did?"

"Yeah. I see the innocence in you, you are clueless at times. It seems as if you see things through the eyes of a child. You think your life was hard. It's a lot you haven't seen, especially dealing with men. Greg is going to be your blueprint for life. Now let's focus on going to Hollywood."

"Yes, Linda, I want to be able to carry my own bags." Both Linda and John had their own idea about my life and how I would live it with a husband, home, and future. One thing she said was true. I was naïve when I arrived. It was time for a change. Linda is focused on pushing me out into the world. I am not mad at her.

"Let's do this. Let's have dinner and call it a night."

I was too excited to really eat, and there was more to think about other than the offer that was made. Then there was Greg. I'd think about him until I fell asleep.

Chapter 21

WDAH Conditions

I arrived at the radio station bright and early. I was prepared and dressed, feeling like a celebrity.

"Good Morning Ms. James. How are you?" I met the same supervisor in the hall by his office. I smiled when he spoke, ready to talk about the position.

"I am doing well. I did a lot of thinking about your offer last night."

"Please have a sit in my office and give me some feedback."

"The offer sounds good. I say, yes."

"I instinctively knew you were going to say yes. I already had the paperwork drawn up the day we offered you the intern position. I saw you talking to the owner when you applied for a position at the station. We needed to be able to slide someone in the slot temporary when our permanent person goes on leave. The owner is on board with my request."

"Sir, you don't know the terms and conditions of what I want. Everything is moving so fast."

"Please look at all the paperwork it's legitimate. I'll have our staff driver take you to your own attorney. I'll be honest with you. I find you to be very attractive. You would be someone I would date. The man in your life should feel very lucky."

I know my face changed the mood of the impromptu meeting. I didn't lift my head from the paperwork, I raised my eyes. I could tell he got the message. I wanted it to be clear.

"Ms. James, what's wrong? Please let me know if I am overstepping my boundaries."

"Yes. You are. I prefer not to have this discussion with you."

"I going to be direct with you. I want to date you."

"Mr. Austin Reynolds there appears to be conditions with this transitional position."

"You can call me Austin, and what about you?" *Is he listening to me?*

"Are we on first names now?" *I can't believe what I am hearing.* "Sir, I hope I haven't given you a wrong impression. I don't date people I work with. I can hear my grandmother saying, "Don't lay where you make your bread.""*

"You should never limit yourself." *I felt sick, violated. I wasn't the child that left the only home I knew anymore.*

"Excuse me, I need to be leaving. Let's table our conversation." This man is looking at me as dating material. Dating at this point is not even on my mind. I'm not even attracted to him. I can feel the tension in the room.

I worked that day in silence. There had to be more to life than back door promises. I left the station and walked to the bus stop. I'm beginning to look forward to taking public transportation. I get to take a nap each day on my long commutes. I wake up just in time to get off the bus and make it to the apartment.

"Hey, how is it going?" Linda won't understand how disappointed I am. Again, she's the only one I can tell about these mishaps.

"The guy at the radio station wants to date me."

"Girl, I know you said yes. We are working on going to Hollywood."

"To be honest with you I told him I don't date people I work with."

"D'Alise here you go again messing everything up for us. Can't you just pretend with him a little? I bet he's furious with you as I am."

"No, I am not attracted to him." I give her the same expression I gave him. What did she really think I was? I didn't sleep around, and I wasn't interested in mixing business with pleasure.

"You need to learn how to relax. You're a little too uptight. Nothing like a long drag of a cigarette and a glass of champagne to top off the day."

"Walking helps me to relax. I don't need anything to alter my state. I always want to be sober." *My grandmother says you always, always need to be sober.* She would emphasize 'always.'

I make my way to the radio station feeling good about standing up for myself. Since having that conversation with Austin, he has been giving me the cold shoulder. He's treating me like I am invisible. He's having me do his and my duties.

"Good Morning, Sir." I wouldn't let his attitude change my work ethics.

"Hi, D'Alise James. You really don't date at work?"

"No."

"Who made that rule?"

"My grandmother and I talked about it."

"It's time for a change." Austin is not happy with the way our conversation is turning out.

Again, I felt a stab at my character. He didn't need to keep prodding me. I am thinking about telling the owner Mr. Taylor about Austin Reynolds. He probably won't believe me. I am beginning to question some of the rules I've set up for myself. I am not a quitter, but I won't deal with harassment at the station every day. Austin Reynolds energy makes me feel uneasy. He's on a power and manipulation trip; there are men like that.

I decided to talk to Mr. Taylor. I thanked him for everything he offered me at the station. I told him I made the decision to resign. He was very sad and inquired why I was leaving? I told him I couldn't work with an employee that was there, and it would be best that I leave. He told me he knew what was going on. He said stay, and he would handle it. I asked him to keep it confidential. I had to leave. He told me to call him if I ever needed a reference or anything.

I trust in the powers that be. I felt I was making the appropriate decision. Goodbye Hollywood.

Chapter 22

Afraid of The Dark

When I reflect back to my dream journals, I noticed its always night. I am surrounded by darkness in the front, back, and on both sides of me. I'm afraid because something is chasing me. I refuse to look back at the demonic forces that are chasing me. I am always trying to find a place to hide, and, in some instances, I am falling and see all that is below and above me. In the dreams where I am falling, I realize at that time in space, I am free and letting go I have no control over the fall. I am flying through space and time free.

My mind and spirit is not at ease. I am conflicted about returning to Alabama. This new life that I am experiencing is nothing like I expected. My cousin and his wife are so different than I imagined them to be. They live with different values and standards. It's their life, I can't say anything about how they live. I am trying to figure out a way to escape from this situation. The atmosphere has changed. On many occasions, when I arrive home, no one is happy to see me. There are constant mood swings. It's like a roller coaster ride for me.

From the front door of the apartment, the corridor leads into the living room. I must pass Linda and her friends before I can get to the room where I sleep. I speak and keep it moving to the bedroom where I am still sleeping on the floor. I see a white powdery substance on the living room table. No one speaks they just stare at me. I hope they don't think I am going to join them in the drinking, smoking, and whatever their choice of drugging is. I will never be like them. Our lifestyles are totally different; we are not a fit. I finally figured out what's been going on in the bedroom.

I hear Linda's voice in the next room saying. "I am going to send my sister in there for you."

I am fed up. I told Linda I am not into women. I have given her many chances to show me respect. At this point, I'm done with her. I don't want to deal with her or any of her friends. I am wearing my feelings on my face and can't hide how I feel about her.

I'm sitting on the floor in the corner of the empty room facing the locked bedroom door holding my pillow in my stomach. It's just me, the walls, carpet, and a window. I am thinking about escaping through the window. *No, I am a big girl now.* I am ready to fight and will not run away. I am trying to find the courage to stand up for myself.

This moment takes me back to a moment when I was a child afraid to go to my bedroom. I learned I had nyctophobia, a fear of the dark.

I slowly walked down the long hallway in my pink night-gown to my bedroom. I felt a sense of anxiety. I didn't want to go to bed. My bedroom didn't really look like a child's room. The large room contained a full-size bed. Too big for a small child. The white brick walls had one single picture. Two windows were covered with beige curtains facing the headboard. The cherry wood sleigh bed was covered with a yellow spread. My room had lots of toys and stuffed animals from my grandmother. She purchased a red bike for me, which was stored in my closet out of sight. My favorite Barbie dolls and paper dolls were stored in the lower dresser drawer in my bedroom. Over the years I've suffered from nightmares. I would wake up in the middle of the night screening yelling and crying. I was awakened to scary faces lions, tigers, and bears. I recall many nights I was afraid. The windows were closed. The window shades were down, and the heavy-duty curtains were closed. No nightstand was in my room. I would open my closed door to exit the terror. I walked down the hallway by myself. I would be searching for my mother, and I couldn't find her. The door to my brother's room was closed. The entrance to my mother's room was closed and locked. I recall each night the monsters would come for me. No one was available to save me.

Now I'm in my cousin's house feeling unsafe, not knowing what is waiting for me on the other side of the door. I feel sad, disappointed, and disgusted with this façade of a family trying to help one another. I realize if I am not as strong as I thought I could get caught in this family cycle of drugs, drinking, and smoking. I could even go to prison by just being in the house with people that have controlled substances in a home, even though I am not a user. There is so much to tell my mother and grandmother. If I told them they would want me to come home.

My thoughts rationalize the situation quickly. *I can't go back to my mother's house. I was furious with her for not believing me when I told her live-in boyfriend was sitting in the chair next to the bed I shared with my sister. I woke up and saw him sitting in the chair. He leaned in and asked me to kiss him. My grandmother didn't like him. He was one of her clients. Each night before I went to bed, I would sleep with my panties and shorts to safeguard my body. Each night I would barricade me and my sister in our room to keep the pervert out of our bedroom. I pushed the dresser up to the door every night before I went to sleep. I sometimes wonder what happens to my sister after I left for college. I recall her telling me she lost her best friend when I left. Often, I felt like she was angry with me for leaving her. I don't know her feelings because we have never talked about her experiences after I left.*

I get up the next day, unlock the door to my room and stick my head out. I look to my left, and right the coast is clear. I make my way to the bathroom quietly.

"Good Morning, D'Alise." I hear the sweetest voice. It was in the moment that I realized she had another personality.

"Good Morning, Linda." Yesterday she was rolling her eyes at me like a demon.

"I'm a little pissed out at you. I thought we were going to Hollywood. You didn't even tell me you quit the radio station. Austin Reynolds called and left a message on the answering machine. You can listen to the message. He was apologizing for his behavior. The offer is still good. He said something about having a meeting with the owner. I want you to call him back and take that offer. Oh, by the way, someone from Wig World offered you a job too. The radio station is the better of the two."

"Is that why you were looking at me that way yesterday. Linda, I am going to leave my options open. It's early; I will be guided to what is best for me. The decision is mine to make regarding where I would like to work and be happy." Linda's eyes are red with fire. *She'll get over it.*

I phoned the radio station talk to the owner and made plans to come in to pick up my personal effects, items I really needed to pick up. Upon my arrival at the radio station, I was greeted by the receptionist who escorted me to the conference room. The owner and Mr. Reynolds were seated at the table, waiting for me. I accepted the apology and declined the offer of employment.

<h1 style="text-align:center">Chapter 23</h1>

Another Job

I jumped on the bus and headed to Canal Street to see about another job offer. I met with Joy Chang and was offered a full-time sales position working from nine in the morning until five in the afternoon. It would be a weekly paycheck every Friday. The staff was friendly and engaging. The energy was upbeat, and this job feels like home.

"Yes, I'll take the job offer, and I can start when the paperwork is finalized."

"We really need help. One of our employees is relocating to another state. We need someone to run the T-shirt print shop, manage the sales floor, put merchandise out. We also need help with visual merchandising for the window display. Can you start tomorrow?"

The dialect is foreign to me, her version of English. I have to listen carefully. It's going to take a minute for me to repeat what she said.

"Mrs. Chang, I only have experience in sales and merchandising. I am familiar with wigs. My grandmother had hair but wore wigs. I never ran a print shop, but I am willing to learn."

I could never understand why my grandmother wore wigs. The wigs were displayed on Styrofoam heads with female faces in her master bedroom. Some of the wigs were long, short, curly, and wavy. I enjoyed visiting her and staying with her in the summer or even long term when my mother was away. It was so much fun for me because I played with them. I would shake my head and brush the hair away from my face. My grandmother had lots of beautiful clothes. I was a curious child. I would go through her jewelry box pretend and make-believe I was grown trying on her big hats, eye-glasses, and jewelry. My grandmother never got angry when she saw me in her personal items. She would look at me and smile. She let me embrace my feminine self. Now I get to take in all the things I did as a child working at this store.

"D'Alise that's good to know you have some knowledge about wigs. Everyone has their designated areas. Pat, Kim and I run the wig area. Mr. Joe takes the payments and orders the supplies. You will manage the areas I mentioned to you. You will work closely with Mr. Joe. Can you start tomorrow?"

"Yes, see you tomorrow." I had to make the best of what I was offered. I am becoming a seasoned bus commuter. I know the bus schedules and routes. I keep my bus passes and always have exact change in my change purse.

I took the time to pray daily, but today was special. *Thank you, God, for opening another door for me I am filled with much gratitude.* Now I can finally go to the French Quarter and put my brass bed on layaway and begin to pay my student loans. I am taking this position for me, not for Linda. Linda made it very clear. I had to leave in a year.

As I approach the apartment door there's silence, no one is home. I see a note on the table Linda is gone on a trip. I wonder when John is coming home. I feel instant peace and decide to lock the door and write in my journal before I retire for the evening.

I patiently wait at the designated bus stop in front of the apartment complex on West Bend Parkway for my commute to Canal Street. I'm headed to my new job at Wig Express-General Shopping Center.

I listen to the conversations of the day; sports, politics, and women talking about their experiences with their children. The atmosphere changes with the arrival of the bus. The passengers line up to take their seats. On many occasions, I have crossed the bridge in either my cousin's vehicle or when Greg had his personal driver pick me up and chauffeur me around. As I reflect, I'm filled with so many warm thoughts about the first day I met Greg. I remember him saying, "When you know you know." He was fighting hard for me. The next relationship I will fight for. I won't let it slip through my fingers. I never fought for him. Not even when he placed me in the back seat of the car and sent me home.

I resigned from two jobs when I probably should have exposed the men who were conducting unethical treatment of women on the job. Indecent proposals and harassment are frowned upon in the workplace. On those two occasions, I had valid reasons to file a complaint. I know the companies would have been investigated, and I would have been compensated favorably. Sometimes you must choose your battles. I am convinced I did the right thing by just letting it go.

I am going to be my own boss one day. I'll be in authority with no one over me. I often wonder how 'Old Greg' is doing. He had his business plan all mapped out for his career. Greg could have been my happy ending. I think I unconsciously didn't believe love was available for me. I sabotaged the whole relationship by letting my thoughts get the best of me. The encounter with Greg has made me realize communication is essential in a relationship. You must talk with your partner to be clear on any misunderstandings.

I realize no one individual has all the attributes we desire in our hearts. We go through cycles where we meet people that have pieces that remind us of that one particular person in our lives. Greg was a bundle of all the pieces of men that I met in the past that made a whole man for me. He is all the good guys I didn't recognize in the past. I am moving on with the expectations to spiral upward in my new relationships.

Chapter 24

Meet Obie Bushman
Cycle #1 - The Bus Stop On the West Bank - Rescue Me

As I wait at that bus stop on West Bend Parkway, I take in the nature that surrounds me. I breathe in, and I breathe out slowly. I am having a difficult time adjusting to my living arrangements with my cousin and his wife. I feel as if they have targeted me. I get the feeling they want to pull me into their addictions. I realize what was supposed to be good isn't good at all. This is not the lifestyle I would have voluntarily selected for myself. I want to be away from the noise, in a quiet place, by myself, in my own apartment.

I ran away from home in search of a new life only to get intimate glimpses of my old home environment. The hope for a new life is fragmented. I wanted to be an adult badly. I still feel like a child. I wanted to leave home now. I want to go back home. I wanted to leave the pain behind me. The pain and remorse are still here with me. Every day I wake up. Every day I pray. I am trying to figure out the mysteries of the world; the untold stories my mother and grandmother have never shared with me. Those things that have held them captive in their life cycles. I don't understand why they're choosing to take their stories to the grave. I guess it's just too much pain to remember and to tell the story. The cycles of abuse, addiction, alcohol, drugs, rape, smoking, and mental illness needs to end. For some reason, I feel as if small aspects of my life are mirroring my mother and my grandmother's life. I am getting their karma. They are my family. My mother once told me her father had mental illness and was an alcoholic. She even told me a family member said to her that her mother left home because of an incident of molestation. God, I do not want to be a statistic. When I left home, I prayed for God to send me a good man. I am not sure if I was specific. I prayed to be in a relationship forever, unconditionally. I realize some relationships are conditional. I am not sure when Linda is returning from her trip. I feel this new job is going to work out for me to support myself.

Each day as I waited for the bus I feel as if someone was watching me. Each time I looked back, I see the blinds fall close. It's as if someone was watching and waiting for me every day. I am happy I have the sense to check my surroundings and environment. You never know who's watching you, calculating and understanding your daily schedule. Sometimes a stalker knows a person's routine better than they do. The stalker watches and studies you and know you better than yourself.

This day I am approached by this big husky guy. He isn't visually pleasing to me. He has a big nappy afro, and his stomach is protruding from his loose-fitting t-shirt. I would say if he was a woman, he would be ready to deliver at any second. His loud odor tagged my nose before he got close. He's walking with a wobble, but he's moving with a purpose to make that money. When he spoke, he spoke with authority.

"Hello, my name is Obie Bushman. O-B-I-E, B-U-S-H-M-A-N. I live in this apartment complex."

"Hi." *I am minding my own business, and I really don't want to be bothered.*

"What is your name?" The intense deep accent is from an island. I'm not sure which one. I'm listening attentively trying to figure out what he is saying. He might be more from an island, possibly Africa.

I looked directly into his eyes and said. "My name is Danielle Alise James; you can call me D'Alise." I saw a twinkle in his eyes. It's as if his eyes were sparkling and dancing in delight. Then his big round thick lips fell apart to my discovery I saw a beautiful smile on his dark chocolate face. In his mouth were a beautiful set of white teeth. I have always been fascinated by a man that takes care of his oral health. I notice how people take care of outside. I guess it's easy to fix up the external because when you start working on the inside it takes a lot of work. Purchasing fancy clothing is easy to put on than making an investment internally.

"Where are you going?"

"Why are you asking?"

"I am a taxi driver. He assumes where I am going. I will take you to work. That's my yellow taxi over there with the number 409 displayed." He shows me his identification and guides me over to the back seat and secures me in for the ride. I can't believe I am trusting this guy.

"It's funny riding in a taxi." I am not sure why I made that statement. I had been in taxi cabs many times before but not under the circumstances today.

"Do you know how much people pay to ride in a taxi? He sounds intimidating.

"No!" I had never given any thought to his question until to-day.

"People normally pay for this service. You should appreciate this."

I do not comment and sit quietly in the back seat. *I pay to take the bus. This guy is so arrogant. This guy is so full of him-self; he don't what to do.*

"D'Alise James where will I be taking you today?"

"Wig Express on Canal Street across from Krauss. Do you need the address?"

"No, I've picked patrons up from the area in the past." He turns to me and smiles. I must look like a piece of pie. He paused long enough for me to wonder what was on his mind. Memories of Greg's driver crossed my mind. I thought about the times he picked me up and took me around. The ride wasn't that long. I am accustomed to the bus making stops to pick up and drop off pas-sengers. It had been a while since I rode to work in a car.

"We are here."

"How much do I owe you?"

"Nothing. It was my pleasure."

"No, sir. Everything cost something. I am paying my way. Thank you for the ride" I've had enough drama over the past weeks. I am paying my way. I handed the money over to the taxi driver to pay for the services.

"D'Alise the money you have given me isn't enough. Look at the meter. Please keep your money. I will pick you up. What time do you get off?"

"Today is my first day at work I get off at five."

"Is it okay if I pick you up? Enjoy your day." He waited patiently. He was still sitting with the window down as I approached the door. *He's waiting for an answer.* I couldn't believe it. I shouted the answer. What is this guy going to mean to me?

"I'll let you pick me up. Thank you." He appeared to be shy and aggressive at the same time.

Wig Express - General Shopping Center

I open the door and walked into my new job with my head held high. I say to myself, "I got this." "When one door closes, another opens; but we often look long and so regretfully upon the closed door that we don't see the one which has open for us. Alexander Graham Bell." The door closes behind me.

I walk through the corridor of the store that leads to a huge store. The store is compartmentalized for all the exclusive services it offers. The store is brightly lit with nice background music.

I make a right and go to the counter, "Good Morning Mrs. Chang."

"Good Morning, D'Alise. I am glad you were able to start today. I am going to let you shadow each of the employees in the three areas of the store. You'll be starting in wigs with Kim and Pat. Mr. Joe will be training you in the print shop, which consists of all the decals and letter designs for the T-Shirts. Alot of tourist makes special shirts purchases with the New Orleans logos. You'll need to be organized and prepared for daily rush hour. The print shop is a busy area. You'll also be working with Mr. Joe handling all the merchandising. I'll give you a discount on any items you purchase. We can use someone to advertise our merchandise. You have a small body type, and the clothes would fit you nicely. You'll have the keys to the jewelry cases. Make sure you take all merchandise to the cash register, Mr. Joe handles all the money." This reminds me of my grandmother saying. "*Keep your eyes on your money at all times.*" This new life everybody is watching their money and brand, even Greg.

"Excuse me, Mrs. Chang, could you speak slowly. I am having trouble trying to keep up. One moment you're speaking English and the next you're speaking a foreign language I'm unable to understand." I hope I didn't offend her. Mrs. Chang laughs. I must have been funny.

"Ha, Ha, Ha D'Alise everyone in the store speaks Korean fluently except for Pat. She knows the basics. I apologize and will try to be mindful. If you are here long enough, you will pick up on the language. Oh, by the way, I won't be at this store every day I operator two other locations throughout the city. I have to check on."

Mrs. Chang is a real businesswoman. I am going to take notes so I can learn how to set up my future business. She doesn't appear to have had a hard life. You can never judge a book by its cover you have to open it up and read the chapters. Looking at my mother, you would never know all the drama she's had in her life. My mother experienced hell in her life. Who would have thought Greg was a doctor? I just realized I am the tallest employee in the store. Most of the employees have similar pale features with straight black hair, thin lips, and small bodies. Everyone smokes cigarette except Mrs. Chang and me.

"Mrs. Chang, thank you for this opportunity. You will never regret it."

"You're welcome. I've been around all types of people. I've seen the good the bad and the ugly. This store gets a lot of foot passage it's busy. I watch the customers and listen closely they will tell you who they are. I have a good feeling about you."

I heard something similar from Greg. This is something I must pay close attention too when I meet people. "Mrs. Chang I am always open to advice." My grandmother and mother always had a lot of advice for me built around stories.

Mrs. Chang walks me over to the wig department, and I get a chance to experience wigs as an adult.

"Hi, ladies do you remember D'Alise from yesterday?"

"Yes,"

"I hired her. I want you to give her a short tutorial on wigs and sales. Ladies if you are good, I need to go visit my other stores."

Everyone says goodbye. "Goodbye."

"Hey, Mrs. Kim, I want D'Alise to start with you first bye."

Mrs. Kim had the most serious expression on her face when I first met her. I wasn't sure if she liked people. Listening to the interaction between her and Pat, I heard quick responses and lots of joking and laughter. I realize my perception of her was wrong. She seems to be friendly; it's just a matter of me getting to know her. Mrs. Kim had long, straight waist-length hair. She wore fitted clothing and could walk without any difficulty in eight-inch heels. The heels gave her height as she is very short. I recall my cousin's wife, suggesting I wear that type of height heel when she was helping me get ready for my date with Greg. I am most compatible wearing three to four-inch heels. I have height and don't need anything to increase my height.

"Hi D'Alise, I think you are going to enjoy working in this store. We are beauty professionals. The team in this department are licensed, cosmetologists. Many clients visit the store because they have hair loss due to radiation and medical challenge conditions. We also have entertainers, and fashion-conscious people coming in to change their looks. Women need to change their appearance sometimes to keep their man interested but nothing extreme. "

"My mother said a man likes a natural woman."

"Even natural women need to add a little something. You don't want to be one dimensional all the time."

"I am listening." My thoughts are no one needs to change themselves for a man.

"The wigs displayed in the window are for sale, and the price tags are on each wig. We have a wide selection of name brand wigs, ponytails and clip-on's in our stores. The wigs are short, mid-length, and long. We carry curly, straight, and wavy. The Human Hair, Remy Human Hair, and Synthetic Hair wigs and extension are displayed behind the counter. We carry accessories for the hair. We also wash and style wigs. When helping someone select a wig, be aware of the hair color, skin tone, and eye color."

"This is much different than playing wigs at my grandmother's house."

"I am going to take a break and let Mrs. Pat talk to you."

"D'Alise, I am styling this wig right here for a client watch me. Mrs. Chang must like you. She gave you the keys to the display case on the first day. She doesn't trust anybody. I am surprised they have kept me around this long. Mrs. Chang husband is a real businessman. Before he got sick, he had restaurants, spas, liquor stores, and wig stores like this one. Mrs. Chang was forced into the business. We are like family here. We look out for one another. She has one son. Mrs. Chang is good to her employees. My husband is in prison, and this job is the best thing for me."

I am listening to Mrs. Pat. She has all the tea as Greg would say. I am not sure if I want to tell her too much about myself. I get the impression she likes to gossip. Mrs. Pat is an African American woman in her forties. Her complexion is dark brown. She has the big protruding brown eyes. When she smokes her cigarette, her heart-shaped lips blow out. I am not sure how she manages to hold the wigs with her long-curved fingernails. Her body is well developed big breast and a lot of cushion on her butt. She wears those tight-fitting clothes on her hourglass body.

"How do you remember all of this stuff?"

"It will come in time. You'll be spending a lot of your time with Mr. Joe. Doesn't he look like Bruce Lee? Giggle. This lady comes around here looking for him every month. I think he married her for his green card." She is talking non-stop. "We have to clean up at the end of the day."

Cleaning up has been a part of my routine since I was a child. "Mrs. Pat, I have no problem cleaning. I am a team player."

"What do you for lunch?" I hope my facial expression isn't showing again. It's only 10:00 am, and she is talking about lunch. "Mrs. Chang has a refrigerator in the back. She shares the rice, tofu, seaweed, kimchi, soup, vegetables and roasted meat or fish with the employees. We use chopsticks for eating utensils. Feel free to help yourself to the variety of teas."

"I plan on bringing my lunch and walking on my breaks. I like fried chicken and might go to Popeyes for lunch."

Mr. Joe comes over. "We have a customer in the print shop; let me take D'Alise over to that area to explain the set-up." Mrs. Pat frowns at Mr. Joe. I am glad he saved me. I hope Mrs. Chang doesn't ask me what I learned from Mrs. Pat today. She styled the wig but didn't explain anything to me. That's probably why she wanted me to work with Mrs. Kim first.

After Mr. Joe showed me everything in the print shop, we stocked the shelves, ticketed, and put merchandise out on the sales floor. I helped a few customers in the fitting room and gave my opinion when I was asked. Mrs. Kim mentioned she had to pick up extra supplies from another store and asks Mr. Joe to bring the supplies in for the wig shop. All the associates were pretty laid back. I mentioned I wanted to take my lunch around one each day. I wouldn't have to worry about the lunch rush on canal street. The store was centrally located by everything. The store is continuously busy throughout the day. The time went by so fast I can't believe I get off in fifteen minutes.

Everyone is interested in how my first day went. "D'Alise how was your first day in the store."

"I enjoyed it. I'm going to finish cleaning up I get off soon." I looked out the window and saw my yellow taxi waiting for me. "Goodbye, everyone I will see you tomorrow.

Taxicab Conversations with Obie Bushman

I must say I am impressed Obie Bushman is prompt he shows up on time and is waiting outside to take me home. This gives me an indication he is a dependable man.

Obie greets me with a big smile. "Hi, D'Alise, I told you I would pick you up."

"Thank you. I appreciate your generosity."

"How was your day?"

This man seems to be interested in my day. "I had an awesome day at work. It was a bit challenging because of the language barriers with my co-workers. I have difficulties understanding the dialect even yours. Where are you originally from?"

"I am from Nigeria. The capital is in Lagos. Do you know anything about Africa?"

"I know you are from "Negroland" and the geography maps were changed. We both laugh at my little joke. I attended a historically black college in my freshman year of college and met a few people from Africa. I only learned about things they cared to share with me. I 've heard a lot about Africa.

"Hopefully, good things."

Humm. I don't want to base my opinions on someone else's experiences or the history that has been erased. You've lived over there. Why don't you educate me on the culture and tell me about yourself? I am curious.

"I am twenty-two years old, and I know who I am. I played soccer back home. Some people call it football."

His body type doesn't look like a soccer player. "You and I are the same age." For some reason, I thought he was much older. I wonder if he actively plays soccer now? My facial expression must have given me away.

"I've gained a little weight and want to play more. I came to the United States to study accounting at Pennsylvania State University. I am currently working on my master's degree in New Orleans. I am going to be a CPA like my uncle, Charles. He is a partner at Price Water House in the United Kingdom. I came over here for a better life. I plan on getting all I can from the land of opportunity. When I reach retirement age, I am moving back to Africa. I have family and friends spread out in different areas of the united states. Everyone in my family is college-educated and has professional careers. I have cousins that live in Atlanta in the Buckhead area. I have a cousin that owns an African store on Buford Highway and one past the Airport. I think that's considered the Southside?"

"It seems you already have your life planned out."

"I had no choice my family was very involved in my life. My job was to study anything below A was not acceptable."

"I am self-motivated and have had mentors. I had a variety of grades ranging from A's, B's, and C's. I wasn't a straight-A student. It seems like you are an overachiever. Please continue. I apologize for interrupting you."

"D'Alise have you ever been to Atlanta?"

"I visited Atlanta when I was in the Upward Bound program. My college roommate had an aunt that lived in Forest Park. I visited that area during Spring Break. Atlanta would have been my first preference because it's closer to my family." My home town is still in my subconscious thoughts, even though I wanted to leave so badly.

"Atlanta is where I am going to move eventually. You can visit my family and me."

"Don't you think that's a little pre-mature I just met you." These days my thoughts are being verbalized. It seems like this guy is trying to snatch me up.

"Sometimes, when you meet a person, you automatically have a good feeling about them. It's called intuition. When you know you know?" "Have you ever traveled outside the United States?"

This conversation sounds familiar to me.   "No. I am afraid not."

"I've been traveling since I was a child. My parents sent me to a boarding school. Do you speak any foreign languages?"

This conversation still sounds familiar to me. No, not really a little Spanish from high school. I picked up a little from my mother, who studied French in high school.

"I speak eight languages in addition to my native languages. Being able to speak other languages is important. You need to be multidimensional to walk through different doors."

I speak a secret language that no one knows about. It feels as if Greg's presence is right here with me trying to speak to me through Obie Bushman. "I'm taking in everything that you are saying."

"I have an older brother that lives here. My sister is still back home. My father has other children outside his marriage. I eat a lot of spicy food. I'll have to make some of my cultural food for you. I make stews with chicken, beef, and goat. I make egusi soup, rice, fufu, and fried plantains. I eat rice with everything." *Now I am getting to hear how other people eat.*

"It important for a woman respect their man. Some of my friends say they wouldn't date an African American woman because they show no respect for their men.   I am a traditional man. I am not a dominant type of man, but I do require respect. I don't think a woman should pay for nothing. You offended me when you offered to pay. If it comes a time where I don't have money to pay for something, I will let you know in advance."

"I am glad to hear about your cultural upbringing. I'll try not to offend you. I was raised to have my own money and to pay my way. My mother had a controlling partner. I don't plan on being in that type of relationship. No one is ever going to control me. I am an independent thinker."

"Do you care to tell me about you:"

"It's nothing much to tell. I have a dysfunctional family. I grew up poor. I've had quite a few adverse childhood experiences. I have a real business plan for my life."

"That's it. It seems like you could tell me more."

I don't plan on disclosing a lot about myself to this stranger. He is not a love interest. I am not interested in being a friend to a man that comes from a background where women are treated as mere possessions. My gut is telling me to keep him at a distance. Obie will learn more about me as the days go back. He is going to have to prove me his cultural values are not imprinted in him. I am going to study him, listen, and watch his body language.

"That's it. I have nothing more to say. Everybody doesn't deserve to hear your story because they aren't ready."

"Would you like to stop at Shoney's for dinner before I take you home?"

"Why"

"Everybody has to eat. Plus, I want to get to know you."

"So, are you trying to take me on an informal date or something like that?"

"You are a sassy little something. Obie laughs. I am trying to be friendly with you. What do you say?"

I feel a little hesitant about riding in this taxi. "What do I say about what?"

"A bite to eat. Please…"

"Okay. But I can pay for my food."

The dinner at Shoney's went well. Obie got me to talk a little more.

Over the weeks, he picked me up every day and took me to work the conversations continue to grow I began to trust him. I tell him about my living situation with my cousin and his wife. I explain I am co-existing with my family here in the city. Obie invites me to his two-bedroom apartment. I get to meet his cousin. Obie cooks for me, and I help clean up after dinner. The apartment is lightly furnished with a floor lamp, sofa, and coffee table. The kitchen area has a four-piece dining table perfect for a small apartment. The apartment is simply nothing over the top. He has an overflow of books in his study area. He mentions he paid his apartment rent for the year.

I don't recall any of my family members paying their rent for a full year. "D'Alise has your cousin ever asked you how you and his wife get alone?"

"No, he hasn't."

He has a look of concern on his face. "You are his family, and he hasn't asked."

"He works overseas. When he's home, the two of them are drinking, smoking, and dealing with those controlled substances. I stay out of their way because they have mood swings. I'm sleeping on the floor. I don't plan on bringing any furniture in that apartment. I am going to purchase my own bedding so I won't be using theirs anymore."

"Girl, who is that dropping you off every day?"

"Pat, it's just a friend."

"Looks like one of those African men has taking a liking to you. Be careful girl. I have been told some of them are really possessive. I don't want your body to get cut up. My friend was dating a Jamaican man girl. He came after her with ax. They are controlling and will kill you. He doesn't even look like your type. He is trying to come up. Do you see him? You must be blind.

"Oh, Pat, he's really nice. We are friends. I am so attractive to his brain. He is full of knowledge. He explains things to me and doesn't judge me for not having a lot of worldly experiences."

"I am telling you D'Alise run and don't look back. All the staff was looking out the window. We had a meeting and decided you need to leave him alone. He has plans for you. You have something that he wants."

"Pat, I have nothing materially to offer him." Pat is pointing her long fingernails in my face.

"You have class. Class is something a person can't purchase. He's upgrading himself with you."   Everyone in the store overhears Pat and begins to laugh.

Returning from Overseas

It appears John and Linda are not on good terms. I overheard them fighting in the bedroom over money. John is upset because Linda was supposed to purchase a quality mattress. This is a side of John I have never seen before because he's always so laid back. I could tell John about Linda's booster friends but It's none of my business. I'm glad I was able to locate a store that would let me layaway my brass bed and china dinnerware. At least, I know it will be mine and honest purchase. I am trying to co-exist with Linda. I am sure she's told John all kinds of lies on me. I am not even going to have a conversation with him to defend my truth. I see her lies are catching up with her. It's easier, to tell the truth, because you must remember the lies you tell. Linda has the best of two worlds; sometimes, she disappears for a week. I am beginning to think John wanted me to come live with them so I could keep an eye on Linda and report out to him. Obie wants to meet my cousin and wife. I'm a little hesitant because Greg made such a lasting impression on them.

"Hi, cousin. How is everything going for you?" I surprised he's concerned.

"It's going okay. How are you and Linda doing?"

"You must have overheard us arguing."

"Yes. But it's none of my business."

"I'm gone a lot; it's important I need to know I can trust Linda with my life."

"John, I trust God and myself. That's all I have."

"I am beginning to question Linda's character when it comes to our money. We both have addictions we are functional addicts we go to work every day. Addictions can drain your bank account. I am proud of you by the simple fact you aren't using anything to alter your mental state. Remember one person in the relationship needs to be sober." This conversation reminds me of Clara Rosa and Greg.

"Thank you for giving me the opportunity to leave Alabama. I met a guy and want you to meet him before you travel again."

"Sure." John is up on the game and can give me some good advice.

John and Linda met Obie. Their personalities did not connect. Linda and John felt Obie had more exposure to the world than me and felt it would not be a good fit. My tribe didn't talk bad about Obie. I am not going to ask them to explain a fit because we'll be talking forever. My tribe is seeing something I don't see. The more people try telling me Obie is not a fit, the more I am drawn in to want to know more about this man from Africa. It's like your parents telling you not to put your hands on the hot stove. The more I want to go into the fire to have the experience for myself. One day Obie came to visit me and advised I needed to get out that apartment. He was concerned because I could go to prison for associating with people that did drugs. I realize everyone has an addiction to something or someone. I am making good decisions and maintaining self-control. The young stages of my life are important. It's the foundation for everything after. My mother and grandmother said if you have good credit, you can get anything you want. I am going to save my money for the deposit on my apartment and have at least three months of an emergency fund. It would be nice to pay my rent for a year. I could always use the money that Greg set-up in the safe deposit box for me, but I am not. I am a big girl. I'm going to mail the key to his home. I've looked for the key high and low and not about to locate the key. I guess I lost it during the move. It was good seeing John. I hope he and Linda are on better terms when he returns home again.

Getting to Know Obie

Obie and I are becoming good friends. We talk a lot about education, family and traditions. We are collecting data on each other. He and I have something in common we both have been helping with our family at an early age. That melts my heart because I thought I was the only person in my previous situation. Sometimes I feel like I am in school. He's the teacher, and I am a student. He tells me a lot about his travels. I am fascinated. I have experienced the world through books and television. He has had real-life experiences. I, on the other hand, have been wearing my white gloves, never getting too dirty, being very careful about things in life. If I mess up, I have no one to rescue me. I feel as if he has a desire to improve me or is grooming me for something great. He is presenting his best self to me. Obie laughs and smiles at everything. He even laughs at himself. He doesn't seem to take life seriously. He is predictable. I know he is going to show up on time at least thirty minutes early. He encourages me to improve myself through reading. He looks very intimidating but is a big teddy bear. I feel safe around him, except for the times he grabs for me. I am not sure what his intentions are at the time. I immediately grab my personal items to make a dash for the door and head for home. When this happens, my favorite word is "I am going home." He laughs in a jolly tone opens the door, and I exit. Sometimes when I am in my room I hear a tapping on the window pane. I go to the window and to my discovery it's Obie in the bushes signaling for me to come outside so he can talk to me. I've even witnessed him standing in the rain just to get a glimpse of me through the window soaking wet I can't recall a time where I didn't shield myself from the rain.

"Hi, Obie." I wonder what he wants today.

"D'Alise I made a lot of money today. I want to give you some money to purchase a nice outfit and go to the hair salon. I want you to attend a party with me and meet some of my friends on Saturday."

I've been around the party scene all my life and have been trying to escape that lifestyle. My grandmother had a bootleg house. My cousin managed a night club in my hometown. Another family member-owned a night club in another state. I've had the experience of setting up for a happy hour. I didn't really care to hang out in college. I recall my freshmen year my four roommates dragged me out of bed drugged me down the dorm hallways around 9:30 p.m. on a Friday night chatting you're going to hang out with us. I was the mama bear in the group watching everyone's purses and making sure everybody got back to the dorm safely. There was the fraternity houses and the Party Barn right next to the railroad tracks. They supported me and cheered me on in pageants, so I felt obligated to hang out with them.

"What time is this party?"

"The day party starts around 4:00 pm and ends later in the night."

"What time do you plan on leaving the party?"

"We can leave whenever you like."

"I am going to return your money. I will not be able to attend the party. I appreciate the invitation."

"The money is a gift you can't return the money. May I ask why you're not going to attend the party with me."

"I'm not really a party or club person. I have my own adult curfew."

"What's your curfew time."

"It's midnight. I try to stay within the watches of the night. Growing up, I always had to be home before midnight. I was one-minute late once and got locked out of the house."

"Really. Girl. You are grown now. If I agree to have you home by 11:00 pm will you go?"

"I'll get back with you tomorrow." That's nice to know he's flexible.

The next day I am at the bus stop waiting to catch my bus to work. Obie is right on time like clockwork waiting for me.

"D'Alise I'll take you to work."

"Thank you, not this morning." I don't need any distractions in my thoughts today. I am trying to figure out where I am going to move and how much I want to pay for rent. My cousin's wife is giving me the cold shoulder."

"I would like to pick you up when you get off. Is that's okay? I want you to meet my brother and his family."

"Sure." I guess he's trying to impress me. His family education is not his. Greg was well established but much older than Obie. We are both starting out right out of college. Hopeful I can endure the struggle. I really want my family to be proud of me.

I am really enjoying my job. It feels like home. I am becoming a pro in the print shop. I walk to the stores to make payments on my layaways during my lunch. Mrs. Chang is the best boss. She trusts I will do the right thing when she's not looking. I manage and pace myself to give the best customer service in the store. I pick lunch up from Popeyes as a surprise for my co-workers. Everyone appreciates me bringing lunch for them. The conversation of the day is me hanging out with a man from Africa. The employees are expressing their feeling I am listening and ignoring everything they are saying. The language barriers aren't so difficult any more I am paying attention, listening closely, and being present.

"Girl, your man here to pick you up." Laughing.

"He is not my man; we are friends."

"Can't you see he's claimed you."

"Bye Pat, Kim, and Joe."

"Hi, D'Alise." Obie is always greeting me with a big smile. I feel safe with him. If he asks me, I am going to say yes; I will meet his brother and attend the party. I look forward to seeing how other people live.

"Hi Obie, thank you for picking me up."

"I have a question for you."

"What is your question?"

"I want you to meet my brother and attend the party with me. Please say yes, I will be the happiest man in the world."

"Yes, to all your question."

"Thank you D'Alise, you are so beautiful. I want you to meet all my friends." I like hearing those words. Greg is coming to my thoughts. I remember those words coming from him. I am going to push those thoughts out of my mind, for we have both moved on. "Let me help you in the car. My brother lives in Metairie. The commute shouldn't belong." I am assuming Obie likes Reggae music every time I get in the car Bob Marley is playing "One Love." He is true to his culture and doesn't deviate or compromise.

"I can't wait to meet all of them."

"I am going to take you to TJ Maxx so you can purchase a comforter before we go to my brother's house."

I end up selecting two items, a peach king-size spread and a light blue ruffled lace queen comforter for my room. We spent a lot of time in the store Obie suggest we visit his brother another day. I focus on picking my outfit for the party. I am pleased with my selections. Obie insists on paying for my purchases, and I let him.

"D'Alise I like you. I will always protect and stand up for you."

"Obie. Those words sound so sweet to my ears." I didn't get a lot of protection growing up. Honestly, trust and feeling safe means a lot to me.

Obie has stacks of money in his taxi and carries a firearm in the glove compartment. He is an excellent driver. He knows this city like the back of his hands.

"D'Alise let me help you get your purchases to your apartment."

"Thanks, Obie." Linda opens the front door.

We both speak to Linda. She extends a welcome and invites us in. She's in a good mood tonight. Obie mentions he must study and leaves. Tensions are in the air.

"Bye, Obie."

"D'Alise we have been passing each other up. What been going on with you?"

"I've been working."

"When are you going to invite me to come to the store to take advantage of your discount?"

Linda always has a motive when she is nice. "We'll work something out the day I am off from the store."

"D'Alise you got another hookup. Don't blow this with the store and the African fellow. Girl if we do this correctly, we could be visiting Africa. He doesn't look like much, but you can cultivate him by encouraging him to get his hair cut, lose weight, and upgrade his clothing style. You have excellent taste for the finer things in life. You know how to put things together classy. If you play your cards right, you could marry this guy. You're both young and can struggle together he will never forget you. You will make him a success and reap the rewards." Here she goes again; she will not stop with her scheming.

"I hear you, Linda."

"So, what you got in those bags."

"Just bedding. Girl, he makes a lot of money driving that taxi. I never would have thought."

"I could have told you that. This is a tourist city. Girl, those people know how to hide the money. They are crooks. Plus, he is going to be a CPA watch out now." Sounds like Linda has dated someone from the Islands.

We arrive at an event hall. Everyone is dressed in their traditional clothing. The music is loud. I wish I had brought earplugs to shield my ears from all the noise. The sponsor has enough food to feed one-hundred people. I have never seen so much food in one sitting. This is the first time I have felt like a foreigner in my own country in a circle of men speaking. I witness no one speaking English at this party. Obie was not translating for me. One of his friend's steps in to explain the conversation in the group. It was suggested I take a course to study the language and visit Africa. This is the first time I've seen Obie dressed up. He is wearing a tan suit with a white shirt and yellow tie. He has a fresh haircut. I am beginning to see him with a different set of eyes. He introduces me to all his friends. He prepares my food for me and brings me a bottled water to drink and finds a place for me to sit. He is very attentive he checks on me and keeps asking am I okay. This man is a real social butterfly; he knows how to get around the room. I am just sitting observing him. He is very charming and loving towards his tribe. I notice him going to an isolated area with a few people. I can't imagine someone spending over eight hours at a party. Two hours is enough; I'm ready to go home. I search for Obie and find him in a room debating with a group of men. I don't know what to think. They appear to be hostile towards one another. The guys are in each other's faces. Obie spots me and waves me over. I didn't realize he smoked and drank alcohol. "Hi, baby. Everybody this is D'Alise." Everybody's eyes move towards me. Everyone smiles. I get to meet all his career friends.

"Are you okay?"

"Yes."

"D'Alise, you look tired. We can leave at 8:00 p.m.

I am glad Obie is a man of his word I arrive home safely.

It's Official We Are A Couple

I notice Obie only socializes with his tribe of people from Nigeria. Everything is centered around his own culture. He only eats his food and listens to his type of music. We travel in taxi cab 409 everywhere. Today I am scheduled to meet Obie's brother he picks me up in burgundy Benz. Obie's brother home is grander than Greg's home. The home is modern with high-end furniture. It appears his family is well established, not him. I wish he would stop bragging on his family's titles. I am curious about what he is going to make out of his self in the future.

One day Obie and I were hanging out at The Mall at Canal Place. He poses a question...

"D'Alise we have been hanging for a while." It appears Obie is mustering up enough courage to ask me a question. "What does a guy need to do to be your boyfriend. I have been working hard to win you over. I want you to be my girl. We can take care of each other."

"First of all, if a guy wants to be my man or be in a relationship with me, he has to ask me. I'll give a truthful answer, yes or no. I am not playing any elementary childhood stuff. When we both agree, then we will be exclusively dating each other."

"D'Alise James, will you be my girlfriend? I want to be in a relationship with you."

"What? Are you serious? I am still collecting data on you."

"Yes. I am serious about you D'Alise."

"Humm. I need to seriously think about that because we have cultural differences. When do you need an answer?"

"Now."

"That sounds a little demanding."

"You did ask, and I am waiting for my answer."

Laughs. "Obie, I will be your lady but no hanky panky stuff right away. Let's work on getting to know one another more. I want us to be friends first. We'll need to work out what we both expect in the relationship considering we've had conversations in your taxicab. I didn't even know you smoke and drank alcohol."

"It's only in social settings. Is it a problem?"

"No, if it's only in social settings."

"I am the happiest man alive right now. I want to meet your family. I would like your family to visit Africa. Give me your families contact information in Alabama." I can hear Linda's background chatter about visiting Africa.

I write the contact information on a piece of paper and hand it to him. Obie grabs for me, pulls me closer, and gives me a big hug. He kisses the crown of my head. I've always been attracted to a smart guy. He's very intelligent and respectful. I love his accent. I'm trying to figure out what just happen that was fast. I am in a relationship.

"The first time I saw you from the window, I fell in love with you. I knew we would be good for each other. I know we're not sleeping with each other. I want you to promise me when we consummate our relationship; I will be the only man that touches your body. I will go crazy to ever think of another man ever touching you. I respect your body. I am going to be rich one day, and I want a feminine classy woman by my side. Once I get established, I want to marry you. I want to have a big African wedding with 500 people."

"I only want a wedding with fifty people."

"I want to take really good care of you. I don't want you to work." He ignored my mention of small wedding plans. If I permit this, I will be promoting this behavior. I'm going to ignore it because he is too far into the future. I don't understand how I keep attracting men that want to take care of me. Do I look, needy?

Obie's goes in his pocket and pulls out a fist of cash to pay for my v neck yellow sweater and other miscellaneous items I am going to purchase. Most of the people I know carry their cash in their wallets or have a credit card.   Linda is right I am going to have to cultivate Obie. This seems like it's going to be a big project for me. I need to slow down. I am getting ahead of myself trying to help this man bring his dream to life.

Obie goes off to locate a bathroom in the mall. While sitting on the bench in the mall court, a couple approaches me. It's Donald and Crissy looking like two love birds. They come over to speak to me. Donald tells Crissy to go ahead of him. He explains he wants to give me an update on Greg. I feel like Donald is making a confession to me. He explains how his and Crissy's family intervened took her away from him. He admitted he was not honoring their marital vows. He admitted prayer, and self-control has changed him to be a better man to his wife. I was happy to hear they are working on starting a family. I'll never understand how she stayed with him cheating on her with men. Donald was about to give me an update on Greg when Obie walked up. Donald gives me a hug and a kiss on the cheek and races off to catch up with his wife. I did not introduce Obie to Donald.

The Tantrum

Obie's eyes are red as fire; his mood changed all a certain. It's like he's Dr. Jekyll and Mr. Hyde. He was so loving a few minutes ago I have never seen a man so jealous in my life. His personality reminds me of my step-father. I am questioned to the point of no return. Obie sucked the life right out of me. He started accusing me of dating Donald. I should have introduced them. Something inside me didn't want to give Donald the impression I was moving on. I am thinking any those accusations are untrue. I know the truth Donald is gay. Obie's imagination has gone wild. I felt a queasy or achy feeling in my stomach. My face is cupped in my hands to shield the welling of tears that begin falling down my face. I feel so emotional. I've seen enough fussing in my childhood environment to last me a lifetime and didn't want to get into any arguments with anyone over petty stuff. The moment I said yes, he changed. I refuse to ride back with him and told him I would take the bus home. I start marching towards the exit of the mall to catch my bus.

Obie is walking and talking none stop insisting on me riding back in the taxi. The first apology to the mental abuse I suffered appeared to be sincere. I left the items he purchased me on the mall floor and made my way to the bus stop and headed home. On the ride back home, I sit silent hurt and disappointment. I asked myself how in the world did I attract someone like that in my life. I have never been in a situation like that in my adult life. I felt so humiliated.

It's been a couple of days since the blowup I haven't seen Obie at the bus stop waiting for me. There hasn't been any tapping on my window pane. I am glad I saw his radical behavior now I am free we are unofficial I am out of a relationship. Obie's cousin passed me while I was waiting for my bus and mentioned Obie went to Africa and wasn't sure when or if he would be returning to the United States of America. The cousin begins talking some creepy stuff like "I saw you first. You and I are supposed to be together. Obie is not the man for you." I disregarded his comments as my bus was boarding passengers. I got on the bus and waved his cousin off.

There is one person that lives in this state I wish I could sit down with to talk about men. I can't because they told me to never ask them for anything. I'll never be able to have the father-daughter talk. Who's to say he could tell me anything about men because he was never present in my life.

Meeting a New Guy

As the weeks go by, I am back on my bus routine. Things are going well on my job. Linda is happy to take advantage of my discount at the store. I am making friends with the customers that patronize the store. I became fast friends with Angela while designing her shirt in the print shop. We were talking about guys. I told her I wasn't having any luck with men. She told me, "I have just the guy for you." She planned for me to meet Ken Waters one weekend. Linda drove me to the shopping center around the corner from the apartment to meet Ken. I had rollers in my hair, no make-up, a T-shirt, and sweat pants. Ken arrived in an old beat-up hooptie with his brother and Angela. Ken was wearing his construction work clothes. I could see he was firm lean by looking at his arms. When we shook my hands, I could feel the callouses on his hand. His short-sleeve T-shirt displayed scabs on his elbows. I can tell this man did a lot of physical work. During our conversation, I determined Ken was genuine, and family meant a lot to him. I was automatically drawn to his energy and family values. Once again, I find myself drawn to a man that values family.

Linda always has something to say. "Girl, you should date Ken he can build you a house with those hands. I think he likes you. You got the chemical in your body that attracts men. He would not stop smiling. Did you notice all his front teeth were rotten? I know you did because you got a little hang-up on teeth. That's how Obie Bushman trapped you. Come on with it, I know you got something to say."

"Linda, the chemical is called pheromones you said enough for me. Maybe I could guide Ken into getting them fixed. I could make an appointment and ask him to take me."

"D'Alise you got nice teeth I wish you would smile more. Relax girl. Oh, by the way, thanks for hooking me up with your discount at the store. The store is a one-stop store."

"You are welcome."

Angela stops by the store to say Ken is taken away with me. I told her I got a good vibe from him. She confirms he is a decent man. He's only two years older than me. We started hanging out. Much of our time is spent at his aunt's shotgun house inwards. They have two pit bulls on the back of the house. I stay clear because I am allergic to dogs. The aunt is making out like a fat cat. She gets her live-in companion paycheck in addition to Ken's check and the other two brothers that live with her. When Ken purchases a gift for me, and she gets word of it, he has to purchase something for her.

One day Ken comes over to visit, Linda manipulates him into purchasing me a designer purse from Canal Place Mall. I told her that was inappropriate for her to have him purchase me such an expensive item. "Girl get your payday early in the relationship." I am trying to figure out how to donate all the items Greg purchased me without Linda getting upset. I know she would try to sell them and make a profit.

Ken is a wonderful guy; he lives a simple life. On the weekends we usually hang out at Lakefront sit by the water and eat bags of crawfish and listen to music. This is new to me; I have never eaten this type of food before. Ken frequently participates in the Mardi Gras Parade with the Zulu organization. That's all he ever talks about.

I found a beautiful one-bedroom apartment on the Westbank. I placed my deposit with a move date of two months. I am signing a six-month rental lease. I'll tell Linda thirty days before I get ready to move. I've almost finished paying off my brass bed and china set. I am so happy all the new items will arrive to my new living space.

Blow Up

Sometimes Linda can be a bit much. She has that forceful push energy that takes you by surprise. One day I came home from work. Undenounced to me, I was volunteered to go with her cousin to take some of her salon supplies to his shop. "Linda, did you ever think I might have plans with Ken."

"D'Alise go with my cousin all you are doing is sitting with Ken. He not taking you anywhere. Ken is a (COG) come over guy. He does nothing creative with you. Greg was taking you out on the town."

"I will this time but check with me in the future." I went along just to get along the dwarf superfly seems to be harmless. After helping drop the supplies off, he offered to take me out for a bite to eat. I thanked him but declined mentioned I needed to get back. The guy came on strong in the car I had to fight him off. He said Linda wants you out of her house. When I got back to the apartment, I confronted Linda; she said her cousin was lying. Then she said, "you been here almost a year; it's time for you to go." I told her I would be gone within thirty days. Her cousin had no reason to lie to me. All I ever ask of anyone was, to be honest, and I could respect them.

Moving Out

I decided to move out of the apartment when Linda was away. I returned the cable box back to the company because it was in my name. I didn't get a chance to say goodbye to John. It's so much I wanted to tell him about Linda. I am sure he has already figured her out. I did return to the apartment to give them the keys. Linda had a lot to say about me returning the cable box. I ignored her and left. She's told so many lies to my family about me that's okay. I am not going to attempt to defend myself because the truth will come out in the end.

Moving in My Own Apartment

Finally, a place to call my own. I have my own furniture. Thank you, God, for providing a warm, safe place for me to sleep at night. I have so much peace and joy in my life. Ken has been looking out for me. I feel like he could be the one. I appreciate him for listening to the stories of living with my cousin and his wife. Ken spends a lot of time at my apartment. The only thing he wants me to do is to cook for him. He loves to eat. On the weekends we do our rituals of visiting his family, praising God and relaxing. My family is happy that I have my own place now. I speak to my mother and grandmother every other day. My co-workers are happy for me. They purchased a few housewarming gifts for me. I am learning so much from Mrs. Chang about owning a business. Pat and my other co-workers are happy. I have moved on from Obie. She claims a lot of people from the islands are into the dark arts. I ignore Pat because she has a story for every scenario.

Where Did Time Go?

It seems like I moved into my apartment yesterday. Where did the time go? I am happy, but I feel stagnated. I want a professional career with more money. My grandmother called me to tell me my mother was having an episode. I realize I needed to go back home to help support my mother. I talked to Ken, and he's very supportive of me. "Baby, I love you. I support you in whatever you decide." Those words warmed my heart.

"Ken, I would love for you to come with me. Once my mother recovers, I am going to move to Atlanta." This reminds me of the day my brother Bruno asked me to run away with him. Ken is looking like New Orleans is all he knows.

"I can't go."

"Do this for me get your own apartment. I will give you a lot of the items I purchased for my apartment. It's only material items plus you helped me buy a lot."

I break the news to my co-workers that I will be moving back to Alabama. My grandmother is happy and planning for me to come back home. My grandmother and brother move me back to Alabama. My grandmother is singing all the way to Alabama. Just like old times.

Back to Alabama Memories, Emotion, and Confusion

I relocate back to Alabama and place my furniture in U Haul storage. I can't believe Ken didn't want much. Nothing has changed; I am back in my old routine of helping around the house. The skills from the wig store come in handy. I get hired as a merchandising clothing specialist in McFarland Mall. My mother is still with her perverted boyfriend. Every time I think of the night, I awaken to him in my room, I feel sick to my stomach. My siblings are walking around, acting like a victim pregnancy out of wedlock, alcohol, and drug abuse in the family. They got me feeling like I owe them something. They chose their life. It is what it is. I work to bring my check home and purchase food for the house. I go out of my way to renew my relationship with my aunt. John's mother isn't speaking to me. I am trying to figure out why she is angry with me. I can imagine the lies Linda has told her. If she only knew her son's and wife shame of a perfect life, she would be embarrassed. That's okay; I am not going to attempt to renew the relationship. I am out of her face; she doesn't exist anymore. She is invisible to me. She is going to have to change for me to change. Once my mother recovers, I am moving away. The bad dreams haven't changed; I am still running away, hiding and scared in the dark. My dreams reflect my reality.

One day I receive a phone call it's Obie. I can't imagine how he got the number. Now I remember I gave it to him before he had his temper tantrum. "Hi, D'Alise, I went by the store; they told me you moved back to Alabama. I am moving to Georgia and want you to visit me. I want to meet your family in Alabama." This guy is crazy. I can't believe he's calling me acting as nothing has happened. He has a Dr. Jekyll and Mr. Hyde personality. He sounds so loving and caring. I am speechless. "Are you there?"

"Yes." I don't know what to say, so I say nothing.

"How is your mother? Baby I know I messed up bad. I hope you can find it in your heart to forgive me. I apologize." I hear him speaking. I don't know what to say, so I say nothing. I am running away from pain. "You claim to be a Christian, you have to forgive me." I am still listening he's playing the Christian card on me. I say nothing. "You promised me we were going to be together, are you still my girl?" The silence breaks.

"Obie Bushman, you are one crazy African. If I were a loosed lipped woman, I would let you have it. I haven't seen you in close to a year, and you come calling me like it's yesterday. No, I am not your girl. When you disappeared with no communication, you shouldn't expect anything from me." I should have told him how his cousin tried to push up on me at the bus stop.

"I have moved on goodbye." I hang up the phone. It took a lot out of me to say those words I am exhausted. I feel dizzy I need to sit down and collect myself.

I let Greg slip through my fingers. I am not going to let Ken getaway. I am going to fight for Ken I'm throwing my pride out the window. I going to ask him to relocate anywhere somewhere with me just he and me.

My brother drives me to New Orleans in total silence to visit Ken. Ken is expecting me and tells me things aren't the same since I left. He mentions he's thinking about giving up his apartment moving back to his aunt's house. I begged and pleaded with him not to move back in with her. I gave him all the reason we could have a good life and be happy together; he didn't hear it. I wish he would cut the cord with his aunt and create a life with me. She has him brained washed. Ken has a good heart, always giving selflessly to his family just like me. I have never seen him angry, nor has he ever disrespected me. He's always pulled me close and held me in his arms lovingly. I like the fact that he's not a smoker. He drinks a beer or two socially. This man could build a house with his hands. This man could be my happily ever after.

I called to check on my mother and grandmother and was told, "There's a man at the house claiming to be your boyfriend. You didn't tell us you had a new boyfriend." Obie is sitting down at the table, having dinner with us right now. When are you coming home? Do you want to speak to him? I am speechless this man is bold.

"No, I don't want to speak to him."

"You should. Obie, here's the phone."

"Hi D'Alise, I miss you and can't wait to see you."

"Hi, Obie. I am not sure when I will be home. I'm trying to work some things out. Please leave my family's house once you finish dinner. How can you invite yourself to a person's family home?"

"Baby. I just wanted to surprise you. I want to lay my eyes on you. I'll leave after dinner. I want you to visit Atlanta. You can have a career. I want you to use your income to pay your student loans off and buy a car. I'll take care of everything else. I just want you by my side. I thought about all the plans you have for my life." I am in awe. This can't be real.

"Obie, I want you to leave my family and me alone. Goodbye." I hung up the phone. I feel confused by the fact Ken isn't saying nothing and Obie is saying all the right words like a smooth operator. I feel a little enticed by Obie's offer. I secretly want to see and do more with my life. Even though I know Obie is crazy, some pieces of him remind me of Greg. He sees my potential just like Greg. Obie reminds me of someone from my past, even before Greg. I can't quite put my finger on who it is.

I am glad I got a chance to see my friends at the wig store. I will forever keep in touch with them. I left New Orleans with a broken heart. I am crying on the inside but will never like Ken see me crying.   I am a big girl now. I have the closure I leave Ken on a good note. He chooses to stay in his birth city. Goodbye, Ken, thank you for loving me.

We finally arrive back in Alabama. My brother doesn't say a thing. I think he wants me to be happy. I'm trying to recover myself from putting all my feelings and emotions on display.

I pour myself into helping at my mom and grandmother's house. Clara Rosa is singing and cooking like old times. My mother is out of the hospital. I manage to get my driver's license. The most challenging part was parallel parking. I am looking for cars. My co-worker wants to sell me her car. I decided I would be purchasing a new car. I hate my grandmother sold her antique car. I bet she collected a nice price for the vehicle. She helped my brother buy a   brand-new car. My grandmother made sure the family always had new stuff. I never had to wear used or second-hand clothing. Thank God for grandmothers.

My mother will not stop talking about Obie. She likes him. He gave her an envelope which contained a large sum of money. My grandmother sees right through Obie. She tells me to be careful and explain a man like him will robe a woman like me of my innocence.   She's preaching and praying saying he's the devil looking to attach his self to the light. Obie doesn't care much for my grandmother.

I am working trying to save for my new car. The student loan payment is killing me. Obie starts calling and the next thing you know he's in Alabama in his red mustang visiting with one of his cousins. All the promises he is making sounds tempting to me.

It seems as if I was in high school yesterday not counting college. My classmates have aged so much marriage and children. I feel like I am getting left behind, some of my classmates are on their second marriage. I accepted several invitations from Obie to visit Atlanta. My plane tickets are always waiting for me at the Birmingham airport. My brother never fails to get me to my destination. Everything is moving fast in Atlanta. I get to meet all of Obie's family and friends; everyone is friendly. I still can't understand a word anyone is saying. Obie is a real charmer. I am drawn in by all the promises he's making me. I put in my resignation from my job, eager to find a better life in Atlanta. I am conflicted because my grandmother is furious that I am leaving again. She is still talking about going back to school. I have dreams of being debt-free and don't want to get any more student loans. Obie sends me several checks to deposit in my bank account the checks bounce. What a mess. This has never happened to me. I am so angry. My mother and grandmother have always stressed the importance of being financially responsible. I am supposed to be leaving Alabama in a few days. My footlocker is packed for Atlanta. I am too embarrassed to tell anyone the state of my bank account. My grandmother is right about Obie if I tell her she might just shoot him. I contact Obie to tell him the checks he wrote to me bounced. He laughs it off as if it's nothing and mentioned he didn't have time to transfer money. He apologies again I forgive him.

Moving to Atlanta

Obie has a nicely furnished apartment in Sandy Springs. I am still traveling with the footlocker my grandmother purchased for me. Obie's cousin lives in the same complex. Obie cooks for me, irons my clothing, and bathe me. I feel safe with him, but I am sad. I'm still upset about the bad checks he wrote. He makes me feel like something is wrong with me because I want to discuss what happened with the bad checks. He makes it seem as if it's unimportant. He mentions over and over again, I should let it go and to stop holding on to the issue with the checks. I did stress to him. His checks aren't any good to me; he would have to give me cash in the future.

We are driving on 285 in traffic, and Obie pops the question out of nowhere. I honestly don't know what to say. Obie gives me all the reason why I should say yes. "You promised me you would be my girl in Louisiana. I want you to be my wife." I am thinking to myself this man left me in a rage and re-appears so differently than he was before. The proposal was so unromantic. I said yes, and we go to Perimeter Mall to get a nice ring engagement ring. I feel like I am being held, hostage. Everything is happening so fast. He wants a large wedding with 500 people. I want a small intimate wedding with 50 people. I am thinking to myself where is all the money coming from to pay for this stuff. He tells me not to worry about anything his family will be covering all the expenses. Obie wants a luxury house, and I want to live in a starter house. I only want one child. We are so opposite of each other. He doesn't want me to work. He wants me to be a stay at home wife and wants to ship the child off to boarding school. We don't agree on a lot of things. Obie is nothing like Greg.

Obie is one jealous man. One day we were riding in the Mustang. I am just looking out the window he turns to me and tell me every time he sees me looking at another man he wants to break my neck. He's upset and demands I look at him. He's not even paying attention to the traffic on 285. I feel mentally abused. His moods change like the wind. I feel like a Siamese twin. This relationship is different. I feel as if I am being suffocated.

Obie is educated but isn't employed in a professional career. He is working as a dishwasher in a restaurant. I can't understand how an educated man with a master's degree can't get a good job.

He blames it on his foreign accent. He is playing the race card. He tries to figure out how I came to Atlanta got connected with a service that places people on temporary to permanent jobs. I learned early in life about volunteering and networking with the right people. Sometimes you have to do something for free in order to get a return on your investment. I started working the second week I arrived in Georgia. I worked in customer service, sales, insurance, collections, and for the credit bureau. I finally got a permanent job as a receptionist and moved up the ladder to an operator to the supervisor of the department. The managers and staff liked me because I was loyal and fair to everyone. I came to work did my job and went home no drama. Obie lets me save my money. I pay on my student loans and send money to my mother. When Obie goes to work, I normally hop on the bus to explore the city. This particular day I arrive home I see Obie sitting in the corner foaming at the mouth. His eyes are red as fire again.

"D'Alise where have you been? I have been calling you, and you never answered the phone. I was worried about you. I am responsible for you. If anything happens to you, I know your grandmother will be looking for me. Where have you been?"

I answer in a pleasant calm tone, "Obie, I've been exploring the city on the bus."

"Are you sure that's all you've been doing?"

"Yes, Obie don't you trust me?"

"D'Alise I can't imagine another man hands on you. If I ever catch you cheating on me, I will kill you."

"Obie, don't you trust me? I have no reason to lie. If you ever think about physically abusing me I will kill you in your sleep, and you will never wake up." As a child, I saw my mother beaten time after time, and I promised myself this will never happen to me.

This reminds me of the time Greg asked me a similar question regarding trust. Obie doesn't answer. I am not angry with him because I've been spending time with myself.

Car

Obie has his moments, but he is really looking out for his girl. He stands up for me in the car dealership and will not let anyone take advantage of me. I am so thankful for Obie, giving me the opportunity to move to Georgia. I saved my money and put a large down payment on a new blue Toyota Tercel. I get to drive myself to work now. I'm driving Obie crazy because he can't keep his eyes on me. He wants me to check-in with him all the time. He claims I am very secretive and has an issue with me not telling him every detail about my day. I think Obie is going to miss dropping me off and picking me up. He was always on time, never late. He takes great pride in both of our cars by washing and keeping them gassed up.

Nightlife

Obie loves the nightlife. It's all about him - me, me, me. He wants everybody to see him as we make our grand entrance at public events. Obie is a social butterfly. He wants to show me off to the world. He starts to drink and smoke excessively. His once pearly white teeth are stained from the cigarettes. He wants to go out seven days a week. That's just not attractive to me. I enjoy attending church, cinema, museum, theater, concerts, and hang out in the park, exercise, and volunteer. He is never interested in things that are important to me. I complain to my mother, and she advises if I don't go, he might just meet another woman. One day we were hanging out in the daiquiri bar on the south side of time and a man slice his friends face in the bar over a woman. Blood was everywhere. I have never seen such a site. I was terrified and couldn't understand how someone could just walk up to someone in public and slice their face open. The once handsome man's face is scarred for life at such a young age.

Exploring the Idea of A Change in Scenery

I started encouraging Obie to apply for outstanding scholar positions in public service throughout the United States. I filled out his application and typed his resumes and cover letters. I promised him if he gets hired, I would be right by his side where ever his career leads him. Obie wants to marry me. Sometimes I think he wants to own me like a possession. It's time for a change in our mid-twenties. We need to get out of Georgia. All of Obie's colleagues are educated and well established in the community. Most of them have shadow sides, even criminal minds. They know how to get the money and move the money overseas in foreign bank accounts. I thought I was moving fast with my cousin and his wife. I'm only a roller coaster ride. I am thinking maybe I should have started my master's degree program. My mother didn't encourage me to join the military; be a flight attendant; or special agent in public service.

Confronted with Questions

One day I get a knock on the door, it's Obie's cousin's wife. I invite her in, and we start talking like old girlfriends.

"D'Alise you seem like a really nice girl. You need to leave Obie alone." Everyone sees something in this man I don't. "Obie is married he has a wife in New Orleans. Go back home. Don't tell him I told you just go back home. Obie is a bad guy. He is a lying dog." I begin to cry disappointed again in love.

"Thanks, I won't say anything."

"Bye."

That day I begin going through every inch of the apartment. I find wedding pictures stored away in a box in the back of the closet. I learned from the past you need to ask the question and find out if it's true. I go directly to the source. I find a name on the program and start making phone calls. I finally speak to a lady who confirms she is married, and Obie is going to purchase her a house one day. The worst thing a person can do is lie to me. I begin reaching out to my college classmates, planning my escape. I move my personal belonging out of the apartment. I leave no note message or nothing. The following day the receptionist keeps transferring calls to my office. I am a nervous wreck; I can't function at work. Upon me getting off from work, Obie is waiting outside my job. I tell him everything I found out about him. He told me he only got married for his citizenship; he never loved the lady. He promises me he is divorced and could show me the papers. I can't believe I disclosed the true source of my information. Obie was upset with me. He made me tell him who planted those thoughts in my head. He is furious with his cousin's wife. I think he wanted to kill her for disrupting his house.

I never would have thought I would be in a situation like this. I was always the strong one in college advises and telling my girl-friends what to do. As the weeks progress the flowers and phone calls don't stop. I am so frightened on the inside and return to Obie once he shows me the divorce papers. I've lost my friends. They stopped speaking to me. I am isolated from my friends and family.

Relocating to Virginia

"D'Alise I got a job offer in accounting. They are going to train me and pay for me to study and take the CPA examination. I am ready to start my career. We can get married and move to Virginia. Are you going to Virginia with me?"

"Obie, I have a career I am almost making six figures." I always wanted to be well established before I turned twenty-five.

"D'Alise a promise is a promise. I can't do this without you. You are my lucky charm. I need you. I am leaving less than thirty days. You will find a job."

"I can't go."

"You promise." For the next couple of days, that's all I am hearing is relocating. There is no peace. I am being hounded and badgered. Obie is bullying me.

I go into my job and turn in my notice to resign. The management staff isn't taking it well because I did all the reports, training, and put the training material together for staff. They ask me to take a leave of absence just in case it doesn't work out. My adventures or frighten side isn't thinking logically. I know in my heart I probably should take a leave, but I don't.

The Apartment

The mountains are so beautiful in Virginia. I get Obie on a plan to lose weight. I attend weight watchers' classes with him. He loses a lot of weight. He has a new body. We settle into our new apartment. The apartment feels so much like home. I am glad I was able to see my family and get my furniture out of storage. Obie is doing well in his new position as an auditor for white-collar crimes. I manage to get hired on in the school system. They have good benefits. I replace my silver fillings with white fillings. I only need twelve hours to get my teachers certification. Prior to graduation from college, I was asked if I wanted my teachers certificate. I said no because I never wanted to teach or be a training coordinate. It's seems like the universe keeps placing me in teaching positions. Obie travels an awful lot. I am left home alone a lot. I miss my job and friends and longing to return to Georgia. We travel to DC almost every other weekend to see his friends. One day out of the blue Obie asks me to make a small contribution to house spending expenses. He's never asked me to pay for anything. He mentions he wants to travel to Africa for a month to see his family and extends the invitation to me to travel with him.

Seasons Changed

Hip, Hip Hooray school is out. It's summertime, and the living is easy. Since Obie travels a lot for work, I decided to take a job in a retail store. I get a hefty thirty percent discount and able to get really nice home accessories. The doorbell rings. I can't image who would be visiting other than the neighbors. I open the door, and a woman is looking for Obie.

"Hi, I am looking for Obie."

"May I ask why?"

"Obie is my boyfriend."

"Really, Obie there is a woman at the front door looking for you." Obie is in the bedroom and doesn't say anything. He doesn't even acknowledge my voice. The lady is standing at the front entrance of the apartment as if she has been in the apartment before. I face her off and tell her she can have him if he would go with her. She eventually leaves, and I close the door. I go into the bedroom to address Obie. He ignores me as nothing has just happened. I have never used profanity in my life until I met Obie. I call him a black ass mother fucker. I quit a decent job to travel halfway around the world with him. I helped him lose weight. I typed his resumes and cover letters and told him what to wear.

"Obie, I am leaving you."

"Where are you gonna go? I am the only one that cares about you. I moved you from that depressed country town. I helped you. I let you use all your money to save for a new car and pay on your student loans and helped your crazy mother. You aren't leaving me. I will tell you when to leave. You promised me we were going to get married. Your gonna marry me. You got the ring. It's for better or worst baby. You promised me. My boss likes you. You will marry me, and you will be a good wife. You're going to keep your weight down, and you will look flawless everywhere we go. We will be the perfect couple, and everyone will be envious of us. I'm going to ride this meal ticket with my job until it runs dry. I am going to be the boss on my job and even make partner in another company. Do you hear me?"

I ignore Obie. It drives him crazy when I don't respond to him. He likes a big debate. I'm giving him nothing.

"You're not leaving." I know people that do bad things. I know where your family lives. D'Alise, do you like your life? Don't you like living? Don't you?"

Obie can be one mean man when he's angry. I don't get the last word in. Obie leaves to go on a business trip. I am beginning to question everything he tells me.

Stalked

I noticed the woman that showed up at my apartment is frequently shopping the store. The woman is the total opposite of me. When I look at her, I see all her flaws yet Obie want me to be flawless for his business colleagues. The woman finally approaches me to tell me Obie told her I was his sister. She begins to spill all the tea. She verbally tells me she had been inside the apartment. She had been in my bed. At this point, I feel totally violated. My first thought was he brought another woman in our apartment while I was in Alabama. He called to make sure I made it. The woman started coming to my place of employment with her friends trying to intimidate me. I had security escort me out to my car the days I worked late. This woman friends were increasing in numbers some days four or six. I call Obie to tell him he needed to get his side chick under control. I started carrying self-defense weapons. I had to become very aware of my environment. I was looking over my shoulders everywhere I went. The last time a female stalker pursued me, was when I was in college dating a jock.

Liar

I speak to my family and friend but can't tell them what's going on in Virginia. I am a liar pretending everything is okay, but it isn't. I've lied so much I don't what is the truth. I don't even want him to touch me anymore. He forces himself on me. I get the cards, flowers and beautiful gifts they mean nothing to me. Everything is for show and make-believe. It's not romantic. He's not romantic. It's all about him (me, me, me, me). I want to wake up from this horrible dream. How did I get here? This man feels the world owes him everything. He's not physically abusive. Obie plays dirty mentally.

Losing My Edges

I am on edge. I'm a nervous wreck. My health is falling me. My beautiful hair is falling out by the hand full. I never thought I would be losing my edges. I never thought I would have bald patches in my hair. This relationship is killing me. Every month I am losing lot of blood. I am bleeding. Obie has disappeared and left me in Virginia by myself. The friends I made at work listen but really don't want to get involved. I decided in the future, I will never discuss my relationship issues at work. One day a young lady suggested I cut my hair off and start treatments. The best hair cut ever. I was rocking my Hallie Berry haircut.

Exit Strategy

It's time for me to make some hard decisions. My grandmother always told me I needed to be sober at all time. I haven't been sober in this relationship. I have been intoxicated by Obie's dream. I've put my dreams down to help a man that doesn't even respect me. Let alone I don't even respect myself. I am allowing this behavior. Trust and believe when I finally leave Obie, I am done with him. I have given him many chances to be a good person. At the end of the day, he is looking out for himself. A low variation woman would probably kill him. I have self-control and better than that. I threw my pride to the waste side and contact my old job.

"D'Alise we asked you to take a leave the position is filled. We don't have any management position available or any openings at this time. Check-in with us once you relocate back to Georgia. You were a good employee if anything comes open, we'll try to hold it for you.

"Thanks."

"By the way did you marry that crazy guy that was calling and showing up at the job every day."

I pause. "No." I am too embarrassed to say I am still with him.

"Great. Good for you."

"Bye."

Obie is due to return home today. I will discuss our issues and tell him of my plans to leave. I've saved up a nice sum of money. I can pay for my apartment for at least six months. I'm glad I never had a bank account with him. I understand now why Obie wanted me to make a contribution toward the house. He was cheating on me. Obie needs a lot of adoration. I guess I wasn't giving it to him. I am still trying to figure out how I ended up in this relationship. I believed in him and had the right attitude. It's time for me to serve myself.

Return to Georgia

When I returned to Georgia, I had the feeling that everything was going to be alright. Obie convinced me he was going to do right by me. He asked me to forgive him, and he put in for a transfer to return to Georgia with me. We are still together living in Dunwoody. He's doing well on his job. He's on his best behavior. We are dating like old times. I am supporting him mingling at all the social events with him. He is so full of his self. He has a new body that comes with a new attitude. I mentioned to him I've been getting a lot of calls, then they hang up. He brushes it off as if it's nothing or he did not hear me.

Date Night

Now, headed to the Luther Vandross concert. We look like the perfect couple on our date. After the concert is over, I hear a voice from the crowd calling me. An old classmate from college. I introduce them to Obie. They give both of us their business card we exchange hugs and go on our separate way. Once we get to the car, Obie starts to drill me. I am upset and ask him to let me out the car. I open the door to a moving car to get out. He manages to snatch me back in the car. I tell him his jealousy is too much and the spotlight isn't going to always be on him. It's not always about him. I told him it wasn't working out.

"D'Alise, you want to leave me?"

"Yes."

"I see now you want to get with your attorney classmate."

"It's not like that."

"You want to leave me. I want everything back that I ever gave you starting right now."

I can't believe I am in downtown Atlanta pulling my shoes off in the middle of the street in addition to other clothing accessory Obie gave me. Thank God he didn't purchase my outfit. I would be nude. He collected the items and threw them in the back seat.

"D'Alise you make me crazy. I can't think of another man looking at you. Please forgive me. I am sorry. You have to forgive me you are a Christian."

I have a lot to say just don't want to argue, fuss, or fight. I am trying not to trigger my asthma. I was thinking, Obie is an Indian Giver. I decide today, I will never let him give me anything else.

Blindsided

"Baby, you never tell me how good I look. When I am at work, the ladies in the cafeteria tell me how handsome I am every day. They have my coffee ready for me every day. You never tell me how strong I am. Look at this body. Look at my abs. Everyone is catering to me."

"Obie. Did you want to hear that every day?"

"Yes. You are supposed to worship me."

"Obie, you aren't God." Why did I say that?

"D'Alise I don't want to live with you anymore. I don't want to marry you. I got options."

I hope I'm hearing him correctly. No woman ever looked twice at him. I helped him build his financial empire. He's a risk-taker and would have made a lot of bad decisions without doing the research. I gave him the road map and plan. He was a project that I helped to build up. "Obie when are you moving out?"

"I'm not leaving you are moving out the apartment within the next week."

"What?" The feeling of being safe and protected is gone. Starting over. How do I do that?

"D'Alise you are boring. You need to get some experience."

"Obie, I believed in you when you didn't believe in yourself. I sacrificed for you." I am crying uncontrollably. I had an asthma attack and fell to the floor.

"D'Alise you are such a good actress, always crying. It's nothing wrong with you. Get up." Obie throws my inhaler at me as I lay on the floor, trying to collect myself. I manage to recover.

Moving On

I never thought I would have to fight for the furniture I purchased prior to being in a relationship or even moving in with Obie. This man is the biggest clown. Really, he wants the vacuum cleaner such a small, petty item. I remove my name from the lease. I am preparing to trash any pictures of he and I together. I am taking my mother's position and move on with class. I'm not going to fued, fight, or make a public scene. I am going to let Obie's karma deal with his narcissistic personality. I was on the fast track prior to me quitting my job.

"Okay, Obie. I am leaving, and I will be suing you for palimony." I never saw Obie's eyes get so big. "This will be the day I will be using my classmate's business card." It is a good day he agrees to pay me off. I scared myself not sure where those words came from inside me (*Virginia and Georgia don't recognize common law marriage*). I am filled with sadness because I wanted to believe he would change. I want to believe human beings are good.

Settling in my new place – A new me

My new apartment is peaceful. I'm not worried about people dropping in all times of the day on the weekend. My home is alcohol-free and no cigarette smoke. I can breathe. I have no stress in my life. I am happy for the first time. I am celibate just doing me. My hair is beginning to grow back. I am doing well on my job saving to purchase my first home. I'm reconnecting with friends and have a strong support group around me. I am in the company of whole decent men that give me good advice.

The Chase

Like a theft in the night, Obie walks up on me in the parking lot at my office. I thought I had got away from him. I haven't seen or heard from him in a while. In my mind, I'm thinking what does he want or has he come to kill me. Obie has the type of energy that's in and out. Just when you think he's gone, he comes back. He is talking sweet nothings in my ear. Obie's family started to seek me out stating he's a mad man and obsessed with me. They have been begging and pleading for me to return to him. I can't understand why they are telling me all this.

The young lady in his family that once reached out to me found me and told me what was really going on. She told me he was bringing ghetto women to the company functions. A couple of women stole all his money out of his bank account. Someone stole high ticket items from his apartment. He got a DUI in Dekalb County and was arrested. She asked me if I had been watching the news. Obie was arrested for the soliciting of a prostitute for sex while traveling for work. I was told he has a wife in Africa and in the United States. I had to sit down on that because I remember him once telling me he could pay for sex. I never took anything from Obie. I know she took a risk to tell me all these things. This time I will remain silent.

I got one of my male friends to help me purchase a gun. The gun was too beautiful to shoot anyone. I love the pink mother of pearl handle. I don't need to take any classes. I got all the training from living with my grandmother and ROTC in high school on how to shoot a gun.

I was traveling to Alabama to check on my family and almost got killed. The tire from an eighteen-wheeler came through my windshield. I realized life is precious. I managed to get towed back to Georgia. The near-death accident was my wake-up call. I gave my time to a man that never cared about me or even loved me. I must admit, through all the difficult times I still loved him unconditionally. I remember the words from Greg. If a man doesn't have self-control, he will cheat on you. The red flags were always there in addition to my own red flags of just wanting to feel safe and secure. Obie never loved me. I was his competition. We were never equal. In this day and age, he wanted me to be his slave woman.

Obie likes the chase.

It got so bad I had to file a restraining order from Fulton County and send it to his job. Strangely enough, his own secretary was trying to tell me what was going on when I was with Obie. This man didn't want me because I was boring and he is chasing me like there's no tomorrow. Goodbye Obie. It's been an experience.

Lessons to Learn

Approaching phrase - attractive-attraction. Are you giving a chance to the wrong guys? We run towards the familiar and run away from what's not familiar.

Red flags - Gives us the spirit of discernment. Red tells us when to stop. Why do we ignore the red flags and continued to date the wrong guys? We normally don't pay attention because we don't feel worthy or we feel no other guys are out there to date.

Recognizing my own red flags - The things that draw you into the relationship.

Levels of confidence – When you have low confidence, you have poor self-esteem deep down inside. Low respect leads to not honoring yourself and knowing thy self. A woman with low values will attract bad guys. Women, how are you treating yourself? Evaluate the relationship you have with yourself.

Chapter 25

Transitioning from the late '80s to '90s is an amazing Joyous Expansion of myself. I am filled with peace and harmony and being celibate. God is answering all my prayers. He is giving me everything that I need in the right place and time. I'm reading the bible. It's a new day. I am leaving the past behind me and living in the present and looking forward to the future every day.

"Tina, Thanks for hooking my hair up. I'll tell everybody you are my stylist."

"Do you remember how we met?"

"Yea, I was in the beauty supply store looking for a pressing comb because I was letting the perm grow out my hair. I wanted my hair to be free of chemicals."

"Too bad you're going home to get in the bed. You should be out on the town."

"Tina, it's nothing out there in those streets. I keep running across men who are narcissist. They come in cycles. I've met the ones who are preoccupied with success and power, entitlement, lack of empathy. Some men have the attitude that it's all about them. Demonstration of arrogant behaviors. I have everything I need at home.

Reflecting back on dating-talk. I'm choosing to just be with me for now.

"The next time you travel to Virginia, tell your mother I say hello."

"Bye."

After I leave Tina's salon, I run into the grocery store to pick up a few items. I can't help to notice it, but a man is following me around the store. I had no intentions of picking up anything extra tonight. I just want to go home and get ready for work tomorrow. I make my way to the checkout. This guy is in my foot tracks following me.

"Hi, my name is Earnest." I look around, trying to see who he's talking to. The people in the check-out line look at me and start pointing at me. I look in front of me. I guess this man is talking to me.

"Hi."

"I wanted to know if I can give you my number?" The people in the check-out line are waiting for a response.

"You want me to call you? I am not calling you." I blasted out. Everyone in the check-out stopped what they were doing. Listening and waiting patiently for a response.

"Well, can I have your number?" I just wrote the number on a piece of paper, then threw it on the counter. I notice everyone in the checkout jump back.

"I'm traveling to celebrate my birthday. I will give you a call once I return in May." My eyes trace from the floor where his feet were placed, then move up he has height and he was in shape. Everything he has on is new as if he has worn his business suite for the first time. Finally, his facial features. I move out of my trance. I paid the cashier and left not to look behind. I made it to my car, eager to get home and ready to drive. I look back seeing him standing in the exit of the store. I drove out of the parking lot into the traffic on Jimmy Carter to head towards the interstate.

Home Alone

Ring, ring, ring. The answering machine picks up. " D'Alise I know you're home. Girl pick-up the phone".

"Hello, Hello."

"D'Alise you never answer your home phone. Are you screening your calls," What are you doing?"

"I am in my office, meditating and working on a few projects."

"Girl, when are you going to stop dating yourself?"

"I enjoy my own company. Oh, check this out I met a guy in the grocery store a few days ago after my hair appointment."

"I hope you didn't give him an intimidating or irritated facial expression."

"What are you talking about?"

"You're always mugging guys. I recognize the strong Alpha male type men aren't afraid of you."

"Yea, Dee that's my secret weapon to scare the weak men away. Especially the ones that don't have any confidence in themselves."

"D'Alise you got game."

"Game know game." The two friends giggle.

"I remember when I first saw you, I was shopping in a retail store. You were a striking businesswoman. I was joking and smiling. I recall you was serious and made no small talk.   I met you again when you registered to take the real estate license course for Georgia. I knew you were a good person. I decided I was going to make you my friend. It took a lot of work to knock your wall down. I started to take it personally because you would never hang out with me. Then I begin to understand your values and what you expected from people and friends.   I would sit and talk with you for hours after we studied for class. You never told me any of your business."

"Dee, you are one of my ride or die, friends. I appreciate your loyalty. You stand up and fight for me when I'm not present. Thanks for supporting and believing that I would finally get away from Obie Bushman. I never in this lifetime thought I would put up with so much craziness. I've abandoned friends in the past because they didn't know better. I was judging them. I never thought the table would have been turned on me. I am strong, but it's something about when you get with a man you will either lose yourself or get stuck. I don't wish anything bad for Obie."

"D'Alise. You were there for me when I divorced my husband. Let's stop reminiscing about the past. So, when is the first date?"

"I don't think he is going to call me."

"Why?"

"I really wasn't thinking about meeting a man. I was going about my day. He interrupted me in the check-out line. I was trying to get home because I was tired and needed to get organized for the next day."

"Really, to a big empty house. Tell me, how did he look?"

"Dee, something about him, reminded me of someone in my past."

"How does he look? You got me in suspense."

"Dee, I looked him over. He looked like he stepped out of GQ magazine."

"You are killing me. How does he look?"

"Girl, he was masculine. I could tell underneath that suit he was sculpted. I could see anything bugging out. He was very tall, bronze skin tone, salt, and pepper wavy hair. He had a beard and a mustache. His teeth were perfect, and I loved his smile. I got out of my trance and left. I didn't even look back."

"How does he look?"

"He was handsome. I didn't give him any encouragement."

"D'Alise you've attracted an older accomplished man. How do you do that?"

"Do what?"

"Get the men with the money."

"Stop making assumptions, Dee."

"You could get married one day and never have to work."

"That's not a life for me. I never want to end up like my mother. I like my own money." Sometimes the way Dee talks, remind me of Linda.

"D'Alise, I am going to Du Bai to visit my friend's family. I want you to check on my house and two girls while I am gone. Please go on a date. Stop being so uptight."

"Okay."

Dee Miller is one of the closest people in my circle. She's a real businesswoman in real estate and other business throughout the United States. She comes from a legacy of money. Her family has land, businesses, and funeral homes. She's always with the people constantly networking and findings ways to grow her money. Dee is bi-racial. She has straight waist-length hair and has curves in all the right places. We are never in competition with one another. We support and uplift one another with our own unique appearance to attract the men for our personality type. Dee keeps me up on all the latest fashion trends. She lives in one of the estate communities around the corner from me. We are always looking out for each other. It's nice to know I have a friend that lives that close to me.

The Telephone Call

Ring. Ring. Ring. "Hello."

"Hi, this is Earnest Baptiste, may I speak to D'Alise."

"This is she."

"How are you doing? I met you in the grocery store." Pause, silence. "Are you there."

"Yes. I wasn't expecting to get a call from you."

"I told you I would call you after I returned from my birthday celebration travels. How are you?"

"I am well."

"Do you still have my business card."

"Yes."

"I wrote my home telephone number on the back of the card. I would love to get to know you. We can start by talking on the telephone. Once you feel compatible, I will invite you to my home here in Georgia. You can visit my place of employment you have the address. Are you still there?"

"Yes. I am listening. I have a few questions for you. Are you married? Do you have a girlfriend?" Rambling questions.

"No, I am not married. I am divorced. My girlfriend died a few years ago. She was taking this diet supplement to lose weight and died all of a sudden. I have a grown son."

Over the weeks, I talk to Earnest on the phone almost every day. He is a very good listener, always interested in my day. He's a bundle of knowledge. He knows everything about everything very smart and knows how to invest his money. I feel like I am in school again. He talks about his job and family a lot. I get the impression he is very close to all of his family members.

Invitation

"Hi, D'Alise. Do you have any plans when you get off from work today?"

"No, why."

"I want you to see where I live. I'd love to prepare dinner for you."

"I purchased a box of fish and have it on ice. It needs to be refrigerated."

"You can place it in my refrigerator."

"It's a lot of fish for one person. I'll share it with you."

"What about coming over at 5:00 p.m. Here's my address…give it to one of your family members and friends, so they will know where you're going today. Tell them to call you to make sure you've arrived home around 8:00 p.m." I'm feeling impressed by Mr. Baptiste ways. My gut feeling is telling me to go. Yes.

Prior to leaving work, I research the area I will be visiting. I arrive one hour early and realize Mr. Baptiste lives in the historic Norcross. While in the area, I familiarize myself with the dining, shopping, parks, and the community. He lives in a nice secured community.

I called to confirm my arrival time. "Hi, Earnest. I'm in the area and should arrive on time."

"I will be looking out for you. I have a burgundy Lexus parked out front."

Earnest helps me to get the cooler of fish inside the townhome and place his share in freezer bags. He gives me a tour of all the three levels. He opens closet doors and drawers. I am feeling this because I am a curious woman. I have need to know everything. The townhome has 10 ft ceilings on main. The floor plan has an open layout w/exquisite molding. New paint, granite counters, stainless steel appliances, light fixtures, architectural windows, front doors, custom closets. The oversized master w/sitting room & his/her custom closets. The private side patio is perfect for outdoor entertaining. Earnest home is immaculate just like him. I think he has obsessive cleaning disorder (OCD). There is nothing out of place in his apartment. I thought I was clean. I am outdone today.

"Thank you for inviting me over for dinner and giving me the grand tour. I see you are very organized."

"Yes. I was in the military for a number of years. I believe in order. Let me walk you to your car so you can arrive home on time. Oh, let me grab the fish. Call me to let me know you made it home safe."

"Okay," This come over date was good. Earnest was the perfect gentlemen.

"D'Alise, I would love to see you again. I would love to continue to call you. Is it okay?"

"Yes."

"Goodnight."

Investing

My communication with Earnest continues over the phone. I visit his office and meet his employees. He loves for me to visit his place of residence. We sit in his home office at his computer for hours watching the stock market. I watch him trade online moving money around. He is teaching me how to invest money. He talks about credit, insurance, wills, and saving. He's happy I have a good job and have my own money. He takes me to one of the top brokerage firms to invest my money. I have made some wise investments with his guidance. I look forward to collecting on my returns. Earnest takes a lot of risk with money. I explained to him I grew up poor and don't take a lot of risk with money. He explains if I ever lose any money, he will reimburse me. He explains I will be better off financially since I met him. He loves money and the finer things in life. Listening to him talk, he believes he deserves to have the best of everything. He believes you must have money to be happy. This man has a portfolio and trust me to let me look at his assets. He really knows where to invest his money. He has a legacy, and his parent have trained him well. He has a career and is a CEO in the public sector. Money comes naturally to him. He has his money invested everywhere. He has franchises, rentals properties, homes, and cars in multiple states. I am not sure if I have the courage to take such risk. He is encouraging me to do more investing. He knows everything about everything.

The First Official Date

Earnest lets me select our first official date on the town. He arrives at my home looking dapper. I get the impression he is always looking to have an audience so he can show his dapperness. He was dressed in all white carrying a dozen of yellow roses. This happy color yellow symbolizes friendship and joy. This is appropriate because we are getting to know each other as friends.

We arrive at Sambuca's for dinner and live entertainment. He gives the valet a tip for parking the car. He's carrying a lot of cash money in his wallet. He loves the selection of the upscale jazz café in Buckhead. Everything is appealing to his five senses. Earnest is laid back, slow to move, still and quiet taking everything in at the venue. He tells me to order whatever I want. I order pineapple juice, and he order alcohol. This man is traditional he believes the man should pay for everything. He holds door and gets the car door. He's predictable, kind, loyal, and romantic. He reminds me of someone I have met before I can't quite put my finger on who it is.

Earnest claims to be a little older than me but won't tell me his exact age. I don't have any grey hairs in my head. I am trying to do the calculation in my head as I did with Greg. Earnest has accomplished a lot in the short time he's been living. He talks fondly of his best friends it appears they are financially wealthy.

Emergency

"D'Alise I know we are friends. I would like to be more to you in the future. I am happy you have your own job and money. I want you to carry at least $100 a day in your pocket. I want to pay for your hair and nails every two weeks. I realize your time is valuable."

"Earnest, that's very kind of you but I can't. We are dating."

"I want you to be my lady. I have to get myself right for you."

"What do you mean?"

"I can't talk about it right now."

Mind Chatter

I feel guilty about hanging out with Earnest. I have home projects that I been neglecting. I discuss my dilemma. I can't believe he wants to help. He said he would pay someone to do the jobs but wanted to work alongside me to help me complete those jobs. I never thought he would get his hand dirty. He organizes my garage beautifully. He helps me hang pictures that have been on the floor for years. I came home one day, and he was cutting my yard. I am impressed. Earnest later tells he learned how to perform repairs on his building because people were charging an arm and a leg. He's licensed in electrical, plumbing and heating and air. Who would have thought? Thank God for Earnest he saved me a lot of money.

Asking and Receiving an Answer

"D'Alise, I love being with you. I want to be with you every day."

"Earnest, I enjoy your company. You are a perfect gentleman."

"I want you to be my lady."

"Earnest, Yes. I thought you would never ask."

"I want to marry you. I want you to have a baby for me."

"Earnest…" Tears begin to fall.

On that specific day, I tell Earnest my life story from beginning to end. We cry together. He tells me he loves me, and it will be okay. He appears to be the happiest man in the world. He takes me to the jewelry store, and I select my engagement ring. It's breathtaking. We get our physical examination. I get to meet his family and friends.

Dating and Gifts

Over the months, Earnest is courting me. He wants me with him everywhere he goes. He loves good company, food, and sex. We are going to all the upscale restaurants, comedy shows, plays, and movies. Earnest is a jewelry and purse man. He surprises me with the best quality accessories.

Exploring Me

One day I was visiting Earnest at his apartment, he seems to be sad. I tried to comfort him, and I asked him what was wrong. He explained he had to go away on a business trip in a few days. He wanted me to go with him, but it was last minute. I didn't see it as a reason to be sad. He said he was going to be gone for two weeks. He never wants me to sleep with anyone but him. I have self-control and was celibate for years before I got with him. This is taking me back and reminds me of a conversation I had with Obie when we were together.

That night Earnest ask me if I had ever explored my body by touching myself. I told him no. He asked me if I would be willing to engage in the experiment of exploring me. I was hesitant and told him yes. He told me my body was mine, and I should touch it. He explained self-pleasure was not a bad thing.

That night Earnest picked me up and carried me upstairs in his arms to his bedroom. He undressed me put me in a bubble bath surrounded with candles. My favorite jazz was playing on the surround sound. Once clean, he dried me off and laid me in the king-size bed on the white sheets, kissed and caressed me. I laid in the bed as he guided me and held my hand as I was afraid to touch me. I took ownership of my own body. I was scared; it felt good. Earnest guided my fingers to the secret place and watched encouraging me not to stop. I had my first organism through self-pleasuring. Earnest was emotions, and I embraced him sobbing on his shoulder. I have never had that type of experience with a man. He held and embraced. Earnest opened me up sexually. I was afraid to touch my body. I thought it was dirty and a sin.

Can I get a return call?

"D'Alise, the kids said you were checking on them while I was in Du Bai. I got the message you went on your first date. I'm just getting back from Africa. Give me a call."

"Dee, I am calling you back world traveler. Earnest is out of town for two weeks. Maybe we can have movie night at my house like old times with the gang. Bye."

It's been a minute since I talked to Dee. Hopefully, our busy lives will slow down, and we'll be able to connect soon.

The Barrier of Bad News

I'm hanging out with my friends at the Taco lounge having a fantastic time in Buckhead. We are singing and joking. Dee and gang always have a way of getting me to let my hair down and not be so uptight. Dee runs over to me, acting uptight.

"Girl, let's get out of here."

"It's still early. We've only been here an hour." I look up Oh My God (OMG). It's Obie Bushman with his entourage of African friends. He spots me and comes over to our table. I'm feeling really sick to my stomach.

"Danelle Alise James (D'Alise') It's been a long time." My ride or die, Dee steps in between us. He moves her out of the way with his hands.

"Hi Obie, we were just leaving."

"You don't have to leave on my account. Hey, everybody, you see this lady right here. I made her. I took her out of the village and made her a success. To be exact, I took her out of public housing (the projects). She was nothing until she met me. She was a scared little girl when I met her. She was a cry baby. Everything she saw for the first time was with me. She wanted someone to rescue her. I made her grow up. She's the woman she today because of me. We grew up together. I know everything about her and her family. I know all her secrets." Obie laughs and takes a puff of his cigarette. He blows the fog of smoke in my face and turns his head and laughs again.

"Come on, girl let's go you don't have to listen to him. He's a liar."

"Dee, he is not lying."

I am listening to Obie, and I am not going to give him nothing verbally. He lied to me. He cheated on me the entire time I was with him. I relocated to support him, and he tried to control me when I didn't have a lot of money. We helped each other it wasn't just one-sided. I grew when I started dating him. It's true.

"I been following you and watching your every move. I am watching and waiting in the shadows for the relationship to tower over. Then your goanna come back to me D'Alise you can't leave me. You can never leave me. I am the best man you ever had in your life. I know how to push you towards success."

"Dee, let's leave. Gather the gang up and let's head home. Can you drive?"

"Obie, D'Alise is getting married."

"What? It will never happen over my dead body. We're supposed to be together we are a part of each other."

"Dee, why did you have to say that. He's is a crazy man."

"Baby, you are looking dam good to me today," Obie yells out as we exit the building and starts laughing in his deep baritone voice. He toasts his drink in the air and takes another puff of his cigarette. "Baby when it doesn't work out give me a call. I am watching and waiting for you baby."

"Girl you might have to get a restraining order for our area."

Love Message

"Hey, baby, give me a call when you get this message. I want to fly you out for the weekend. I love you. I miss you. I wanted to surprise and want you to catch a flight tonight to Los Angeles. You can purchase clothes when you arrive."

"Dee, Earnest left several messages for me last night. We love each other. He's been talking about us having a baby together. This will be my only opportunity the tumors have to be removed, and I lose my organs. I never told him how Obie was obsessed and crazy over me."

"Did you check in with him and tell him we were going out last night?"

"No."

"That's not going to look good. You need to tell him what happened last night."

"Good Morning Earnest."

"Hi, baby, did you get my messages?"

"I got your messages this morning."

"I was worried about you. Felt something was wrong. I am glad you get up early you can catch an early flight and be here around 10:00 a.m. All you have to do is shower and bring your purse. I will take care of everything once you arrive."

"Earnest."

"What is it."

"I went to the Taco lounge last night with Dee and some other friends. My ex-fiancé came in."

"What? Ex-fiancé. Let's not talk about this over the telephone. Can you catch the early flight out to Los Angles?"

"Yes."

"I'll book the flight your ticket will be waiting at the airport for you. I have a driver to pick you up and bring you to the hotel."

I make my way to the airport and make the flight to California. I tell Earnest everything about the relationship with Obie. Earnest is willing to fight for me. This is the first time in my life I've seen someone fight for me. I am determined to be with Earnest. Sometimes I get the impression he wants to control me with his money. I am determined not to end up like my mother. I want to have my own money. I discovered Earnest is about the same age as Greg. On my way to the airport, I get a call from Obie.

"D'Alise I apologize for making that scene last night at Taco Bar. I need to share something with you. I know you think I am a bad person. I am not that bad. The guy you are dating is not for you. Leave him alone he has someone else. You are in a third-party situation he lie to you. Obie gives all the details; this is a sad day for me. I know God has someone for me. I'm trying to understand all the things Obie is telling me about the love of my life it can't be true. I am disappointed once again. I meet with Earnest confirms everything Obie told me. Once again, I am alone not dating anyone.

Chapter 26

Meet Corey Knight
Cycle #3 Jumper Cables – Quality Time & Role Plays

On a warm Sunday day, I was rushing to the post office to mail my mother her weekly allowance. Upon my return to my car I find my perfect new battery had died. My car would not start. A kind man parked next to me offered to help. He offered his assistance by using jumper cables to start my battery. This tall man had a warm kind energy about himself. He appeared to genuinely care about people, so we exchanged information. Over the course of a few days, he called to check on me. At that moment when talking to him on the phone, something sparked inside of me. My inner voice said this man could be my companion. I knew right away. Over conversations extended beyond the phone, we decided to meet at Red Robins for dinner after a month. Corey Knight was self-employed and was the perfect gentlemen. He told me he had been married 18 years and had two small children. I could tell this man was not the type of man that dated around and this man was looking for a real relationship. He made it very clear to me up-front. I decided it would be best that we take our time to get to know each other because he was fresh out of a marriage. When I heard him speak about his marriage, I was under the impression he didn't want a divorce. I've never been married and didn't have any children. I did a lot of listening. I gathered the wife was ready for the marriage to end. My schedule was pretty busy.

I later invited Corey into my space. We spent quality time together and exchanged words of appreciation. We both help each other around the house. I occasionally gave Corey a warm embrace and purchased him a gift to show how much I appreciated him.

A year later. Corey knocks on my door. I let him in to find out he wanted to have a serious conversation. He expressed we had been hanging out in a platonic relationship for a year, and he needed to know how I felt about him. I said, can't you see how I feel about you?

Corey said D'Alise I need to hear the words inside your head before I leave here tonight. I told him I am finding my voice and really didn't know how to express myself.

Corey said you implied how you feel! "I need to hear the words. I LOVE YOU. I need to hear those words. Speak!"

I couldn't understand what Corey wanted from me because I was raised by my mother and grandmother, who edified expressions of love with acts of service and gifts.

I realized for our relationship to work, we must communicate.

I had to revisit Dr. Gary Chapman's five love languages. Four of the love languages acts of service, quality time, receiving gifts, and physical touch has nothing to do with the spoken word only words of affirmation.

I realized my love language was acts of service. What do you think my partners love language is?

It's a new day his voice speaks out and says I need to hear the words inside your head. I need to hear the words inside your head a man needs to hear those words sometimes. My heart and my voice say I love you.

My companions love language is words of affirmation.

After a year, I met the two adorable kids, a boy, and a girl.

I received a beautiful promise. We did everything together. We talked on the phone every day for hours. He wanted to know my every move, where I was going, and what I was doing.

The relationship started out good we talked on the phone every day for hours... When we verbally agreed to be in a relationship, things started to change.

When I didn't answer the phone right away, I could hear the tone in his voice of being upset. He talked badly about the ex-spouse, so I thought it was the ex-spouse. I later found out he was still married to her.

He blamed her for a lot of stuff like not paying her bills on time. He blamed her for his failing business claims. He said he never wanted to get married at such a young age, but since he got married, he could not finish college. He claims he could never realize his dreams because he had to take care of his family.

I had been lied too.

Breaking the CYCLES!

When you know yourself, you can be by yourself with God in prayer. You can sit alone away in a quiet space. There will be no need for third-party entities to influence and program the mind, body, and spirit. You are no longer on the passenger's side. You are on the driver's side driving your life. You become an independent thinker and can stand on your own. No one will own you. The holy spirit has all the answers. The holy spirit will lead and direct your life. The holy spirit will never tell a lie. If you ask, you will get answers to all the secrets in life. The holy spirit will reveal who should be in your life, and who shouldn't be in your life. The holy spirit will see the hearts of your contacts. You will know all the answers before you walk through the closed doors. It is truly a blessing to be able to speak to the holy spirit. We are united in peace and one love.

Love of God

Love of Self

Knowing One Self

It's called Telling the "Truth" - Stop Hiding Behind the Lie

Only when we surrender to God will the holy spirit come into our lives. You have a choice to be with God or be with the people. There are infinite possibilities of what life has in store for us. You can choose to be in an unequally yoked relationship or be in a relationship with a God-man or God woman. All things are possible, be patient; God answers all prayers. He is listening. Love waits for us in this world. The past does not equal the future. The lies that we tell ourselves and truths we want the public to believe is a fragment of our imagination. When we know the truth in our hearts. It's no need to lie when we chose to stay in a lie. Sometimes we lie to make ourselves look better and make the other person look bad. The good, bad, and ugly in the relationship is a mirrored reflection of us. We are only reflecting ourselves. If we point the finger by magnifying negative traits in others, those traits are us. Our experiences force us to look at ourselves and to help us grow by making healthier choices for the next relationship.

Breaking Attachments

For a long time, I felt angry at Obie for wanting all the things back that he purchased for me. I looked at him as an Indian giver. I have matured and realized those things were attachments and would have been holding me bonded to him. I am free. I have nothing in my life that belongs to him or any of my other relationships. Anything I had is no longer in my possession. I am free to move on to my new life.

Amen

Doing the work of healing my life for the past two years has been a fantastic journey.

Who, What, When, Where and Why

"D'Alise James, we have unfinished business we need to talk. I am in Georgia for a conference give me a call." Cycle II coming soon.